DEATH OF A NARCISSIST

DEATH OF A NARCISSIST

A Death Motors Mystery

Book 2

MICHELLE HARING

For Jason and Riley

Contents

ONE

"I'm Gene Johnson, the owner of Genius Used Cars!"

Staying cocooned in a gorgeous media room watching many episodes of *Supernatural* hasn't erased the image of a dead blonde in a convertible from my memory. I've been able to watch it because I'm unemployed and living with my grandfather. No job recruiters are headhunting a twenty-seven year old woman with a doctorate in Popular Culture and less than a month of work experience in car sales. The axiom no publicity is bad publicity must not apply to murders because Roar Motors, the family owned dealership where I worked prior to finding my deceased coworker, closed. The national brand pulled the franchise because an onsite murder broke the morals clause. I don't think any car brand wants their products to star in a true crime podcast or *Lifetime* movie.

Thinking about my grandfather, Lando, makes him appear. He bursts into the darkened room by throwing open the closed door and bringing light and energy with him. He knocks his cane on the wall and starts lecturing me. "I want you to reenter society. Your friends have been calling and texting, but you stay wrapped in a blanket in the middle of summer staring at those boys while they save the world."

He jabs toward the television with the cane, "You need a car and I heard a good one slipped through one of the dealerships. It's an older car with low mileage which makes pricing it through Kelly Blue Book tough. I think it'll be the perfect first car for you. It's a 2005 Ford Thunderbird in the special 50th anniversary cashmere. I know a guy at the dealership who traded it in, and he called me last week. I didn't get back to him right away. Anyway, they passed it to one of the used car lots because they thought it was too specialized. You need out of this house. We're going to check it out now."

I sigh and rise from the couch. Arguing with Lando when he's acting bossy is futile. When he embraces an idea, he resembles Richard Castle following Beckett around in the first season of *Castle*. I follow him in silence to his magnificent land barge of a Lincoln Town Car. My grandfather, Lando, the car salesman extraordinaire, loves gigantic cars. He believes vehicles should reflect the personality of their drivers. He's a faithful fan of the American manufacturers.

On the twenty minute drive to Whitehall to check out this car, he lectures me about the history of the Ford Thunderbird telling me about how the cars started production in the 1950s but went through various incarnations and body styles.

During my weeks as a salesperson at Roar Motors, I never saw a Thunderbird, the last production year was 2005. My former employer focused on new cars and late model used cars. During my childhood, cars served as reliable transportation. My parents purchased practical, beige new cars every five years. They weren't devoted to any particular brand. They wanted reliable cars which blended into traffic. We lived over five hours away from my grandfather, and they never bought cars from him.

We arrive at Genius Used Cars and a giant inflatable purple figure blowing in the wind greets us. The yellow text on the midsection states good cars, cheap. I wrinkle my nose at the ostentatiousness until I catch sight of the Thunderbird. I throw my hands to my mouth.

Lando grins and says, "Isn't she a beauty? I love the color and the retro style. It seems like the type of car a woman who helped solve murders would drive."

I shake my head and tears well in my eyes. "I'm so sorry, Lando, but the gorgeous convertible flashes me back to finding Tiffany's body even if that convertible was blue not gold."

He runs his hand through his luxurious silver hair. "I'm sorry, Violet. It never occurred to me. We can leave."

My eyes shift to the left of the convertible, and I spy my future car. It's adorable and sized right for me. The light tan color and sporty bubbly design looks nothing like the car where I found a dead body a few weeks ago.

I wave toward the cute car and whisper to Lando, "I love it. I'm afraid to go look at it because too much enthusiasm is the kiss of death in negotiating a good deal, especially on a used car like her. How should I play this?"

He glances between the elegant Thunderbird convertible and the car I'm pointing at and asks, "Do you even know what type of car it is?"

I shrug. "I only learned the Ford brands and she doesn't look like a Ford. The emblem is small and unfamiliar to me. What is she?"

Lando shakes his head, "That's a Fiat. We called them Fix It Again Tony." He smirks, "at least it'll probably be cheap. Which brings up your original plan to pretend to be uninterested, those are good instincts and training from your weeks in the car business, kid. Never let the salesperson realize you love a specific used car. Play on your phone and act bored. I'll handle this."

Lando worked for about fifty years selling cars. Pittsburgh is a city but it's a city where people know people. He spent his career in the South Hills a few miles from this dingy car lot. He walks onto the lot with his knowledge of car sales as his shield.

He taps his cane and moves around the car, inspecting the body for dings and scratches. He peers into the interior to check the dark upholstery. I hide behind my long brown hair to observe Lando and watch the lot.

My last manager, Carmine would've been screaming at someone by this point. Lando's been surveying the car for over five minutes, and no salespeople have appeared to talk to him yet. If a prospective buyer was on the lot for over sixty seconds without anyone approaching them, Carmine would grab the closest salesperson and hiss at them to help the customer and then berate anyone else who missed a possible sale. At the ten minute mark with no one in evidence, I join Lando and we approach the sales office. Unlike the glass enclosed showroom at my former job, this car lot office is lodged in what appears to be a converted house trailer.

Lando strides across the used car lot. He throws open the trailer door and asks, "Is there anyone who can help me with a car? Or is everyone too busy?"

The three people in the trailer look at him and then glance at each other. The only woman, continues filing her nails and rolls her eyes. "Sales isn't my job. I just do the titles."

A gigantic bald guy sprawls in a folding chair wearing a sleeveless black shirt with ripped jeans. The rips are in horrifying areas and when I glance at him, I think no one wants to see that much of his hairy legs. He glares with protruding blue eyes and grunts, "I get the cars back, I don't put them on the road. Not my job."

The oldest person in the room pulls himself to his feet and says with a wheeze, "I'm Walter. I can help you if you needs it. I don't want to go out there in the heat if yinz are just looky loos."

I defer to Lando and observe his response to this guy. Walter's sales pitch is the worst I've ever seen. He should star in training videos on how to not sell a car.

Lando points toward the lot, "If the price is right and the car is solid, I'm buying a car today. Get up off your lazy butt and get out here and show me a car. Since you didn't ask which car I want and I'm sure you don't know the details on all or maybe any of your stock, I'll tell you I'm only interested in the Fiat. Grab the keys and the car's file and come out here to show me the vehicle."

Lando's contemptuous reply doesn't encourage Walter to move faster. I wonder if these people have a manager. Even with his cane and bad hip, Lando and I beat the worthless salesman to the Fiat.

Lando runs a hand over the back of the car and asks, "What's the best price? We'll do a test drive because it'll be fun to watch you try to squeeze into the backseat of a two door car."

Walter mops his brow with a rumpled handkerchief and asks, "Why can't the girl climb into the back. She's much smaller than me and probably in better shape."

My head snaps up when this sloth says I'm probably in better shape than him. Looking at his blank expression, I realize he's utterly clueless, not trying to insult me.

I lean down to peer into the back window, "I can crawl into the back, no big deal."

Lando gives me a questioning look, but he puts his hand out for the keys and says, "I'll drive."

Walter says with a sigh, "Gene doesn't like it when the customers drive the cars. You might drive off and take the car. This here's an expensive vehicle."

Lando shakes his head and says, "Look, you'll be in the passenger seat. If I was going to bother to steal a car, would I take the lazy salesman with me? Here are my keys to the Lincoln. Take them inside and let your clerk hold them on the test drive. My car's easily worth more than this car and any two others on the lot."

Walter points back at the trailer. "I just came outside. Can't the girl run the keys into the office? My knees ache."

If my pretty little car wasn't singing her siren's call to me, we would disappear faster than Walter could finish a sentence. At least Walter makes me feel like I wasn't the worst salesperson during my time at Roar Motors. I want to see how much more awful he can be. I grab the keys from his hand, "I'll take them in. No problem."

The bald guy's sitting on the woman's desk when I open the door. I must startle them as the door slips out of my hand and slams against the metal siding of the building. I take the keys to the woman, "Walter told me to bring these to you. He's taking us on a test drive and is worried about being carjacked. Please leave the Lincoln alone while we're gone."

Based upon their intimate proximity and his hands on her, they'll be busy with each other during our test drive. I don't wait for a response because none of these people seem to be familiar with social niceties or basic manners.

When I arrive at the car, both men are waiting for me to climb into the back. I dislike riding in the back of a two door car. If my lovely girl comes home with me, I never plan to sit in the back. I'm relieved she rides like a dream even from the back seat. Throughout the drive, Lando interrogates Walter about the service history, former owners and the Carfax. Walter can't be aware Lando had a friend at another dealership pull the Carfax while we were looking at the car and waiting for someone to help us. Lando discovered it was a single owner vehicle with no accidents and regular maintenance.

Walter doesn't seem to care enough to be flustered by Lando. Walter replies, "We don't do dat Carfax thing, it costs too much money."

When we return to Genius Used Cars, Walter looks uncomfortable as he tugs at his frayed cuffs and grimaces.

A bright yellow sports car sits in front of the sales office blocking the door.

Walter stares at the yellow car and whispers, "Gene's back early from auction. Crap on a cracker." He swivels to look at Lando and asks, "Are ya buying it or not?"

Lando tilts his head and asks, "Can your boss give me a better deal? I'm not paying over eight grand. I'm using cash. It's a gift."

Walter rubs his hand over his bald head exposing the sweat stains under the arms of his creased sports coat, "I'll give you a hint since you've been a stand up guy. He'll go lower if you don't tell him you're paying cash til the last minute. Please don't tell him about me. I need this job. I been a salesman all my life. I used to sell booze to the bars, but now all the good old bars are gone replaced by clubs and stuff. I lost my job, and I had to come here. He fired someone yesterday. I can't lose this one, too. He'd rather negotiate with customers on price anyways."

Walter gingerly opens the trailer door, and Gene Johnson dominates the room. His suit looks like it was expensive when he purchased it, but the suit's losing the battle to contain a few pounds more than its design parameters. Unlike many men in the car business, he still has what appears to be his original hair. His shiny, whitened teeth and well maintained hair cut don't align with the dingy trailer framing him.

His mouth flashes a wide smile but his flat eyes contradict it, "Sir, welcome to my little dealership, can I sell you a car? I'm Gene Johnson, the Genius."

Gene focuses on Lando. I fight to suppress my eye roll. He thrusts his hand out to shake with Lando and points at Walter, "Why don't you entertain this gentleman's young companion out here? It can be so cramped in the office."

Walter hustles me outside the trailer. As the door slams in my face, my jaw drops. I say, "This is the weirdest customer service in the world. Why did he assume Lando was buying the car and I wasn't?"

Walter pats my shoulder and winks, "Sweetie, you don't want to be alone in a room with him. I'm safe because my get up and go has got up and gone but he might bother you if he thinks he can. Let him deal with your old man."

I shudder, "Eww, my old man. Do you think I'm with him in a dating way? That is so gross. He's my grandfather. I've never been interested in a man who's over thirty much less a person over seventy."

Walter grins and says, "At a dealership like this, we see a lot of young girls with older men and the way they hang on them, they ain't their grandads. Some of them call the men daddy but not in a family way if you get my drift. Your clothes are two sizes bigger than most of what those girls wear, and your face isn't caked with makeup." He waves at my ears, "Them diamonds earrings look real, and his Lincoln is sharp. I'll admit, I took you for a higher class version of them chicks." He wrinkles his brow. "The car you picked didn't fit that, Thunderbirds are expensive lookin' rides but Fiats are just silly toys."

I stare at Walter. This isn't the type of conversation I expect. I've got no response. Not only, does he think my grandfather is my sugar daddy but he believes he's complimenting me. I remain quiet because I don't want to mess up Lando's wheeling and dealing. My silence must unnerve Walter because he starts talking again.

He wraps his arms around his middle, "Please don't be mad at me. I didn't mean to get you upset. Please don't say anythin' to Gene. He'll fire me in a heartbeat. He loves to fire people. He'd fire us all but not many people want to sell at a dealership like this. Everyone wants to work in the big dealerships. Course those dealerships have issues too. Did you hear two people got whacked at Roar Motors? I heard they might make a movie about it."

"Where did you hear about a possible movie? I don't know anything about a movie of the case," I ask as I step away from him.

Lando and I kept our names out of the newspaper accounts of the murder and the solving of it. We solved Tiffany's case for the sake of justice not notoriety. Tiffany's best friend, Mac, has made sure she's interviewed for every story. Detective Rousch represents the official voice of the police, and I have no desire to tangle with him again.

Walter pulls on the sleeves of his frayed suit jacket and replies, "Car people talk and I sometimes go to the club where the dead girl used to wait tables. A lot of car salesmen go to that club. Some of the girls who work there buy cars here. The girls notice a guy like me in a suit. Some of them dealerships have their guys wear shirts like they're going golfin'. That ain't the way to look like a professional."

Bringing attention to his attire isn't the way to impress me. Walter's grey suit wasn't expensive when he bought it. It doesn't appear that he cleans it on a regular basis based on the spots on his lapels and the grease marks on this thighs. The fabric is also worn at the elbows and stepped on at the heels.

I don't want to talk about Tiffany's murder ever again. I almost died investigating her case and the memories haunt me.

As I attempt to escape this conversation, my text message notification beeps. Before looking at the screen, I say, "Excuse me, I've been waiting for this text. It's been nice talking to you. I'm going to go back to my grandfather's car to take care of this."

The text that saves me is a notification about Barnes and Noble offering a special buy one, get one free coupon for coffee. I've spent the last few weeks ignoring any and all texts from actual people. After the first week, contact from my new potential friends slowed.

During the weeks after the murder when I wasn't watching *Supernatural*, Lando and I watched *Buffy the Vampire Slayer*. I've seen it many times because it was the subject of my doctoral dissertation in Popular Culture. Lando never watched it because he didn't own a television until my arrival in Pittsburgh. After facing death, I needed to decompress and Lando wanted to comfort me in the only way I'd accept.

During our television viewing, Lando mentioned he's worried if I move back to the eastern part of the state with my parents, my dad might put him in a nursing home. I haven't told Lando that I think his concern about my dad's plans are justified. Whenever my parents call, they tell me Lando would be happier around people his own age. I don't want to abandon Lando, who has been my rock since I moved to Pittsburgh. He loves his gorgeous book-filled house and his independence.

I concentrate on my phone until the trailer door bangs open and Lando emerges with Gene.

Gene addresses me before Lando speaks, "Well little lady, your grandfather here is a legend in the business, and he drives a hard bargain. But you my girl are about to be the proud owner of this lovely car right here." He waves toward the mocha colored Fiat, "Congratulations. I just need you to sign a few papers. He wants to put the car in your name."

When I enter the dealership office trailer, Lando follows me. I guess now that I have to sign paperwork, I'm allowed into the cramped trailer. Gene runs his eyes over me and asks, "What do you do for a job?"

I reply, "I'm currently between positions. I sold cars at my last job."

He points his fingers at me like they're a gun, "It must be fate. I just lost an employee. He didn't die like that girl at Roar Motors, he just left here." He shrugs, "Sorry to mention the tragedy. We're down to two salespeople and very busy. After talking to your grandfather, I'm sure you can do this. Do you want to sell cars here?"

Lando and I've been the only customers for the hour or two we've been looking at the Fiat. However, two salespeople to cover the six days of a car dealership seems to be too few. Lando got me my last job but I didn't think he had set this up for me. I need to get out of the house. How bad could another job selling cars be? This is the easiest interview I've ever heard of. He hasn't asked me for a resume or curriculum vitae.

I hesitate and ask, "Can I get back to you in ten minutes? I want to talk to my grandfather first."

Gene nods and opens the door for me, "I like your style, kid. Family's important and your granddad knows a bunch."

Lando's leaning against his Lincoln Town Car, and I rush over to him, "So Gene Johnson just offered me a job selling cars here. I don't want to give him an answer until I discuss it with you."

"Good instincts, my dear." Lando waves toward the trailer. "Gene got in real trouble for taking pocket shots and some other economic abnormalities like some missing cash at his last dealership job. I heard he could be an arrogant jerk but no worse than your last boss, Carmine. Neither of those things make him unusual in the car business. I've been talking to some of my contacts at the big dealer groups about hiring you but they move slow. I'm pretty sure Gene will watch himself around my granddaughter. If you don't like it here, you can always quit."

"What are pocket shots?" I ask.

Lando looks around the empty lot as if he's checking to make sure no one can overhear us. "Pocket shots are car business lingo for taking kickbacks from wholesale car buyers. The big dealer groups stopped using wholesalers because of scandals like Gene's. I might've heard of some other monetary shenanigans involving Gene. I'll ask around."

Lando winks, "I know what your parents have been pushing you about. I figure you getting a job here will quiet them down for a little bit. Those two always act like having a job's next to godliness."

With Lando's approval ringing in my ears, I return to the trailer and open the door. Gene grins at me and this time his eyes smile. I say, "I'd be happy to work here."

Gene reaches out and gives my hand a firm shake. "Welcome to Genius Used Cars. From what your grandfather told me about you, I'm looking forward to working with another smart person, Dr. Landovic."

TWO

"I'm an actual genius, and I have the
papers to prove it!"

I bounce out of bed on my first day at Genius Used Cars. After spending the weekend watching *Supernatural* and petting my cat, Annika, I need to do something. The unpleasant attitude of Walter, the salesman, and those two people in the office bother me, but Gene welcomed me and hired me because I impressed him. The sun's shining on this June day.

I get ready and run over to Lando's side of the house to grab breakfast. Lando's at the kitchen table reading *Virgin River* by Robyn Carr. I plop into the seat and ask, "Is that a romance novel?"

He glances up from his book, "Romance is hopeful because the main characters always get their happily ever after and today feels like it's going to be a good day for you."

Nodding at his logic, I say, "I've never read one, because my mom made fun of them. College and graduate school certainly never included a romance novel on the required reading list. Maybe I'll start one tonight because I need some tips on relating to guys. *Supernatural* failed to show me how to develop a relationship with a guy that didn't end in someone's premature, bloody death, "

Flinging open the refrigerator door, I find a paper bag with a label stating Violet's lunch. Lando smiles at me, "I figure you won't have to leave the car lot for lunch on your first day. There's even a snack bag of popcorn, so you won't offend anyone with microwave popcorn smell."

I grab mini carrots, the pitcher of iced tea and a bagel. I check the time on my watch. I have an hour before I need to be at work, but I don't know how to judge the traffic. I walked to my last car sales job. Lando appears to be reading but he must catch my movement. "Don't worry, you've got plenty of time to make it for your first day. You'll face some traffic but you'll turn off before the tunnels and miss the worst of it."

Annika, my gorgeous fluffy cat, arrives in the doorway of the kitchen as I sit down to eat. I jump up to give her wet food. She twines around my ankles as I open the cupboard.

Lando laughs, "She's trying to scam you. I fed her fifty pages ago. Annika must have learned manipulation from her original owner, Tiffany."

Lando waves toward the backdoor and the partially completed addition to his house. He says, "Speaking of Annika, Sean's building her a catwalk system in the book annex. I visited a cool bookstore in the middle of the state that had catwalks above the bookshelves for their bookstore cats. I loved the idea and now that we have a cat, I told him to implement the plan. Everything is almost done in the addition. Sean's been working like a champ. I'm sure he'd love it if you stopped in to see it. He misses you."

Rubbing my hand over my face, I avoid looking toward the backyard because I don't have the emotional energy to deal with Sean on my first day at my new job. I ignore Lando's opening. I gesture at my dark blue t-shirt dress and black flats, "Does this outfit look okay for Genius Used Cars?"

He shrugs, "Based on the title clerk's mini skirt and halter top, the scary ripped jeans on the repo guy, and Walter's rumpled suit, I don't think appearance is important to anyone other than Gene Johnson, himself. I'm not sure he even notices other people."

I shove my bagged lunch into my crossbody messenger bag and hurry out to my adorable new car. The mocha latte Fiat glistens in the morning light, and I name her Dawn. I love my first car and naming a car is a mark of ownership. I pick Dawn because she's the most underrated character on *Buffy*.

My drive proves to be as easy as Lando promised, and I arrive at Genius Used Cars half an hour early. I pull in front of the office trailer and knock on the door. No one answers and I hesitate with my hand on the door handle. I stumble back when the door hits me.

Gene emerges with a glare which turns into a grin. "Good morning, Violet. I'm delighted to discover a sales professional who understands being early is a fantastic way to start the day."

Waving toward my vehicle I say, "I wasn't sure where employee parking was."

Rather than telling me anything, he takes the keys from my hand and gets into the driver's seat. He slides it back. "Wow, you're petite. I guess good things do come in small packages." He says with a wink.

Stiffening, I step further away from my car. He leans across my car and opens my passenger door from the inside. He pats the seat, "Please don't worry, I'm not hitting on you. I respect your intellect too much. You remind me of the type of young woman I want my daughter to grow up to be."

Getting into the car, I smile and ask, "How old is your daughter?"

"She's about sixteen, and she reminds me of myself at her age. She talks, moves and thinks fast." He replies with smirk as he starts my car. He taps the dashboard, "I like Fiats. The brand conveys a joie de vivre. You can park your car behind the service building next to my baby."

He pulls into a spot three feet away from the bright, yellow sports car. He touches my shoulder, "Remember, you're the only other person I'm allowing back here. Always make sure you stay a few feet away. Your doors are longer than usual. You have a two-door car."

He drops my keys on the driver's seat and walks toward the trailer with a wave. I follow him across the lot, avoiding the numerous potholes. The condition of the lot and the trailer contradict the impression he conveys with his spotless car and fastidious clothing. I hesitate before entering with Walter's warnings about being alone with Gene rushing through my memory. Lando didn't seem to be worried, and Gene's acted like a gentleman with me.

I take a deep breath and open the door. Gene's

leaning on the door to his office and he tells me to fill out the paperwork on the reception desk. "You better sit on the customer side because Phoebe's weird about her chair."

Filling out new employment paperwork for the second time in two months at a car dealership seems like deja vu. As I write my name and all of my important data, the trailer door flies open, and the woman who I presume is Phoebe teeters into the room on five inch heels with skintight ripped jeans and a cropped top. Her platinum blond hair with pink streaks is in pigtails.

I stand up to shake her hand, and she rolls her eyes and walks past me to Gene's office. She yells, "Gene, did you hire a new girl? I like salesmen better."

Gene pulls her into his office and slams the door. As I hover on the other side of the door, I think about how much I hate the term "new girl." The woman calling me girl looks like she's still in her twenties.

Walter creeps into the trailer and sighs at me. "I told you to stay away from this place, little girl."

I shake my head at him because I despise the phrase "little girl" even more than "new girl," "You aren't going to scare me away from this job. I think you're afraid I'll outsell you."

The door opens again and a young man bursts into the room. He waves at me, "Hi, I'm Dalton. I'm sure you'll slay it here." He points to Walter and then himself, "It's not like the sales competition's exactly legit."

He doesn't call me girl for a refreshing change of pace. Since he looks years younger than my twenty-seven, it would be odd. His light brown hair is pulled into a man bun, and he's wearing cargo shorts, t-shirt and hiking boots. Between Gene's crisp white shirt, khaki pants and sports jacket, Walter's dirty suit which appears to be the same one he wore Friday when we bought the car from him and Dalton and Phoebe's outfits, I don't think Genius Used Cars enforces a strict dress code.

Phoebe exits Gene's office and slams the door. She stomps to her desk and throws herself into her chair. When I hand her all my paperwork, I ask, "Is there any type of training manual or a dress code?"

She cackles and replies, "Seriously? Just go out to the lot and sell cars to anyone dumb or desperate enough to come to dis here place."

She looks me over and points at my legs, "Gene don't care what the men wear, but he likes us girls in skirts, just sayin."

Taking her advice and escaping her overpowering musky perfume, I rush into the fresh air and run into a young couple with a preschool age child, a toddler and an infant. They approach me and ask about one of the two door cars. I glance around the lot for their current car and when I ask they tell me they rode the bus to get to Genius Used Cars.

We talk for a few minutes and discuss the logistics of three car seats in the back of a tiny car. The mother avoids my eyes as she explains they need the cheapest car they can find because they don't have any credit. She tells me the last place they tried, one of the big dealerships, told them they were ghosts because they paid cash for everything. I learned the term at my last job and I explain to them it isn't an insult.

I point to the gigantic sign on the trailer office building which proclaims "No Credit, Bad Credit, No Problem, We Can Get You in a Car." Those letters are five feet high. In print on the bottom of the sign in six inch letters, there's the caveat. The infinitesimal print states "with down payment."

I tell the couple I don't know all the rules because they are my first customers at Genius Used Cars. I dash to the trailer, ignore Phoebe and knock on Gene's closed door. He shouts, "What?"

Phoebe giggles and I reply, "Gene, I have some customers out in the lot with questions." After a minute, he swings open the door and says, "Violet, I'm sorry for my tone. I assumed you were one of these incompetents. Please come into my office."

"My customers told me they don't have any credit at all, but they need a car. How does it work for people the other dealerships call ghosts?" I ask.

Gene says with a smirk, "We can put them in a car as long as they've got a down payment. Bring them in to talk with me."

After retrieving the people and depositing them in Gene's office, I wander the lot and examine the cars. Roar Motors, my last job, sold new and attractive late model used cars, trucks, and SUVs. These vehicles encompass a variety of car brands but many of the cars display imperfections including scratches and dents. A few trucks sit on the lot but most of the forty or so automobiles are sedans with a sprinkling of boxy minivans.

I become familiar with the inventory by peering into windows and inspecting each car. Walter and Dalton watch me from the service building where they sit on lawn chairs with a floor fan blowing from the open garage door. There's no service technician in evidence, just the two salesmen.

Gene brings the family out and hands them the keys to the car. I join them, thank them and wish them the best of luck. I clench my jaw when the mother buckles the preschooler and the toddler into the backseat and then gets into the front seat holding the baby. She rolls down the window and says, "Miss, I promise we got car seats at home. I couldn't carry them and the babies on the bus."

When they pull away, Gene turns to me and says, "You did a marvelous job with the family today, Violet." He waves toward the salesmen observing us from the garage, "During your doctoral work, you learned a work ethic unlike those two fools. Good help's difficult to find. I'll leave you to it because someone else is pulling onto the lot. Remember the key to selling cars here, is down payment."

As Gene heads back to the air conditioned trailer, I rub my hand over my glistening face and turn to greet the two male customers. Their current beater car must've given him a clue to their situation because I discover they don't have any type of down payment. Rather than trying to work with them for a long time, I return to the trailer and ask Gene what to do about people without down money. He replies, "I'll launch them. I love tossing losers."

Gene comes out and I watch him talk to the prospective customers. One of the men points to the sign on the trailer and Gene walks over and jabs at the small words stating "with down payment." The men jump back into their car, slam the doors and peel out of the lot.

After witnessing the uncomfortable interaction I ask about the procedure and meaning of "Buy Here, Pay Here," I think my new boss might try to sugarcoat it.

Instead Gene smiles with his veneers glistening in the sun and says, "The most important caveat is "with a down payment." I own a "Buy Here, Pay Here" lot. I acquire all of the cars at auction or from reputable dealerships that don't bother with cheap cars. I'm aware of exactly how much money I invest in each car. That's the amount I demand for the down payment. The price of the car is about three times what I paid for it. The customer pays the down money and finances the rest of the car. According to Pennsylvania law, twenty-one percent is the highest interest rate that can be charged on vehicles older than two years."

"How does financing work? Do I need to do anything with that end of the business?" I ask.

Gene replies, "All you need to do is ask about the size of their down payment. If someone comes to Genius Used Cars and doesn't have all of the cash to buy the car, I charge them twenty-one percent interest. If they make all of their payments, they can rebuild their credit. I make most of my money off the financing, not necessarily the car. I charge a late fee of fifty dollars a week in addition to the interest rate. After one month of missed payments, the repo guy retrieves the car." He says, "We don't tell the customers about my repo guy. I'm telling you because you work here and your granddad bought your car outright."

Cocking my head to the side, I ask, "Does the repo guy works for you?"

"In a manner of speaking because I'm his best customer. Not really, he's an independent contractor, and he grabs cars for other "Buy Here, Pay Here" lots, too. Gene says with a grin.

I nod at Gene and thank him for the information. For the first time, I feel a little uncomfortable about this new job. I understand people need cars, but I don't want to be involved in taking advantage of them.

Gene pats me on the arm, "I have to go to auction to buy more cars. You're doing an amazing job, Violet. You are my best hire since I started my own car lot. You keep up the great work, and we will work stupendously together. I love working with someone who gets me."

I wander the car lot but with less than fifty vehicles and no customers, there isn't much I can do. When I try to go into the trailer, the door's locked. Dalton and Walter cross their arms and laugh at my attempt to enter the trailer. Dalton runs over to me and says, "Don't bother Butch and Phoebe are locked in there and believe me you don't want to see what they might be doing. I got in it one time and I felt like I needed bleach for my eyes."

Dalton strolls back to the service building so I follow him and ask, "Why is the repo guy even here? What's the deal with him?"

Based on my brief interaction on Friday, I fear the repo guy. His bald head shines like he waxes it every morning. He possesses more muscles than teeth, chews tobacco and spits into a gross, filthy soda bottle.

At my last dealership, I never learned about repossessing cars. Lando, my grandfather an authority on the car business, told me that it happened but it rarely impacted salespeople. Gene just told me the creep isn't an employee of Genius Used Cars.

Dalton explains, "The repo guy's name is Butch, and he hangs out at Genius Used Cars lots of days. He brings in at least a car a day. Since I've been here, I've sold about a car a day. Walter sell a car every other day. About two or three cars a day is the average for the dealership. With Butch repossessing a car a day, it means almost half the cars we sell from this lot get repossessed."

Dalton plops back into his chair and expounds on the car lot gossip, Butch's in some type of a relationship with the title clerk, Phoebe. When they're in the trailer together, and Gene's at the car auctions, the door's usually locked. When one of the salespeople needs to go in to retrieve keys, we have to bang on the door. Phoebe always appears disheveled when she opens it. She pats her hair and claims the door sticks. Magically it never sticks when Gene's on the property.

Walter struggles to rise from his lawn chair and offers it to me. I thank him but I can't take a seat from someone in obvious pain. Instead I lean on the work bench and ask, "Where's the service technician?"

Dalton replies, "Iggy, the mechanic, has a day job. When he shows up, he works here nights and weekends so Walter and me hang out here to shoot the bull and keep on eye on the lot."

The two guys delight in having a new audience for their stories and the rest of the afternoon passes with them telling me about their lives. Walter focuses on his years in liquor sales and some of the weird things he witnessed. Dalton talks about his family and tales from his childhood. When a customer arrives, the two of them do rock, paper, scissors and the loser has to help the person. I laugh the first time it happens because it reminds me of the boys' games on *Supernatural.* Neither of them are aware of the show so when that customer's a bust, I tell them the story of two brothers and their family business of saving people and hunting things. I don't share stories about my own life but I can always talk about television.

Gene doesn't have any training program. I learn about my pay and hours from Dalton and Walter. I work every day from 11 am to 8 pm except Sunday. In Pennsylvania, car dealerships aren't allowed to sell cars on Sundays. This rather antiquated blue law gives car salesmen one day guaranteed off every week. Lando told me most of the dealerships love this law. People come to check out the car lots on Sundays and avoid salespeople. I asked if this wasn't a tad old-fashioned with the Internet as a way to look at cars without leaving one's house. He explained most people want to see the cars because it's not like the dealers take pictures of the flaws and put those online.

At Genius Used Cars, there's not a sophisticated formula for getting paid. Every salesperson gets seventy-five dollars for selling a car plus ten percent of gross profit. There's no backend money, no warranty or unit bonus and no pay per hour.

Dalton quotes what Gene told him about the pay plan, "I like to make my pay scale easy for everyone to understand. You get paid for production. I get paid for production. Everyone gets paid for production. You deliver a car and you earn seventy-five dollars plus ten percent of gross profit. If you don't like it, feel free to leave."

I decide to stay at the job in spite of the low pay because I don't need the money. I can't fail at another job. Lando insists on covering all of the household expenses because he pays those if I live with him or if he's alone. He paid off his beautiful house a decade ago, so it's just utilities, taxes, the cleaning lady, food and books. He has enough extra money to build an addition so his books will have more space.

Listening to Walter and Dalton and talking to my customers, I observe different lives than graduate school or television shows.

Gene treats me like a star and a professional without making me uncomfortable. He brought me flowers the day of my first sale, and he has a new coffee drink waiting for me every morning. He insists he'll figure out which type I like best. I always thank him and then pour it behind the building. I don't want to offend him but I dislike coffee. After my experience with my dismissive manager, Carmine, at Roar Motors, I appreciate feeling valued.

THREE

"Try to be smart like me and buy a car at Genius Used Cars."

Gene spends my first week of work trying to charm me and insisting he wants to be my mentor. Sometimes when I catch his intense gaze out of the corner of my eye, I worry he wants more than a work relationship. I don't want to offend Gene, so the best way to discourage any possible interest is to produce a semi-imaginary boyfriend.

I ask Lando's friend Sean for a ride to work on my first Friday to avoid any awkwardness from Gene. Sean's a gigantic guy, over six foot, four inches. Working as a contractor, he's also built like an action hero. His dark red hair and blue eyes don't radiate menace but his size, tattoos and the way he carries himself discourage poor behavior. My relationship with Sean developed while we were investigating Tiffany's murder. During my hibernation month, he persevered by showing up to watch an occasional *Supernatural* episode. I didn't answer calls or texts but he was working on my grandfather's property and a longtime family friend so I talked to him several times during my hiding time. He proved to be difficult to avoid.

Friday's the first chance we have for me to show off my new car because of his work on the backyard library addition for Lando. I pick him up at the house he shares with his grandparents. Both of us live with senior citizens which gives us something in common. When I pull in front of his house, I jump out of my cute Fiat and dash over to open the passenger door for him.

He laughs, "I love the courtesy, but you know I like to open your door for you."

Waving away his comment, I slide back into the driver's seat, "This morning, breakfast at Eat N' Park is my treat as long as you don't mind driving my car and then picking me up tonight."

He points to the road, "Do you need directions?"

Shrugging my shoulders, I say, "The second time we talked was when I got lost in your neighborhood, but I've memorized the route. I need to concentrate."

When I park, I turn to him and say, "Gene, my new boss, has been so nice to me this week, almost too nice. The other salesmen seem to hate him but they won't tell me why. Last night Dalton, the young one, stood at his car with his arms crossed and watched me talk to Gene. He didn't leave until I drove away.

Looking down, I put my hand on my forehead, "At my last job, Carmine SanDelgado and Oliver Roar were a little creepy, but I never worried that they would try anything with me because of Lando. I hate using you as a shield, but maybe Gene wouldn't misunderstand me if he thinks I have a big, burly guy like you as my boyfriend."

Sean nods, "I've got no problem pretending to be your boyfriend because I'm your friend. I need to be honest, I'd like to be your boyfriend when you're ready to take that step. I've left you alone for the last few weeks, because you needed to recharge, but this might be a good time to talk about us."

This conversation makes the small car feel like it's shrinking, "This job is a way for me to regain some confidence back after being threatened by a murderer and saved by my cat. You're one of the most trustworthy people I've met in Pittsburgh, but I need to get some of my confidence back after that fiasco."

He reaches over to pat my shoulder, "You act like Roar Motors was a disaster but you solved the murder and the killer is in jail because you kept a clear head and recorded the bad guy monologue. I'm happy to wait for you." He runs his hand through his hair, "I don't know how I feel about you taking a job with a guy who makes your coworkers uncomfortable. Have you mentioned this to Lando?"

I shake my head, "I need to make decisions about my own life. I let my parents compel me to come to Pittsburgh. Lando got me my last job. Mac pushed Lando and me to investigate Tiffany's murder. I was impulsive, but I decided to try to work at Genius Used Cars. Even if it's the wrong choice, it's my choice."

At breakfast, we talk about inconsequential things like our favorite television shows. Sean drives my car to Genius Used Cars. He makes a production of getting out of the car and hugging me. I'm five minutes early rather than my usual fifteen and Dalton and Gene witness our goodbye.

Dalton asks, "Who's the big guy?"

I wave to Sean as he drives away in my car. I glance at Gene, "He's my boyfriend."

Gene flashes me an inscrutable look and enters the trailer. Dalton pulls me into the service building and peppers me with questions. Gene goes to the auction and doesn't bring me back a drink, but he's cordial to me.

At five o'clock, I up a young woman wearing black leggings and an oversized white t-shirt with a baby covered in a red blanket in a heavy infant car seat with a base. Ups are customers in the traditional car business. At this dealership, Dalton and Walter let me take most of the customers. It's like they don't care about making money.

She introduces herself as Shelby and her baby's name is Ruby. She explains she needs a car to go to work and her current car won't pass inspection. She shares with me she rode the bus to get to Genius Used Cars and asks if she can leave the infant carrier in the car she plans to buy. She has some money down, but I'm not sure if it's enough to buy the car. Gene never tells the salespeople what he pays for cars at auction. I take her into the trailer to talk to Gene. He flashes his shiny teeth, takes her arm and asks me to take the baby for a while.

Shelby gives me her baby with a shrug and kisses her daughter's fluffy blond head. I walk the baby around the lot and talk to her about the cars. Ruby coos at me and the cars, but she's not wearing a hat so I worry about her getting burned by the late afternoon sun.

We join Dalton and Walter in the garage. Walter

grunts and Dalton covers his eyes to play peek a boo with the baby. After about an hour, the baby starts to whimper a little and I say, "It seems like they're taking a long time."

Dalton glares at the building and says, "I'm not surprised. I saw the mom and I bet she needed the car. It shouldn't be long now."

Within five minutes, Shelby dashes out of the building and slams the trailer door. She yells, "Where's my baby?"

I rush over to her. She looks disheveled with her dirty blond hair falling around her face and her mascara streaming. She's rubbing her mouth. When I meet her at her new car, she leans over and vomits. I ask, "Can I help you with anything? Do you want me to grab you a water from the trailer?"

She glares at me and shakes her head. I ask again, "What's wrong? Can I help you?"

"Don't you think you've done enough?" She yells in my face.

The baby starts to cry and I rock her while stepping away from Shelby. "I don't know how to help you, and I don't know what's going on. I'm sorry but you're scaring Ruby."

Shelby starts to laugh but it's shrill rather than amused. "You stupid idiot, you can't figure out what he does to women like me who need cars. You stand there with your diamond earrings shining in your ears and ask if you can help me. I bet you never needed anything in your spoiled life. Just give me my baby. I don't need anything from you!"

I hand her the baby and even given Shelby's hysteria, she attaches the carrier and checks it before placing Ruby in it. I watch her without a word. I have no response to her as I start to realize what happened in the trailer. I remember another female customer a few days ago who slammed out of the trailer and left screaming curses about not being desperate enough to buy anything at this place. At the time I chalked it up to anger at the interest rates. I feel queasy, and I can't bear the thought of facing Gene again.

Sean's white F-350 work truck appears in the lot as if he's arriving on a white horse to take me away from this place. To avoid Phoebe and Butch, I keep my messenger bag in the service building. I jog over to grab it. Walter and Dalton stare at me from their matching lawn chairs.

Dalton asks, "How'd that sale go? She looked upset when she peeled outta here. Now you look a little off, too."

I'm not having this conversation until I've processed everything. I tilt my chin up and point at Sean's truck, "My boyfriend's here to pick me up. I delivered a car, and this place closes in half an hour. I'm done."

Sean parks next to the building, and he walks into the shadowy bay that smells of old motor oil with a faint overlay of decay. He introduces himself.

Before he can start a conversation, I grab his arm and say, "I'm hungry. Can we get out of here before my boss makes an appearance?"

Sean walks over to open my door, and I slide into the truck without another glance at my coworkers.

He asks how my day went. I don't want to deal with his thoughts on the subject. I reply with fine and deflect to dinner plans. We grab dinner at a German restaurant on the South Side. I avoid talking about my day by asking Sean about the mystery series he's reading and the work on the addition he's building for Lando.

When we return to my grandfather's house, I open my truck door before he can open it for me. I don't want to deal with any awkward discussions about our dating status or my day at work. I say, "I'll talk to you tomorrow. I need to wake up early for work."

I enter Lando's side of the house and scurry down the hallway to the stairs. Lando yells, "Did you go on a date with Sean?"

I shout back, "I need to clean the cat's litter box."

Lando must be engrossed in a novel because he doesn't try to follow me. He doesn't come over to my side of the double house. During my difficult time, he told me he wanted to give me my own space. He keeps the human and the cat food on his side, as well as the media room. My side of the house contains my bedroom, my gorgeous bathroom and rooms of Lando's books. He feels his books need proper space to be displayed.

After cleaning the litter box and taking a hot shower, I text Lando so he won't worry about me not coming over to see him. I stare at my phone for several minutes, working on my courage to text Quentin, the cute EMT.

He was there for me during the drama at Roar Motors. We went on a single date, and he told me wanted to spend time with me. He's texted a few times, but I haven't replied. I've avoided him since the night of my confrontation with the murderer. He might think I only contact him when I want something, but I need his perspective.

I text.

> Hi, I've been silent for a while, but I was wondering if you were free tomorrow for breakfast. We could meet at Eat N'Park at 9 AM.

The bubbles of writing appear within a minute. He replies,

> I'd love to meet you. That sounds great. I want to catch up with you.

His swift reply makes me feel awkward. I don't want him to think I'm asking him on a date. Another perspective about the legality of Gene's behavior toward women who need cars would help. I don't contact Mac, the lawyer who encouraged Lando and I to investigate her best friend, Tiffany's murder. She'd either ignore me, tease me or confront Gene.

I text again,

> If your uncle is free, could you please bring him, too?

I stare at the phone and no bubbles appear for a few minutes. Annika jumps onto the bed and glances at me. I lean over to pet her as embarrassment rages through me.

Finally my text notification beeps, Quentin replies.

> He's free tomorrow and I understand this isn't a date.

I retrieve *An Offer from a Gentleman* by Julia Quinn from Lando's romance library. I need to read something entertaining and removed from my world. Since Lando told me to try romance I devoured the first two books in the Bridgeton series. Lando recommended the entire series of eight books. He mentioned wanting to watch the show when it finally releases but he doesn't want to sign up for a streaming service. Everything we've watched since I arrived in Pittsburgh has been on DVD. Based upon my *TV Guide* research, it's not a show to watch with my grandfather. The plot of the third novel reenforces my realization about the lack of power women have if they don't have family or money.

FOUR

"No credit, no problem!"

The cloudy, humid day reflects my mood as I drive to Eat N' Park to meet Quentin and his uncle, Detective Rousch. I park next to Quentin's car. I sold it to him at Roar Motors. The car provides physical proof that I've been brave since moving to Pittsburgh. Telling Quentin and his uncle about the things I learned last night about Gene Johnson and Genius Used Cars demands my courage.

Upon entering, I search for them and Quentin jumps out of his seat to pull out a chair for me. He opens his arms and in spite of my discomfort with touching, I walk into his hug.

He whispers into my hair, "It's so good to see you."

I pull away from him and stumble into the seat.

Detective Rousch shakes his head, "I'm assuming this isn't about the murders at Roar Motors. You asked me to be here, so it isn't an attempt to date my nephew." He points at Quentin. "What crime are you involved with now?"

I take a deep breath and say, "I'm not sure if it's a

crime. I got a job at Genius Used Cars and started last Monday. Last night I found out my boss, Gene Johnson, has been either assaulting or perhaps extorting women for sex to sell them cars they wouldn't qualify for under normal circumstances."

Quentin takes my hand and squeezes it. Detective Rousch sighs and says, "Assault is definitely a crime, but the extortion is a different, difficult situation. Why don't you tell me what makes you suspicious?"

I explain my interaction with Shelby last evening. Then I tell them about the cursing woman from earlier in the week. During my explanation, Quentin holds my hand, and Rousch takes notes on his iPad. Rousch asks, "Why would you take a job at a slimy used car lot? Didn't your overprotective grandfather discourage you?"

A waitress interrupts by asking for our order. After she leaves, I answer, "Lando told me Gene used to work for a corporate dealership. Apparently he got in some trouble for embezzlement or kickbacks, but Lando never heard about anything violent or harassing about his behavior." I look at my lap, "During the week I worked for him, Gene, treated me like a professional. Occasionally, I got an odd feeling but I chalked it up to paranoia. The other two salespeople were both men who hinted I wasn't seeing the real Gene. They both act like they fear him and hate talking about him."

Rousch eyes Quentin and says, "You two talk about something else. I'm going to do some research on this Gene Johnson."

Quentin nods and asks about how I've been. I tell him how I hid and apologize for disappearing. He lets go of my hand and runs his hand through his hair, "Don't worry about me. I'm happy to see you again. I understand what happened at Roar Motors was the worst thing you've ever been involved with. Disappearing to decompress seems like a sensible idea to me. Besides, I've been busy working, driving my new car, and seeing baseball games. I'd still love to take you to one. I can't wait to teach you about the joy of Pittsburgh sports."

The waitress brings our breakfast. While eating, Quentin tells me about the Pittsburgh Pirates and some of his favorite players. It's easy to listen to him. His uncle shovels food into his mouth and stares at his iPad. I check my watch, and I have an hour to get to work if I'm going to show up at all.

After the waitress clears the table, I ask for the bill. Quentin says, "Nope, I've got this. Don't try to argue about inviting us. I sense you're going to be out of work again in the near future."

Rousch glances up from his iPad and says, "He's right. We'll go with you this morning. After what I've discovered I don't think you'll be working at Genius Used Cars this afternoon. I'm not telling you anything until after you talk to Mr. Johnson. I'll be there the whole time observing in case I need to testify. There also might be some evidence of crimes in places that don't require a warrant. "

FIVE

"Bad credit, no problem!"

On my first Saturday morning at Genius Used Cars, I drive to work in my adorable Fiat. I love this vehicle as much as I now loathe my job. I dread walking onto the broken lot and interacting with my horrible boss. Detective Rousch and Quentin follow me in Quentin's practical Ford sedan. They plan to pretend to be customers and serve as my backup when I quit. I don't call Lando or Sean from the car because they would only confuse the situation.

At my last job, Roar Motors, a family owned new car dealership, I sold a few cars. This has been my first experience at a used car lot. This dealership serves people for whom transportation is a need. At Roar Motors, some customers were concerned about the exterior car color clashing with their house if the car had to be in the driveway. At this dealership, most people worry about if the car will get them to work on a regular basis. In the past week, I've talked to about fifteen people who desperately wanted to buy a car but couldn't obtain financing because they didn't have enough down money. The people who couldn't buy a car outnumbered those who could by a power of five.

I park my car behind the single service bay. My fun retro Fiat draws attention on the lot and when people notice it, some try to buy it or touch it. As if they assume, it's on this lot, so it's cheap. I walk around the crumbling block building and swallow a scream. Not again.

The front of Gene's yellow Camaro hovers over his lifeless body. All I can see is his head and shoulders. He's definitely dead. I've found three bodies in a month. It isn't all about me but it feels that way when I'm the one finding dead bodies.

With shaking hands but no screaming, I call 911. "I'm at Genius Used Cars in Whitehall, and I need to report a dead body."

The dispatcher asks, "Can the person be helped?"

I shake my head which she can't see through the phone, "No, he appears to be beyond help. To be honest, I don't want to get too close to the body. I'm pretty sure this time there's blood. I don't want to throw up or pass out. I shouldn't contaminate the crime scene."

The dispatcher says, "Ma'am, are you okay? You sound calm for finding a dead body. Are you a first responder?"

I shake my head, "Not okay but I'm not in shock either. This is my third murder victim this month. I screamed at the first one, tried and failed to save the second one. This time I'm resigned to my bad luck and poor timing"

The 911 dispatcher says, "Please tell me the address. I will send emergency personnel. Stay where you are."

Sliding to the ground, I give the address. I'm wearing a long skirt, but it's black so it shouldn't show dirt. I don't know where my coworkers are. I don't want to interact with a single one of them. The dysfunction at this lot's been so severe that any of them could be the murderer. An outside party is a possibility, but I'm confident the employees hate Gene more than the rest of the world loathes him. I was planning to tell Gene I quit today. I slap my hand to my forehead. Quentin and Rousch are probably out front by now. I dialed 911 automatically but I have my own personal police officer and EMT on site. I call Quentin on his cell. "I'm behind the service building, and I need you and your uncle."

Quentin runs around the building in under thirty seconds. When he sees Gene's body, he crouches and checks for a pulse. He shakes his head as his uncle appears around the corner. Quentin rubs his hands on his pants and sits down next me. His shoulder bumps mine but he doesn't touch me with the hand he used to check Gene's pulse.

Rousch pulls out his phone, and I look up at him. "I called it in to 911. I'm sure the dispatcher thinks I'm a nut because I was so cold when I reported it. In my horror at being on the scene of another body, I forgot you were right behind me."

Rousch says, "I'm leaving you here with Quentin and going to grab my kit. I keep an extra one in his car."

A belief in justice and respect for Tiffany, my first murdered coworker, made me want to solve her murder.

I'm curious about who hated Gene the most and ended his awful life. Even if I want to investigate another murder in the car business, I doubt this ridiculous excuse for a dealership will stay open with Gene gone. This time I'm leaving the detecting to the professionals like Detective Rousch.

I stare toward the road and wait for the sirens. My phone's in my hand, but Quentin's quiet presence keeps me from calling Sean or Lando. They'll interfere and add to the chaos.

Last time at Roar Motors, my screams at finding Tiffany's body led to one of my coworkers, Sally, having a minor heart attack. So this time, I'm not letting any of them know what I've found. With this group, someone might dance over Gene's death and deliberately contaminate the crime scene.

As a distraction from thinking about my dead boss, I focus on my coworkers as I wonder who hated Gene enough to run him over with his own car. Genius Used Cars has a staff of six including me. There is the aforementioned dead Gene, a title clerk and notary who is the only other female, Phoebe, a grumpy old salesman, Walter, a young salesman, Dalton and me. The other two sales people are pleasant enough and welcoming. Dalton treats me like an older sister. Walter, treats me like a niece. The title clerk hates me, but Dalton and Walter have assured me she hates everyone. There is also a single mechanic named Iggy, but I've never seen him. Allegedly, he works late nights and weekends to make the cars appear to be roadworthy. According to Dalton, Iggy's been on vacation for the last two weeks. The repo guy,

Butch, spends an unusual amount of time at Genius, but he's an independent contractor.

The ambulance enters the lot with sirens blaring. The noise pulls me out of my reverie.

When the first EMT gets out of the ambulance, Quentin waves at her. I ask, "Isn't that your company? Is this your uncle's jurisdiction, too?"

He shakes his head, "Sorry, Dormont and Whitehall share Emergency Medical Services, but they have different police forces. A whole new set of police detectives will interview you this time."

As he says this, his uncle returns and starts taking pictures of the scene. The questions about jurisdiction flutter out of my mind as I maintain eye contact with Quentin and refuse to look at the yellow sports car or the body underneath it. "I could tell there was nothing I could do to help Gene when I saw his body under the car. I didn't want to see any blood or anything else disgusting. I also didn't feel like any of these coworkers would be helpful. If you notice, the blaring sirens didn't pull them out of the air conditioned trailer. I'm not in shock. I'm numb."

He talks to me while the EMTs on duty check on the body, "The EMTs arrive in case there's someone who we can help. When you found Tiffany, you were crying. You don't seem nearly as upset this time."

I wrap my arms around my stomach even though the summer morning temperature is already in the low eighties, "Like I told you this morning, Gene Johnson, the guy under the car, was one of the biggest jerks I've ever known. I'm not surprised someone killed him."

My back is to the body as I share my feelings about my dead boss with Quentin. I don't notice the new guy on the scene until he asks, "So miss, did you want to kill the victim?"

The interloper is attractive with brown skin, a well shaped bald head and eyes the color of amber. His clothing fits his tall, well-built frame like he knows how to shop. He might have a kind smile but he isn't smiling when he asks me if I'm a murderer. Last time, I annoyed Detective Rousch by being underfoot during his investigation. I never truly feared he suspected me of murder. I didn't have a motive to kill Tiffany unlike what I just admitted.

I glare at the man I assume to be a detective because of his demeanor and question, "Detective, who hasn't given me his name, this is the third body I've found at a car dealership in less than a month. Quentin's been nearby every time I've found a body. Plus I sold him a car. I'm comfortable with him. I don't know you, but I don't have to answer any questions unless my lawyer is present and you take me in for questioning. I'm invoking my right to remain silent. I learned something during the last murders."

I wobble as I rise from the ground. "This case is none of my business. Policeman, a little hint, you might want to talk to the people in the trailer individually. I'm sure some of them have more experience with questioning by law enforcement than I do. I'm not sure if they're savvy enough to ask for a lawyer."

I fumble in my bag and pull out a business card. "When you need to talk to me, you can call my lawyer to set up an appointment. If nothing else, my unfortunate body finding has taught me to do things officially. I'm sure I'll hear from you."

He dips his head in a quick nod, but he watches my conversation with Quentin. He doesn't seem to have noticed Detective Rousch.

Angling my body toward Quentin I ask, "Are you allowed to give me a ride home in my car? As you can tell, I don't want to drive alone but I don't want to panic Lando either."

He shrugs and glances toward his uncle who's still taking pictures of the area but not talking to the nameless detective, "Maybe you should call Sean. I'm sure he'll leap at the chance to drive up in his white Charger."

"It's an F-350 not a Charger. Only middle age crisis men buy Chargers. Go back to your friends at the ambulance. I promise I will text you back. I'm sorry I've been avoiding you. I've been hiding for the past few weeks. These nasty coincidences show me you and Mac are supposed to be part of my life. Thanks for trying," I reply.

"This isn't professional but neither is our relationship. Of course, I could pretend I'm checking you for shock," he says as he wraps his arms around me.

Darting small glances at the detective, I'm aware he's watching and listening to my conversation with Quentin like he's taking mental notes. I nod at him and make eye contact. He must catch sight of Detective Rousch, because the nameless detective yells, "Who are you and why are you on my crime scene?"

Having no desire to be involved in their confrontation, I pull away from Quentin, walk the long way around the building. Once I'm out of view of Gene's body I dial Lando's number. I don't want to, but I have to call him.

Resting my head on the building, I plead, "I need a ride home. I don't feel up to driving. Can you come get me?"

After hesitating for a second, Lando replies, "I shouldn't have let you face that jerk today alone. I had a bad feeling yesterday when you avoided me. I'm on my way, and I'm grabbing Sean."

A laugh escapes me, and I catch the rude detective crossing his arms at my inappropriate outburst at a crime scene, "Additional rescuers are always welcome. I'll wait for you."

I turn my phone off after my brief conversation with Lando. I don't want to explain what's happened. If I try to talk to Lando, my emotional ice might break. I don't need more emergency personnel watching me collapse. I also don't want the police officer to overhear me say anything he could misconstrue. I need to be strong.

My choices are walking around the sales trailer containing my coworkers or by Gene's sports car with his body underneath it to return to my car. The dead body feels less intimidating than the trailer full of possible killers. I ignore the heated discussion between the Detective Rousch and Detective No Name, and they ignore me. I walk around the back of the Camaro, and catch a flash of orange and white on the back window ledge of the car. I move closer to the death vehicle to check. It's a skinny orange and white cat.

No one else appears to notice the cat. The cat isn't my problem. Gene never talked about a pet, and his empathy quotient was stuck at zero. All of the windows are closed. The cat might be a clue. Even if the cat has nothing to do with Gene's death, I don't want it to die in the hot car. I have to tell the police.

I keep watching the cat as I address the Detective with no name and I point at the car, "Sir, there's a cat in the car on top of Gene."

The Detective replies, "I thought you weren't talking to me without a lawyer present."

Gesturing toward the car, I say, "This isn't my opening conversational gambit. I like animals. I'm not sure how long he's been in the car, and I don't want him to become overheated or further contaminate your crime scene. He could pee on important evidence. I thought you should be aware he's in the car before I leave."

He keeps his attention fixed on me and doesn't look toward the car, "Do you recognize the cat? How do you know it's a male cat? Is it your cat?"

I peer into the back window of the Camaro, moving closer to the murder scene, but not Gene's body, "He's not altered, and I saw him from behind. I rescued a cat last month, so I did some research on cats. I've never seen that animal in the car. He appears skinny. Is he considered evidence?"

He rubs his hand over his temples as if I'm giving him a headache, "Of course the cat is evidence. He's in the crime scene. We'll get him out. This isn't your concern. You can leave now. I'll call your lawyer and set up a meeting."

The stray cat distracts so I don't take the detective's obvious dismissal as my chance to escape the upcoming tense scene. The cat looks pathetic. I want to save him. There's room in Lando's house for another pet. This cat is the opposite of my pampered, spoiled Annika. His fur's orange and white but covered in dirt. He's thin and one of his eyes appears cloudy. This cat's body carries marks of valor with several angry looking bloody scratches from a fight.

I stay at the back of the car as the cat meows at my attention, "What are you going to do with the cat? Can I adopt him after you're done with him?"

The detective waves his hand toward Gene's body, "There is a dead man underneath the car and you're worried about some strange alley cat. What's wrong with you?"

I roll my eyes and say, "Obviously the cat didn't murder him. That animal looks like he's had a hard life, and I'd like to help him."

The detective already seems to suspect me of killing Gene. I don't want to give him any additional ammunition. I keep the thought that sometimes karma catches up with people in my head and off my lips. I'll ask about the cat again during my interview with my lawyer present. I need to disappear before my coworkers bother to vacate the trailer.

I'm out front waiting for Lando and Sean to arrive when one of the police officers opens the door to the sales trailer. I pause to listen to the confrontation. With five police officers on the site, I'm not sure why it took them so long to find the other employees. Dalton, the young sales-man, and Phoebe, the title clerk, emerge into the sunlight when one of the officers opens the door. I watch the confrontation from my position in the shade cast by the trailer and hope my coworkers won't notice me if I stay still and in the shadows.

I overhear an officer ask them, "Why didn't you two come out of the trailer with all of the sirens and the commotion?"

Dalton shrugs and answers, "This isn't the best neighborhood. If something illegal's going down, we don't want to be involved. Gene hates it when we're too busy talking to the cops to talk to the customers."

"How do you discover if customers are trying to buy cars if you hide in the sales trailer all day?" The officer asks.

Phoebe fields this question. "The customers who buy cars here, need cars, so they knock on the door of the trailer or just open it all rude like."

"So this is a car lot where you people are supposed to be selling cars and you think it's rude if customers want to buy a car. How does this place stay open?"

This conversation fascinates me, and I can't resist listening. I don't have anything to contribute. Nothing any of the employees at this lot have done over the past week has made sense to me.

Dalton pats his man bun and replies, "When Gene's here, he makes sure all three salespeople are on the lot and scoping for customers. He's such a monster that when he's gone, we hide."

He tries to glance around the dealership, "By the way, today isn't an auction day, have you seen Gene? He'd be so mad that you people are here talking to us. I'm guessing it's about some trouble around here. I told ya, we stay outta it. You know what, Violet and Walter are missing too. Did something happen to Violet? She's always findin' trouble. Did ya hear she found two bodies at her last job?"

The tall detective with no name glides up to join the uniformed officer, pulls out his tablet, and asks, "I'm not sure who any of the people you are talking about are. Could you please give me a description of the people who you just mentioned?"

I eavesdrop from behind the sales trailer in the shadows as Dalton describes everyone in unflattering terms. "Walter's the old dude who works here. He's tired all the time. He tries to hide from the customers the most. He always yakking about how he sold food and booze wholesale to restaurants for years, but they fired him when he got old. He's lazy. Violet's the opposite of Walter, she's always trying to sell cars. She doesn't like to hang out in the trailer or garage with the rest of us. She grabs all of the customers. She worked at one of them fancy dealerships and went to college so she thinks she's better than us. Gene's the boss, and he makes us work. Genius Used Cars belongs to him, and he makes sure everyone knows it. He's a real jerk."

As Dalton's trashing everyone's character, Walter's beat up old car sputters onto the lot. Something must bother him about the uniformed officers and the two marked police cars. He tries to turn around to leave the lot. Dalton interrupts his apt description of Gene to wave at Walter's car, "Hey, that's Walter's car trying to leave the lot. I wonder what he's running from." The officer who's interviewing Dalton calls one of his coworkers and asks them to apprehend Walter so he can also be interviewed.

Within a minute, Sean and Lando drive into the lot in Sean's white Ford F-350. My hero in a shiny white truck arrives with my faithful protector in the form of my grandfather. I pause my eavesdropping and dash to the truck.

I jump on the running boards and try to open the back door of the extended cab pick-up. Lando rolls down the window and asks, "Violet, what's going on? You called and said you needed a ride as soon as possible. I grabbed Sean and he broke all of the speed limits to get here. Why are police here? What happened?"

I shake my head so vigorously that I risk falling off the running boards, "I gave him Mac's business card and told him I didn't want to talk to him without my counsel present."

I start to cry. I try so hard to be brave but Lando's questions push me over the edge. "I found another dead body. Two bodies should be the limit in a month if someone isn't a cop or an EMT."

Lando pokes his head out of the truck as if he's trying to spot the body, "Honey, why didn't you tell me? After you told me to come get you, I tried to call you back. Why didn't you answer your phone?"

Through my tears I say, "I'd cry, and I didn't want the cops to see me lose it. I hate dead bodies, and I'm sick of the police."

Sean throws the truck into park and comes around to lift me off the running boards, "Was it an accident? Did Walter have a heart attack? Whose body did you find?"

I cuddle into his broad chest and reply, "Gene Johnson was under his bright yellow Camaro. Unless he accidentally ran over himself after adding some random orange and white cat to the interior of his car, it's another murder."

Lando interrupts me and says, "This is obviously stressful. Violet doesn't have to give us a blow by blow account of finding her third body in less than a month. Unlike Tiffany, no one has any loyalty to Gene Johnson. He can rest in as much peace as he deserves. Let's go home."

Lando stops asking questions once I'm tucked into the backseat. If I had any energy remaining, I'd be surprised. I welcome the silence on the ride home. When we reach Lando's lovely Victorian, I feel safe. Even though Tiffany's murderer tried to kill me in this house, and I've only lived here for a couple of months, somehow this place feels more like home than the house where my parents raised me. It's the presence of Lando, my cat Annika, the books, and the DVDs. Sean might factor into the equation, as well, but I'm not ready to deal with that relationship yet.

When we enter the house, I announce to Lando and Sean, "I need to call Mac because I gave the nameless detective her card. I learned that talking to the police without a lawyer present was unpleasant. This time, I'll be smart and use her expertise. Then I'm cuddling my cosseted cat. I should be ready to talk to you guys in an hour or two. Bye."

SIX

"I'll sell a car to anyone who is smart enough to buy a Genius used car."

I enter the bookshelf lined foyer and walk up Lando's dignified staircase with the wide landing. The six foot stained glass window creates beautiful colors on the stairs even on this overcast day. It's Pittsburgh, most of the days are cloudy. I walk to the sliding bookcase and push on the edge to make it move. His house is like living in a Scooby Doo episode with its plethora of bookshelves, including this sliding one that connects the two sides of his house. A regular door connects the two kitchens but today I want the magic of the moving bookshelf.

In her five weeks of residence, Annika has claimed my bed with the wrought iron headboard and light muslin canopy as her own. It's convenient she loves this space. Each side of Lando's merged house is over 3,000 square feet excluding the basements and the attics, so if she wanted to disappear it would be easy.

I clutch Annika to my chest and go to one of the attic libraries. I choose the horror library because it reflects today's mood. I pick Mac's name from the short list of contacts on my phone. I'm surprised when she answers my call. Like Quentin, I've been avoiding Mac since we solved Tiffany's case.

Mac answers the phone, "Hey girl, long time no hear. I've been giving you space but tomorrow I was going to come over to Lando's and pull your butt out of the bed. You've officially passed my time limit for being sorry for yourself. I know you'll be shocked that I don't have many female friends, I decided to make you one. If you've spent the past weeks in bed with the tall glass of yummy carpenter, then I totally understand you ditching me."

I plop into the window seat, "Actually, I tried to get back on the horse of selling cars after weeks of moping. I meant to call you. I tried to prove that I'm strong, but I found another dead body today."

She laughs, "Wow, you're like that teapot from *Beauty and the Beast* on that old person mystery show. Does your grandfather love that show? Did you spill everything to the police again? Or are you calling me in my professional capacity?"

"Of course, Lando loves *Murder She Wrote*. He owns all of the books based on the show in hardcover. I'm not sure if he watched the show. On a different note, are you allowed to be my friend, if you're my lawyer? Hearing your voice reminds me I'd rather have you as a friend than a lawyer. Can you recommend anyone?" I ask.

"If you didn't kill this guy, I can be your lawyer. How hard can it be? Plus I owe you for letting Tiffany rest in peace by catching her killer and almost dying in the process."

I say, "I didn't kill Gene Johnson, but this time I might

be a viable suspect. The detective on the case never gave me his name. He acted annoyed I wouldn't talk to him without my lawyer present. My worry about the cat in the car more than the dead guy under the car made him look at me like I was psychotic or a killer or maybe both. It's like when the boys were accused of being serial killers on *Supernatural* because sometimes the monsters they killed looked human."

Mac interrupts my television tangent and says, "Ohh, Gene Johnson, I knew him. He was a regular at the Club where Tiffany and I worked. He tipped generously in front of people but then right before they left, he would take half the tip money off the table. We weren't allowed to touch the tips until the party left the bar. He always left fifteen percent to the penny, but he wanted his buddies to think he was leaving thirty or forty percent. After a few times of that trick, we avoided him. He stopped coming in after his troubles. I wasn't surprised about his legal issues and we laughed at him for it. Why did you take a job working for him?"

I bury my face in Annika's fur and catch a mouth full of fluff when I try to answer, "I wish I'd talked to you before I took the job. It's like when Buffy took the dumb job at the fast food restaurant." This time I pull out of the fantasy television tsunami, "Anyway, he offered, and I didn't have to interview. I planned to quit today. One week of his nonsense was enough for me. I hope the fact I didn't need the job will help convince the detective I have no reason to kill Gene."

She responds but it sounds like she's talking from the bottom of a well, "Why don't I come over this afternoon?

I went to the gym and I'm free for the rest of the day. Does your cute contractor work on the weekends? I'll bring wine, and we can objectify him as we discuss your case."

"What happened to your voice? Your idea sounds wonderful. I'll hide in a room and read until you arrive because I can tell the story once instead of several times. Do you remember Quentin?" I ask.

She replies, "You're talking through the car, because I'm on my way. Of course, I remember him. He was the other cute guy you managed to enthrall. Wasn't he the nephew of the last detective, Rousch, and also an EMT? Have you heard from him?"

I nod but feel silly because while I can see my reflection in the mirror, she can't see through the phone, "I wouldn't say I enthralled him, but we did go on a date to Station Square. I met him and his uncle for breakfast this morning and he followed me to Genius Used Cars. He's been texting me for the last few weeks, too. I haven't answered him either. The universe must be telling me I need you both in my life."

She says, "Remind me again, is Quentin the tall, dark haired guy who is built long and lean like a swimmer? He and your redheaded contractor were not happy to meet each other the night when Tiffany's murderer almost killed you. I think they only reined it in because they didn't want to add to the drama. Maybe it should be me, Lando, and Sean. As much as I love drama and guys with sculpted bodies, I think talking to him might be something you save for a time when Sean isn't around. We also might need to tap his uncle,

Detective Rousch if we have trouble with your new police officer."

"Yes, that's Quentin. I like him, too. This month's been too confusing for me to concentrate on which boy I like better. You're right, I can call him at a different time. I hate talking to people about finding bodies. His uncle was doing a little investigating at the scene when I ducked out with Lando and Sean." I answer as I tug on my ponytail.

When Mac arrives at Lando's, she rings the doorbell which activates the gong which resonates through both sides of the house. Lando must invite Mac in because we all meet in the receiving library. This front library contains incredible bay windows that limit the number of book cases but welcome beautiful natural light when the sun shines in Pittsburgh. Lando sits at his gigantic, antique desk his cleaning lady keeps polished to a glimmering shine. Sean grabs the red settee, Mac takes the comfortable reading chair with the footstool that matches the red velvet of the settee. Rather than joining Sean on the couch, I pull the wooden high back chair with the faded embroidery on the seat into the center of the room. When I place my chair in the middle of the circle of my closest friends, it's like an old fashioned interrogation chamber from a classic movie without the spotlight.

It's easier to collect my thoughts if I stand and pace. So I jump up and ask, "Lando, do you mind taking notes? Last time this happened, it was so much easier to recall situations from the notes that we took closest to the events. I'm not planning to investigate Gene Johnson's murder, but I want to have my thoughts in order in case the police decide to blame me. This time you're in charge of the notebook to keep the cat from hiding it."

He pulls open a drawer with an ornate handle while he talks, "Sure, I always have extra notebooks around the house. I buy them by the case. Sometimes, I like to take notes on the various books I read. Usually I take notes on a whole series in a single notebook. I then shelve the notebooks next to the book series. I hate writing in the physical books because the inscriptions and notes of the long dead in used books always seem sad to me. There's even a hint of melancholy when the author's left personal notes to friends or family. I hope when I die, the people I love will appreciate my notebooks and my book collection." He points toward the closest bookcase, "That's one of the main reasons I invited you out here Violet. Your father doesn't care about my books but I hoped you would come to care for me and, by extension, my lifelong passion."

I walk over to the bookcase on the opposite wall and run my hand over the colorful dust jacketed spines, "Lando, this isn't the time or the place for this conversation, but I'm honored by this opportunity. This has been one of the most memorable times of my life. You've gotten to know me through my love of television, and I've started reading. I'm looking forward to enjoying more books once the real life mysteries end."

As I walk the room, I tell Lando, Sean, and Mac about my morning, "After one week at Genius Used Cars, I couldn't continue at the job. Most of the other employees make me a little uncomfortable. Gene and his repo guy, Butch, are the most disquieting followed by Phoebe, the miserable title clerk, then Walter the old burned out salesman. The service guy, Iggy, never appeared in his building. Dalton, the young salesman, seemed to be the nicest until I heard him throw the rest of us, especially me, under the bus to the police this afternoon."

Mac interrupts, "Please start at the beginning of your day today. Your impressions of the other staff will sound like hearsay or gossip when the police interview you. It's my job to get you ready for an actual police interview. You think Detective Rousch was hard on you during the Roar Motors case, but he tried to be professional yet pleasant. If you had to find another body, it would have been better in his jurisdiction. Then I'm going to need some background about how you were dumb enough to work for Gene Johnson. If you had asked me, I'd have told you to say 'no way.'"

I tug on my ponytail and turn toward Mac, "This morning, I parked my car behind the service building to keep it away from the lot. Gene doesn't like our personal vehicles to be mistaken for saleable cars. Plus my retro looking Fiat draws attention away from the sea of used budget cars. Even though I bought my car from Genius Used Cars, it isn't their typical vehicle."

Mac interrupts again, "The police are going to cut you off as you begin to talk rapturously about your cute car. Those are details that have no bearing on the case. They simply want the facts as clearly as possible."

I'm getting annoyed with Mac for derailing my train of thought. "I'm trying to tell my friends about finding my third dead body since moving to Pittsburgh. This isn't a police interview."

She shakes her head at me, "You need to be ready for a real police interview. Start thinking like a suspect and not the cute little girl who found the body. They can't pin the last two murders on you because they have a confession, but the cop's theory might be that you snapped from the stress or you thought you could get away with murder because you learned from the last case. Maybe you killed this jerk because you couldn't handle him. You're an easy suspect and cops like easy suspects. They also think anyone who lawyers up has something to hide."

Mac's speech shocks me. I try to be a nice person. In the car business, being nice has been a challenge. I live with my vibrant yet elderly grandfather. Until Pittsburgh, I've hidden from reality and tried to remain as forgettable as possible. I don't understand how people who don't know me could think I killed someone.

I glance at Sean who's being quiet and then look at the floor, "Mac, thanks for the wake-up call. I'm sure I didn't help my case by acting like Gene deserved to die. I probably should have cried and acted upset."

Mac cuts me a break. "It's better that you didn't pull out the fake tears. Some cops have a sixth sense for phony sadness. You might have acted weird but at least when they interview you with me present, you'll be the same person. Continue your account of finding the body."

I walk toward the bay window and spin back to face Mac, "I parked my car behind the service building. When I saw Gene's distinctive yellow Camaro, its front end was smashed. I looked down, and I saw his head and shoulders under the car. At several feet from the body, it was obvious I couldn't help him. The car hid the blood and everything else. I called 911 immediately."

She jabs her finger at me, "Did you approach the body or touch it at any point?"

I shake my head, "No, I have an aversion to blood, and no one could help him."

She stares at me, "Did you touch the car?"

I rub my hands together as if it'll spark my tactile memory, "I may have touched the back of the car to steady myself, but I don't remember touching it."

"Were you ever inside the car?" She asks as she paces the room.

I wrap my arms around my middle, "No, absolutely not. Gene invited me for a ride with him at some future date. After last night, I planned to quit my job today. I took Quentin and Detective Rousch with me for courage this morning."

She lifts her eyebrows at me, "Why would your quit your job of less than a week?"

I run my hand across my forehead. Her questions make me jumpy. I'm worried I won't be able to stop fidgeting tomorrow, making me appear to be guilty. "Starting yesterday, Gene Johnson made my spidey senses tingle. He never touched me inappropriately, but he moved closer into my personal space after Sean dropped me off. He and his repo guy Butch stood on either side of me as if they were trapping me. The Shelby situation pushed me over the edge. Honestly, I didn't need this job. The treatment of the desperate customers made me uncomfortable. Selling cars fills a need, it's not like selling comic books. People need reliable transportation."

Mac opens her mouth to stop my tangent, but I hold up my hand. "This part's critical so the police know about the shady practices that widen the suspect pool significantly. In a week of working at Genius Used Cars, I noticed Gene Johnson might have been scamming customers who needed cars. By my second day, I began documenting the uncomfortable things on my phone. I wasn't sure about the legality but keeping track of irregularities doesn't hurt. The app time stamps everything. I want to share this with the police. I wanted to take a look at the files in the trailer to see if I could catch anything and maybe take some pictures with my phone. I planned to contact the Attorney General's office next week with my observations, especially after Shelby."

"Who's Shelby and why do you keep mentioning her name?" Mac asks.

Taking a deep breath, I reply, "Last night I'm certain Gene forced or maybe coerced a young woman to have sex with him so she could buy a car. I wanted to get a look at her file today. Her name is Shelby, and she has the most adorable baby girl, Ruby."

Lando thumps his fist on the desk and asks, "Way to bury the lead. Why didn't you tell me about the stuff that was bothering you at Genius? I never heard anything like that about him or you wouldn't have been working there."

I pivot toward him and put my hands on my hips, "I wanted to act like an adult and not run to my grandfather to fix everything. It started as a creepy feeling. The last case taught me it doesn't hurt to document stuff. The worst thing was Shelby last night, and I couldn't talk to you about it. I needed to process everything. You would never have let me go back this morning to try to get a look at her file."

Mac says, "You can share the unethical practices you witnessed with the police after you tell them about finding the body. Print out your notes and your resignation letter. I'll take them and give them the evidence. You could still have killed him as a form of vigilante justice or self-defense. However, the fact you didn't need the job helps your case."

Annika saunters into the room and twines around my ankles reminding me about the orange and white cat at the scene, "What about the cat?"

Mac pinches the bridge of her nose, "What are you babbling about now?"

"Someone put a skinny, battered tomcat in Gene's car. I pointed him out to the detective on the scene. The cat might be a clue, but he also probably messed up the crime scene some. I would like to adopt the cat. My fixation on the animal seemed to bother the detective. I kept talking about the cat and acted more worried about the stray than the dead guy under the car. By the way, Lando can I save another cat?" I say as I reach down to pet Annika.

Lando replies, "Sure, a twelve bedroom house can hold more than one cat."

Mac says, "I think the cat's a distraction. It sounds like you hyper-focused on the animal at the crime scene. It might be suspicious if you didn't ask about the animal. Now we wait for the police to call to schedule an interview. At this point, I don't want your responses to sound rehearsed."

Sean remains silent during this entire conversation. He must be thinking I'm such a flake and not worth the time or the work. Lando's stuck with me because I'm family. My drama isn't worth everyone's time. Sean stands up and I expect him to head for the door. Instead, he walks over to me, and enfolds me in his arms.

He buries his face in my hair and says, "I'm so sorry I've been so busy this week that I didn't notice your worries. I'm sorry this happened to you again."

His embrace feels like my invitation to breakdown. He pulls me onto the settee with him and lets me cry.

Mac grabs Lando and says, "We're a third and fourth wheel right now. Let's go order lunch in another room like the kitchen."

I have no idea how much time passes. After I'm finished crying, Sean keeps holding me. We don't talk. I don't try to think. We sit in silence until Mac pops back into the room. "Lunch is here. We ordered burritos, because I want to eat food the size of a brick. Come to the kitchen."

SEVEN

"No need to read that fine print!"

During lunch, Mac tells funny, inconsequential stories about working at a soulless corporate law firm. She says, "I worked in a gentleman's club for several years, while working my way through law school. I can put in several years making stupid money for this corporate firm. At the end, I'll have enough saved to open my own practice and contribute to society.

Mac shakes her head, "Don't get me wrong, I'm not a real do-gooder, but I'd like to use this expensive law degree to help women and children who can't help themselves. Until then, I've started doing a little pro bono work for foster kids. I'm not putting Violet's case through the official firm. They're a waste. I should be able to do this on my own time like our last case."

She waves at us, "All I ask is that you three help me sometimes with things for the foster kids."

Lando puts his hand up in protest and says, "Money isn't an issue for me. I paid off this house years ago, and unlike most car salesman, I saved money my whole career. I'm comfortable, and I want to pay you for your time."

Mac smiles at him, "You cared enough about Tiffany to risk yourselves to solve her murder. I can't pay you back, so I'm paying it forward to other kids caught in the foster care system. Help me do that and we're good. Plus I like hanging out with all of you, I need some new friends, and the law firm only offers demons and vampires."

"Does that mean you work for Wolfram and Hart?" asks Sean with a grin showing his dimple.

She laughs and replies, "As a matter of a fact, I think I passed Spike in the hallway last week."

Lando looks back and forth between them and asks, "What joke am I missing here?"

I wave in the direction of the media room which was another library until I moved to Pittsburgh, "You know how we watched *Buffy*, and I told you *Angel*, the *Buffy* spinoff needed to wait until a happier time. Mac is speaking *Angel* code about her job. I'm so pleased to find another person in my circle who loves my fandom. Did I ever mention to you my graduate work focused on *Buffy the Vampire Slayer*?"

Mac says, "Every time you mention it, I think you're kidding. Who was dumb enough to pay for you to go to college and graduate school to study *Buffy*?"

Lando raises his hand and says, "That would be me. Admittedly, her parents presented her degree as Popular Culture and Media Studies which sounds much more academically rigorous than studying television shows about vampires and cheerleaders."

I swivel my head to look at Lando and ask, "What do you mean you paid for my degrees? My parents always acted as if they were the ones who paid for school."

Lando runs his hand through his thick white hair and says, "Oops. I never needed the recognition or thanks, so I allowed them to pretend they were your funders." He gestures at Sean and Mac, "Can we talk about this another time?"

I need to discuss this new information with Lando, but not in front of an audience. My parents have to answer some questions before I move forward with this particular discussion. I also have to think about the ramifications of Lando paying for my schooling.

Explaining my degree calms me, "My major explored television and fiction as a significator of culture. *Buffy* functions as a modern allegorical epic that explores coming of age at the turn of the millennium. I love television, especially fantasy television."

"But what did your major prepare you to do as a career? Fight demons?" Mac asks while raising her eyebrows.

I shrug, "I wanted to become a tenured Professor of Popular Culture. Then I discovered the current crop of professors love their jobs too much to ever want to retire. I looked for a job in academia for a while but having no health care scared me. Apparently, my Bachelors, Masters, and Doctoral degrees have prepared me to enter the exciting world of car sales and murders."

Mac tosses her long dark hair over her shoulder, "On your snarky note, I should leave and you should rest. I'll call as soon as the police contact me to set up an interview. We should go as soon as they try to schedule it. I want your account to be fresh."

After Mac leaves, I tell Lando and Sean I need some time alone. I leave them and go upstairs and cross to my side of the house. I enter the lovely sanctuary of my personal bathroom and take a shower to wash away the metaphorical stench of finding another body. I wrap my body in a fluffy pink bathrobe, open the bathroom door and scream. Sean's fist hovers in the air as he attempts to knock on the door.

Sean's face flames to match his hair, "I'm sorry to catch you in this situation. Lando sent me up to get you. Mac called before she got back to the city. The police would like to meet with you in an hour. Mac is on her way to pick you up." He points at my bare feet. "You should get dressed."

I clutch the robe closed with one hand and gesture toward it with the other, "So, you don't think I should try to go to the police station in my cute, fuzzy pink robe?"

He runs his hand through his thick red hair and says, "Although I think you look pretty in pink, I wouldn't be able to concentrate on asking you questions if you wore your robe. Lando and I will stay here because we don't want this to turn into a circus."

I get dressed with a smile on my face in spite of knowing I'm about to be interrogated by the police. Sean flirted and I responded. I run down the back staircase that leads to my kitchen which has a door between the two sides of the house.

Lando, Sean, and Mac wait for me in the receiving

library at the front of the house. Lando hugs me and whispers, "Good luck, kid. Just follow Mac's lead."

Sean reaches to hug me but I move away from him. If he hugs me, I won't want to let go of him. I don't want Mac to see me collapse into his arms again. Instead, I awkwardly reach my hand out to him for a handshake.

He shakes his head and says, "Seriously, Violet. If there's any day you need another hug, it's today."

He grabs my hand and pulls me toward him. Rather than hugging me, he tilts my head up so we are looking in each other's eyes.

He gently kisses me on the cheek, "You'll be fine. Tell the truth and listen to Mac."

"It's unanimous. I have to listen to you." I say to Mac as I pull away from Sean.

She crosses her arms over her chest and flips her long dark hair behind her, "Absolutely, listening to me should get you out of this mess. Don't tell the police you hated or feared your boss. People you don't like have a habit of dying around you which tends to make the police suspicious."

"Blaming me for the last murders is totally unfair. I helped find the real killer like Richard Castle." I say and bite my lip.

Mac says, "This is a different jurisdiction and their contention might be that you learned about killing from witnessing the last case. On *Castle*, the mystery writer hero was accused of murder a few times. I spent the last month watching this one because without Tiffany, I got bored. It's not like my new friend was returning my calls."

Her mention of *Castle* impresses me with Mac's excellent taste but the zinger of my avoidance of her makes me feel guilty. I tilt my head and say, "I'm sorry about not getting back to you. I'm not a murderer. Seriously, I'd have to be a complete idiot. The murderer got away with several murders before meeting me, but was convinced by me to confess. This wasn't exactly an example of success."

She strides out the front door and talks over her shoulder, "We can talk more about strategy in my car. We need to leave. I've found it's best not to keep the police waiting on a suspect. It makes them crankier."

EIGHT

"You can trust me over what you read."

Mac's car doesn't fit her personality. She drives a dark blue Ford Taurus. It's mundane and similar to every other sedate four-door sedan. Pointing at the car, I ask, "Did you buy your car from Tiffany?"

She pats the side of the car, "Yes, she got me a fantastic deal on the vehicle. One month's salary paid for this used car with no additional car payments. I've had it for three years, and it runs like a champ. I never worry about leaving it in the parking garage all day. I love my boring car."

I stand next to the passenger side, waiting for her to unlock the vehicle, "It's not the type of car I picture for an up and coming lawyer."

"It's wonderful because it doesn't stand out in the garage or on the roads for being too flamboyant or ostentatious. I adore the camouflage. The way I dress and wear makeup makes people notice me. I don't need anyone to ogle my car." She explains as she gets into it.

She pulls down the visor to check her makeup and

continues, "I'm saving every extra dime to open my own law practice. An expensive lease payment to impress the partners isn't in my game plan. If you want to know a secret, I buy most of my fantastic wardrobe at consignment stores. I find it cute that you do everything to hide in the background with your lackluster clothes and no makeup look, but you got a memorable, cute car. By the way, today's dull ensemble is perfect for your police interview."

I scan my outfit to make sure it's clean, "Hey, my black leggings, long gray tunic, and black sneakers aren't a fashion statement. I picked these clothes for comfort in case the police interrogate me for hours."

Mac sighs as she pulls away from Lando's house, "You have counsel with you, and they think you're paying me by the hour. I doubt they'll interrogate you for hours. Remember in most of your beloved television shows, the questioning takes less than fifteen minutes. This is a preliminary interview because you found the body. Cause of death seems clear with Gene under the car. You weren't covered in his blood or screaming at his corpse. Their main evidence against you is your unemotional reaction. Some fake shock or sadness might have prevented their suspicions."

I rub the back of my neck, "I'm awful at fake tears or pretending to be sad. In college, I took an acting class but dropped it the first week. My true reactions always show on my face. During the mirror exercises, I couldn't ever follow a partner. I can't play poker either, my every emotion flows across my face and through my body language. My best bet is telling the truth."

She lectures me as she drives. "At least you learned to have counsel. People who believe their innocence will protect them sometimes end up in prison or on death row. Listen to Lando and Sean and follow my lead. We aren't going to talk about the case anymore because I don't want you to sound rehearsed."

She distracts me during the ride by asking about how many hours of television I had to watch to earn a television degree. We talk about the type of shows I watched and the ways I interpreted them. I love talking about television to someone who appears to be listening. I feel fine until we pull into the parking lot of the police station. At that point, I start to sweat and my stomach roils.

As we walk into the police station, I observe the layout and the police officers. There are fewer officers and desks than I'm used to seeing on police procedurals like *Law & Order* or *Castle*. During the Roar investigation, Detective Rousch interviewed me at the dealership. I only had to come in to sign my statement after I helped solve the case. That time I was cocooned in a bubble of shock. This interview is my first in an interrogation room, and I'm afraid I'm a suspect.

A uniformed officer escorts us to a room. The paint on the plain block walls is a faded yellow which resembles urine. The room has a faint hint of the acrid scent. The table's bolted to the floor and there's only a single chair in the room. I guess Mac is expected to stand. Maybe I'm supposed to stand. I don't know the protocol, and my anxiety starts to flare. This room is far more intimidating than the dumpy service lounge at Roar Motors. I miss Detective Rousch even if he reminded me of the grim reaper. I wonder if he'll be here since he was looking around this morning at the crime scene.

The detective with no name enters the interview room. Mac says, "I notice only a single chair. I'm sure it's an oversight because you arranged this interview with me rather than my client. Therefore, you knew she planned to bring counsel. I'm not sure the reason for no chair for counsel unless it's an intimidation tactic, a rather amateurish one at that."

He glances down at her from his impressive height and replies, "I hope your client isn't paying you by the word. If she is, she'll soon pay for your condo."

Mac tilts her head back to look him in the eye. "My payment arrangements with my client are not your concern. Sarcastic comments to a client's counsel aren't a professional way to start this interview. I still don't have a chair, and you haven't introduced yourself."

A knock at the door heralds an officer carrying a chair for Mac. Someone or multiple someones are behind the glass watching this interview. The unseen observers in police procedurals always impressed me. Castle cracked jokes if he wasn't allowed in the interview room with Beckett. When I'm the one being interviewed, and I don't know whose watching, it's disquieting.

He stares over the top of her head toward the mirrored wall, "Good afternoon, I'm Detective Andrews. I am the lead investigator on this case."

"I'm Maxine MacAlister counsel for Violet Landovic." She says with a sniff.

He turns to me. "For the record, what is your full name."

I swallow before I answer. "My name is Violet Amelia Landovic. I guess technically it's Dr. Violet Landovic. I have a Ph.D. in Popular Culture. Not that my graduate work has anything to do with this situation. Do you need me to spell my last name? A lot of times people add extra letters, it's the weird translation of Cyrillic letters into the English alphabet, because the letters don't always line up perfectly."

Mac shakes her head and says, "Violet, stop rambling."

"That's okay. It's better to spell your entire name. We wouldn't want any wrong information in the file." He glares at Mac but smiles at me.

Maybe he's trying to play good cop with my lawyer in the role of bad cop. After his annoyance at the crime scene, I'm surprised he's being civil. It seems as if Mac annoys him more than I do.

He says, "Please describe your morning."

My voice quivers as I say, "I arrived at Genius Used Cars at 10:30 in the morning. The dealership opens at 11:00 on Saturdays, but I think being on time is late. I like to be at least fifteen minutes early. I was half an hour early because traffic's lighter on Saturdays. This was my first Saturday working at Genius Used Cars. Anyway, I parked behind the service building so my car didn't seem like an available vehicle. My grandfather bought my car for me last week at Genius which is how I got the job there."

"Violet." Mac interrupts my monologue. If I was a villain, I'd totally do the bad guy monologue. I'm doing one now, and I'm not even guilty. I don't want to leave any details out. Mac warned me about talking too much, but the Detective isn't stopping me.

"Sorry, sir. I'll get back to the point." I say and the heat of a blush rises up my neck.

He waves his hand at me, "Don't limit your response on my account. The more information you give me, the better I'll be able to understand the situation and your role in it."

I glance toward Mac, and she frowns at me. She told me to keep it brief and follow her lead. It's time to obey. "When I got out of my car, I noticed Gene's yellow Camaro with a smashed front end. He always babied his car. My first thought was that he would be so upset about the damage. I looked down, and I saw his head protruding from underneath the car. I realized the front end damage wouldn't bother him since he was dead."

"Why did you think he was dead?" Detective Andrews watches me as he asks the question.

I fidget with my ponytail, "He was underneath a car. His skin was the wrong color even if his shirt was the same color as my name, purple. Thankfully, the car hid the blood and other yucky stuff. His color looked like Tiffany's when I found her. The other person wasn't dead yet when I found him so his color was better."

He gestures like he's rewinding, "Wait, roll it back. Who are Tiffany and the other dead body? We didn't find any other bodies at the scene."

"Didn't you research me or talk to Detective Rousch? My name makes it easy to find me. It's not like I have a common name. I've never met another Violet in person. Ethnic last names seem more common in Pittsburgh but mine's still a weird one. The murders at Roar Motors earlier in the month, I found the bodies. Well, the first one, Tiffany I found alone. The second one, I was with a group of people. Then the killer almost killed me. I'm surprised you didn't do your research." I grimace. I hate talking about the situation at Roar Motors.

The Detective clenches his jaw at my lecture. "Well, I've been busy collecting the evidence on this case. I actually just got back from a vacation. I was catching up on my work, and I didn't follow the Pittsburgh news while I was gone. As far as Rousch goes, this isn't his jurisdiction or his case."

Mac tosses her, long, black hair over her shoulder, "While your vacation is a fabulous topic of conversation, Detective, let's get back to the questions. Can we stipulate that my client may have acted in unusual fashion at the crime scene because of the trauma of discovering a third body in a month? This also explains how she knew he was dead. Perhaps you would like to take some time to read about Miss Landovic's heroism in helping to bring the real killer to justice. The murderer cornered her at her home and Miss Landovic had the presence of mind to tape the killer's confession."

As Mac dresses down the Detective, I hear sounds from the other side of the two way glass. I always thought the observation room was soundproof. However, it's laughter, and it must be loud so some of it can be heard faintly in here.

He takes a deep breath and asks, "Back to my questions. Did you notice anything odd about the scene?"

"Yes, I told you at the time about the cat. By the way,

how is he? I meant what I said about wanting to adopt him. He looked so sad trapped in the car. I wonder who would throw an innocent cat in the car. Even if he was a tomcat like Gene Johnson." I look at my hands.

He tilts his head and asks, "What do you mean a tomcat like Gene Johnson?"

I shudder. "Gene was gross. In fact, I was planning to quit. I had my resignation letter in my purse, and I brought Quentin and Detective Rousch with me. You could tell Gene was awful because he hated animals. The only time he corrected me was when he saw cat hair on my black shirt. Mostly Gene tried to be nice to me. I only figured out how awful he was last night."

I turn toward Mac when I hear her hand hitting her forehead. That's right, I wasn't supposed to volunteer information, especially about disliking Gene.

She sighs and says, "No reason to stop talking now, Violet. Finish telling the Detective about Gene's proclivities."

I put my hands on the table with the palms facing up, "Okay, here's the deal. I couldn't stand Gene. However, that's not a motive for me to kill him. Last night my customer asked me to watch her baby while she went into the trailer to sign paperwork with Gene. She was distraught when she left him and yelled at me about how he treated her. She wasn't clear exactly what happened but she implied he took advantage of her and not just economically. Last night, I realized I needed to quit. I told Detective Rousch and his nephew Quentin all about it at breakfast. They came to the dealership with me today as my backup. If I want another job selling cars, I can have one next week. Gene preyed on desperate people, and I've never been desperate."

"Back up, tell me about Gene's behavior toward women. We will come back to his interactions with you. Did you ever witness him behaving inappropriately to any other women?" He rubs his forehead.

I fiddle with one of my diamond earrings, "Yes, as a salesperson if I can't deliver a car, before I allow the customer to leave the dealership, I'm supposed to turn the customer over to a manager. This is called a TO, and it is standard operation procedure at all dealerships. At Roar Motors, customers often wanted to think about the car because cars for them were wants not needs. At Genius Used Cars, the vast majority of the customers desperately needed to buy cars. Many of them couldn't get financing even with all of the signs that guaranteed they could buy a car. The fine print of the financing is the down payment. Gene would grin when I brought him young or middle aged women who couldn't buy cars. He acted curt when I turned over men, older women, or couples who didn't have the down payments."

He crosses his arms making his significant biceps flex, "Did you ever see anything suspicious?"

Glancing toward the mirrored wall, I shiver, "As I mentioned, yesterday, I turned over a twenty something single mother who needed a car to get to work. I watched the interaction. Gene leaned into her and invaded her personal space on the lot in full view of everyone. I couldn't hear the conversation, but I saw her start to shake her head no. His face hardened, and he pointed at the car angrily. She looked at the car and looked down at her baby. Gene called me over and said he needed me to watch her brat while they went into his office to do the paperwork. This woman left me, a stranger with her baby, to do paperwork on a car."

I wave toward the mirrored wall as if it's a picture window, "At reputable dealerships, the offices where they do paperwork, have gigantic windows that open onto the showroom. Gene's door closes and locks. He took her in there. Forty-five minutes later, they reappeared, she yelled at me, threw up next to her new car, grabbed her baby from me, got in the car, and drove off."

He glances toward Mac and asks, "Did you ask him about the situation?"

I shake my head several times, "No way, I wanted to go home and shower. I felt stupid and a little scared."

Detective Andrews looks up from his tablet, "What happened next?"

"Gene had stood at the door of the trailer and watched me talk to Shelby, the poor customer who Gene hurt in some way. I'd already arranged a ride home from my friend, Sean. Sean stands well over six feet tall, and he's a contractor with tattoos. Gene stood about five feet, eight inches with a paunch. He bragged about being a runner, but Sean's arms appear larger than Gene's legs. Sean got out of the truck, he came over and swept me into his arms. Gene slammed the door of the trailer."

"If you were so upset, why didn't you quit last night?" He taps the table.

"I didn't think it would hurt to look around for some evidence of Gene's coercion of poor women or any other possible scams. Saturdays are busy, and I thought Gene's love of money and fear of Sean and Lando would protect me. I didn't expect to find him dead. I also talked to my friend Quentin and his police officer uncle at breakfast. They followed me to Genius Used Cars." I stare at the table to avoid his penetrating gaze and Mac's disapproval.

Mac sits next to me. I can't see her face. I think she's glaring at me for oversharing. I hope the police discover the evidence they need to find Gene's killer. The murderer in this case deserves a medal not jail time. The police don't like vigilante justice, so they can solve the case.

"So, Miss Landovic, who do you think killed Gene Johnson?"

I lift my gaze from the interview table and say. "Correct me if I'm wrong, but isn't finding the killer your job? I played amateur detective the last time I found a dead body and almost ended up murdered. Detective Rousch told me not to get involved in any more criminal cases. I wish I could have complied. Hopefully, I can be done with this one after today's interview."

Detective Andrews looks at Mac and says, "Thank you for allowing your client to be so cooperative. When she asked for counsel, I thought she would be so much more reticent. Thank you for allowing her to display such candor."

He waves his hand at Mac. "Based on your evocative body language, it bothered all of your lawyerly instincts. I might need to interview her again. She's still a suspect because everyone with opportunity and motive is one. Her honesty and unwillingness to try to place blame has been helpful. Sometimes, honest clients are better than safe ones."

"Detective, thank you so much for your analysis of today's interview. Perhaps we can talk when you finish law school." Mac replies with a glare.

He smiles at her and the light reflects off his gorgeous white teeth, "Interesting that you bring up law school, Miss MacAlister. My vacation was my celebration for passing the bar exam. For now, I'm staying with the police department, but I might see you as a professional colleague. I worked my way through law school as a police officer. How did you work your way through law school?"

Mac explodes at his smirk and his question. "I'm guessing from your sarcastic crack that you know darn well how I worked my way through law school. I'm not ashamed of my past. My job was legal. My client and I are done here. If you need to interview her again. Please call the number on my card. I can't say it's been a pleasure."

Mac grabs my arm and drags me out of the interrogation room and the police station. She's got an iron grip for such a tiny person. The rage must be increasing her strength. If I speak, she might transfer it all to me. After all, I'm the one who brought her into this mess. Her usual cases seem to involve people who never recognize her from her old job or they never have the courage to mention it.

NINE

"I've got cars, cars, cars!"

Mac marches to her sensible sedan, and I follow dragging my feet with a sinking heart. I'm sure she's going to chastise me for ignoring her instructions about the proper behavior of a crime witness. My responses in the interview room were the opposite of her advice.

She slams her car door and screams, "I hate sanctimonious, arrogant men who think they're better than me because of the way I earned money for law school. It wasn't the best job, but I did school work during the boring times. Some of them think I'm less of a lawyer because the last job on my resume was cocktail waitress at a gentleman's club. I don't think he was ever a customer because I'd have remembered him."

She changes the subject saving me from responding, "I don't care if it's only three o'clock in the afternoon, we are going for drinks on the South Side. You can ask one or both of your pretty friends to join us."

I raise my eyebrows, "I don't understand. You're the

only woman who I've come close to becoming friends with since I moved to Pittsburgh."

Mac shakes her head and sighs in exasperation, "The pretty's supposed to be ironic. Sean and Quentin are definitely attractive men, but not pretty. I need some eye candy even if they're both interested in you. Their presence at a bar with me lets me pretend they're chasing me."

"Tons of men must chase you until you're sick of it. You're a gorgeous, brilliant, head turning lawyer with your long, rippling, black hair, bottomless, dark eyes, and tiny perfect body." I look over her as I list her assets.

She snorts at me, "Most men don't want brilliant, because they find it intimidating. The incongruence of looking like a tiny doll and my oversized attitude tends to threaten many men. Guys often really dig damsels in distress. You've been rocking 'the wanna be a hero' demographic."

Shaking my head, I reply, "I find your description unfair. I've worked hard at saving myself. Sean and Quentin generally showed up after the excitement ended. Annika, the cat, was the only real knight in furry armor. We can't take Annika to a bar, and I don't feel like inviting the guys. It might be uncomfortable for everyone."

"Not for me, I think it'd be super entertaining." Mac says and she sighs. "Okay, I guess you and I can go to the South Side without them."

She reaches over and pats my hand, "You're the best type of damsel in distress, because you try so hard not to be. The girly girls who throw their hands in the air and ask men to save them draw the bottom feeders. Your rather pathetic attempts at being your own hero are an awesome tactic to pull in two attractive, employed guys."

I cross my arms, "Nothing I've ever done has been to impress men. I wanted to solve Tiffany's murder. I've also been trying to figure out who I am without the safety net of school."

She gives me the side eye, "I've had to be an adult since I graduated from high school. No one said to me that I was allowed to pick a silly major and hide in academia. I busted my behind for ten years to earn my life, and now I'm alone. I talk to my parents on the phone maybe once a month. I don't interact with either set of grandparents. I have no friends from college or law school, and my only real friend was recently murdered. I'm jealous of you, but I like you anyway."

I exhale, "My life wasn't perfect before Pittsburgh. Shallow described my entire time in school. Since I moved here, no one from school has contacted me. The murder gave my parents a reason to try to force me to come home. They always used paying for school as a way to control me, but I discovered they were taking credit for Lando's generosity. Lando seems to like having me around, but his main concern might be keeping my dad from tossing him in a nursing home and getting rid of his beloved books. In college when I studied every weekend, I dreamed about having one man interested in me. I thought I would've loved having two hot guys like me. Now I'm in the situation, and it's confusing."

She scowls and crosses her arms over her chest, "There's nothing confusing about it. You aren't married to either of them, so you should let them compete for you for a while. When you're done, I might console the loser."

Mac and I spend the ride to the South Side talking about her past relationships. She lectures me about all of the stupid things men do. Her exploits fascinate me more than any reality show. I avoided reality television because my advisor hated the entire genre with the passion of a thousand suns of rage.

Mac parks on a side street and takes me into a long, narrow, rather dingy bar. On a Saturday afternoon, a few older men sit on the retro looking but original fifties stools at the bar that dominates the left side of the single room. About fifteen empty tables are scattered around the rest of the area. The tables are black metal with brown laminate tops and the chairs match with ripped and scratched brown padding on the seats.

Mac walks up to the bar and orders two rum and cokes. Then we grab the table in the farthest corner. I whisper to Mac because I don't want to offend the bartender, "This doesn't seem like your usual type of hangout. I picture you sitting in one of the shiny, new places on Carson or at the South Side Works sipping a colorful drink and tossing your hair."

She rubs her hand over the scarred laminate, "I feel like I spend my whole life on display. I love this place, because no one cares about me or anything else at this time of day. At night, it's more of a college bar, so I avoid it. I discovered it as a college student when I began leading my double life of student by day and cocktail waitress by night."

I grip the metal top of the chair which wobbles under

my hand, "That sounds like a line from an eighties police procedural, like *Hill Street Blues*. Was it really so hard to balance?"

She turns toward the door while she answers me, "Yes. I didn't fit in with my fellow students whose parents were paying their way. Most of them didn't even work part-time jobs. Most of the women at the club avoided me, because they thought I'd look down on them. Tiffany was my only friend. Now I'm living the dream as a respectable attorney. It feels like my past still haunts me, especially when it slaps me in the face like it did today."

Mac turns in her seat and looks me in the eye. "This line of discussion needs to end. Let's talk about my nonprofit and the free work you'll be doing for it."

I play with my ponytail and say, "I'll help any way I can. However, I doubt I'm going to be out of work for long. This week, Lando's been talking to guys he knows about a job at one of the corporate dealerships. I took the job at Genius Used Cars because Gene offered it to me with no interview. Lando's trying to find something better. I wonder what's going to happen to Genius Used Cars with Gene dead. I guess it'll close, and all the cars will go back to auction."

My Buffy ringtone interrupts my prediction. It's an unknown number, but I answer. An anonymous young woman squeals, "Hi, I've never met you, but I think you worked for my dad, Gene Johnson. I need your help."

I pull the phone away from my ear because of the volume of her plea, but I put it back to my ear to reply, "Hi, I'm Violet Landovic, and I started working at Genius

Used Cars on Monday. I worked there for less than a week."

"Awesome, that's even better. Most of the people who I met who worked there for a long time were a little creepy. Do you know who I mean, like the old guy with the bad suits? How old are you? You don't sound old. I'm Gennifer with a G, and I'm sixteen. I meant it about needing your help. I think the car dealership is the only thing my dad left me. He never paid his child support on time. My mom and I are broke. I need someone who I can trust to run it." She continues to shout and Mac smiles as she listens to the conversation.

I interrupt when she slows down, "Whoa, I think you have the wrong person. I'm young, only twenty-seven. I've been selling cars for less than a month total. I have no idea how to run a dealership. I'm not sure how I can help you."

Gennifer starts again as I pause to breathe, "Do you know anyone who might want to help me run this dealership, at least until my dad's stuff starts to free up? My mom has cancer, and she can't work right now. Gene wouldn't pay child support because he claimed he wasn't making any money. He said starting your own business meant no income for extras like child support. Sometimes, I'd guilt him into buying us food and paying the utilities before they got shut off. We live in a house he owned, because it helped him to control us. I'm not sure what to do, and I'm really scared. You're the first person who I called, because I thought your name sounded neat."

Gennifer isn't a quiet talker. The bar's quiet, and Mac

mimes eating popcorn as if she's watching a movie. I don't want to become involved, and I'm afraid if I go back and help Gennifer reopen Genius Used Cars on Monday, I'm in it. I hesitate for a second and then I leap before I look again.

With a sigh I say, "Yes, Gennifer, as a matter of a fact, I know someone who can run the dealership for you with my help. My grandfather worked in the car business for over fifty years. He always told me he was smart enough to never be a manager, but he knows how to do everything. Between the two of us, we should be able to help you. Right now, I'm out with my friend. Do you want my grandfather and I to meet you somewhere and when?"

She yells, "Awesome, can you guys come to my house? I don't have a car or a license. Even though I'm sixteen, I just turned sixteen. My mom hasn't taken me to get my permit, because the chemo lays her low. Mom used have a bunch of friends but they all disappeared when she got sick. My aunt doesn't even help us. Mom takes a bus to chemo."

I interrupt again, "Why don't you text me some times that would be convenient for you and your mother? I don't want to bother her if she's sick or tired. Texting's a great way to contact me."

She shrieks, "Oh, I love to text. I wasn't sure if you would text because you might be old. That's right, you're not old so texting is probably natural for you. My mom even texts, and she's way older than you. She's as much older than you as you are than me. I'll talk to her after she wakes up. It sucks she's in so much pain, and she sleeps all the time. I'm here alone a lot, so I get bored."

I rub my ear because of the loudness of her responses, "Yes, Gennifer texting is wonderful. Sometimes it can save your life. We'll stay in touch. Thanks. Bye now."

I disconnect the call before she can start talking again. Her volume and her desperation make me feel terrible for her.

"What do you think of my conversation with Gennifer with a G?" I ask Mac.

Mac laughs, "You found somebody who talks more and faster than you do. I think that's amazing. I feel sorry for the kid. She officially lost her father today, but it sounds like she actually lost him years ago."

The call from Gennifer changes the tone of our excursion. It's like we went from an episode of *Sex and the City*, dive bar edition to a *Castle* episode in the bar. I'm afraid being back at Genius Used Cars, I'm going to get pulled into investigating Gene's death. Lando and I solved a case before, maybe we can again. There might be some clues at the lot.

Mac says, "I called this drinking meeting to complain about the rude detective today. Listening to that poor kid reminds me I'm lucky to have my life. If you don't mind, let's finish our drinks and go update Lando."

Drinking and complaining isn't my idea of a fun afternoon, so I agree. We finish our drinks and walk to her vehicle. When we reach Mac's car, Sean's parked behind her.

He jumps out of his truck and asks both of us, "Do you mind if I take Violet in my truck, I want to talk to her."

There's no graceful way for me to avoid going to Lando's with Sean. This might be a conversation I don't want to have right now or ever.

Mac smiles impishly and says, "No problem. You two should ride together. You can talk. Violet can give you her interpretation of today's events, or you might discuss all kinds of other things. I'll meet you at Lando's."

TEN

"I love connecting with my customers."

Sean and I don't talk as he opens my door and strides over to slide into the driver seat. I hate this awkward silence. Sometimes silence can be comfortable, but this feels expectant. I ask, "How'd you find us?"

"Don't worry. In spite of Lando's concerns about you getting into trouble, no one's tracking you. Mac texted Lando that you two were getting a drink at this bar on the South Side and would be back soon. I didn't want to interrupt you and was debating coming into the bar," Sean says.

Once we're both settled in the vehicle, Sean starts a speech which sounds rehearsed, "I have no idea what's going on between us. I know you've had a rough month with the murders and all. However, I'm not comfortable feeling like I'm in competition with Quentin. Last night I gave you a ride home. You never mentioned anything about a confrontation with Gene Johnson, then this morning you met Quentin for breakfast and told him all about it. If you would rather date him, please tell me now before I become more invested in us."

I dart a glance at him, but turn straight ahead before I reply, "So, do you think we are on the way to being a couple? I feel buffeted by the changes in my life."

I turn to look at his profile and say, "Since moving to Pittsburgh, I've started two new jobs which is two more than I've ever had in my entire life. Two bosses who were jerks. Two attractive guys who want to date me, which is also a record for me. The number two seems to be a reoccurring theme."

He picks up my hand but keeps his eyes on the road, "I don't want to put you under more pressure. When we're together, just the two of us, I want to spend more time with you. However, it feels like when I start to get too close, you throw up barriers. Pushing me at Mac was a test which I passed. If you tell me today you only want to be friends, I'll respect your decision. I'll be your friend, but we won't be anything more. I don't want you to feel like you're caught between two guys, I'll dial it way back to only casual friendship. Saying that, I'd much prefer you wanting to date me. I don't want to pick your friends, but Quentin wants to date you, too. This makes adding him to your friend circle hard for both of us."

I look at his strong profile and gleaming red hair but I drop his hand, "I've never been in a situation like this. It's another scary change for me, but I caught a killer. That was way scarier than deciding who to date. Thank you for making me choose. I'm an avoider. I've been trying to pretend I can drift along and let my life happen to me.

I shrug and say, "Mac would say I should play coy

and ask for time to think about it. That tactic prolongs the drama for all of us. Quentin is a nice guy. I thought when he came to rescue me at Roar Motors he'd never be interested in me. When he asked me on a date, he seemed like he could be the hero of my story. Meanwhile, I'd been watching you from my window at Lando's for two weeks. I knew a guy like you would never talk to me. I'm comfortable with having crushes on unattainable men, but capturing their interest feels unfamiliar and scary."

Sean runs his hand through his hair and his sleeve rides up to show his muscled bicep with the intriguing tattoos and asks, "Were you really watching me? I kept catching glimpses of you, but I was afraid to approach you. Lando always talked about his college girl granddaughter, and I thought you'd judge me for not having a degree. Ursula never judged me, but we'd been together forever. Her grad school friends certainly didn't accept me. After she left, I met a lot of college girls at the bars on the South Side who turned away from me when my response to where did I go to school was I worked. I guess they thought my build came from lifting weights in the gym not from actual labor. When you came outside, you never made eye contact with me."

Playing with my ponytail, I say, "I couldn't make eye contact with you. It's a skill I'm working on acquiring. I respect you for working to help your family. I hope I wouldn't have been as shallow as an undergraduate. I never went anywhere people other than college students frequented. I might have thought we wouldn't have anything in common. Talking to you, we have so much in common. I want to try dating you. Part of me wants to ghost Quentin, but that's not fair. I'll call him tomorrow and meet him for coffee at Eat'N Park. I think that's the adult way to handle an almost dating situation. This morning with him wasn't a date. I asked him to bring his uncle, Detective Rousch."

He grimaces and says, "I respect your decision. I think it's cute since you only went on one date with him, but I can tell he's definitely interested. I want to follow you tomorrow, but I'm trying to respect boundaries. We should hurry, because our talk's slowed us down. I'm a little afraid of the trouble Mac and Lando might create without supervision."

On the rest of the ride back to the South Hills, Sean and I chat about the surface topic of the television shows we both enjoy like *Buffy the Vampire Slayer, Angel*, and *Firefly*. Our tastes in entertainment are similar in everything but music. Finding a guy who enjoys show tunes and movie scores would've been like finding a unicorn. Sean insists since I don't hate country music which is his favorite, he can try to convert me.

We approach the house and find Lando and Mac sitting next to each other on the spacious porch swing. They both smile and wave.

Mac says while looking at Sean, "I'm guessing from the hand holding you two finally made a decision. I saw from the moment we met that you were into Violet, but a test never hurt anyone. I also love to flirt, and I'm excellent at it. I hope there are no hard feelings from anyone. Just telling you once you date one of my friends, you're off my list forever."

Sean smiles and replies, "I'm sure I'm missing a fabulous opportunity with you, Mac. Violet snagged me before she even talked to me. I've been intrigued by her since I've been seeing her pictures and watching her grow up, but not in a creepy stalker way. We never met when we were young, because her visits to Lando were brief. I found his stories about her intriguing. As she's proven this month, Violet fascinates me."

Mac holds her hand up and says, "That's enough detail on the happy couple. We left the bar at the same time, but I beat you two here by quite a margin. I told Lando all about Gennifer and her plea for assistance."

Lando taps his cane on the wooden porch, "I think it's a lovely idea to help the girl. It sounds like she needs help in a variety of ways. Between the four of us, we can guide her through this transition. I don't think she should try to keep the grimy car lot, but we can keep it going until she can sell it without losing everything. Violet, do you realize we're intersecting with a murder investigation again?"

I bite my lip and say, "I know, but the girl's air of desperation on the phone grabbed me. It's not like we have anything better to do. I'll admit I'm also a little curious about who hated Gene enough to kill him. I don't feel any need to obtain justice for him, but if we stumble on some clues, we can tell Detective Andrews. Gennifer texted me that any time tomorrow works for her and her mom. How about one o'clock?"

Lando and Mac say one works for them. Sean says, "I can fit it into my schedule. How about if you and I go out tonight on our first real solo date?"

"It sounds wonderful to me. This is your city, so I'll let you plan our date." I smile as I reply.

He checks his watch, "Its four o'clock now. I'll return at seven. You should dress comfortably. I think you look cute in your khakis and polo shirts or the leggings you're wearing now. Either one is the proper level of dressiness. Food will be involved, but we'll eat later in the evening. You might want to grab a snack while I disappear to make my plans. I want to surprise you."

Mac and Lando laugh at us as Sean hurries to his truck. Mac points at the truck and says, "You're lucky. It's adorable to see the big guy be excited like a little kid about planning a date for the two of you. The sweetness gives me a slight headache. I'm heading home. Excitement swirls around you, and I need to decompress and plan my revenge on the Detective with no name as you so aptly called him. His arrogance reminds me of Snape from *Harry Potter*. Bye."

I join Lando on the porch swing when Mac vacates it. We swing back and forth in companionable silence for several minutes. Today I found a body, the police interviewed me at the station like a real suspect, I agreed to help a desperate young girl, and I picked a guy. This feels like more excitement in a single day than during an entire year of graduate school.

"I'm heading upstairs to my room to nap or read for an hour or two until it's time to get ready for my date." I say as I jump off the swing.

Lando struggles to dismount the porch swing, but he waves away my arm, "I'm going to one of my libraries. I need to read. Make sure you set your alarm, because if you fall asleep, you'll crash."

I fall asleep the instant my head hits the pillow. My

alarm awakens me at six o'clock which gives me an hour to primp for my date. After a quick shower, I inspect my wardrobe. I choose black cotton pants, a red and black short sleeved silk blouse with a scooped neck and geometric pattern. I like the shirt, but I've never worn it in public. Every time I've put it on, it feels too dramatic and eye catching. Tonight, I want to catch Sean's eye. I should add cool, knee high black boots to the ensemble, but I don't own any. My sedate, comfortable black sneakers are better than the black flats I wear to work.

Makeup and hair are the next hurdles. I've never been good at applying makeup. I'm afraid I'll look like a clown if I try too hard. I apply a little black eyeliner and some mascara. Usually, I wear my hair pulled back in a ponytail, because it's easier. A date's a fantastic opportunity for me to wear it down. It takes me about half an hour to get ready. I have plenty of time to head to Lando's kitchen to grab a quick snack. I don't want to be distracted by extreme hunger since I'm not sure what type of food is part of our date.

As I eat my apple, voices carry from the receiving library. I walk into the room, and Sean's waiting for me. I pull my phone out of my pocket and say, "We agreed on seven, right? It's twenty til seven. Am I late?"

Sean silently looks at me for a few seconds before he replies. "You're not late at all. I'm super early. I'm excited, and I thought I'd talk to Lando until you were ready. Is it weird I'm so comfortable here that I like to talk to your grandfather before we go on date?"

He stops and pops a piece of Big Red gum into his mouth, "You are amazing. You always look really cute, but the hair, the makeup, the clothes are stunning. The caveman part of me is happy you don't dress this way every day. Do I sound like a jerk? I'm trying to compliment you, but the hole I'm digging keeps getting deeper. I'll shut up now."

I run my hand through my hair, "I think it's adorable to see you flustered. I feel like I'm always nervous around you, and you stay so cool. Thank you for the compliments. I prefer to blend into the woodwork. The boring clothes, no makeup, and ponytail help me to do it. I feel like it's lovely of you to appreciate my effort. Am I dressed okay for the surprise evening?"

He runs his eyes over me again, "You look amazing, but you can move in your clothes which is important. Let's go."

We both say goodbye to Lando. Sean opens my door for me and then dashes over to the driver side. He says, "Since we're both early, we should be able to score seats on the earlier sightseeing tour. I thought it would be neat to take a cruise on the Gateway Clipper first. Do you get seasick?"

I shrug, "I've seen the boats on the rivers. It sounds awesome, and I don't think I get seasick. I've never been on a boat. My school's senior prom was held on one, but I didn't go."

During the drive to Station Square where the Gateway Clipper docks, Sean and I talk about books. He loves books. Being around Lando, bibliomania feels contagious. The longer I live in this book-filled house the more enamored I become with books. He suggests we start a private book club and read the same book to discuss it. Before he helps me out of the truck, Sean insists since this date is his idea he's going to pay for it.

On the one hour evening tour of the rivers, we listen to the tour guide and appreciate the cool breeze. We hold hands and check out the sights rather than each other. After the cruise, Sean takes me to dinner in the Strip District at Spaghetti Warehouse. The décor encompasses early twentieth century eclectic antiques with stained glass, old advertising signs, and the obligatory nonfunctioning telephone booth. Some of the tables are inside a complete trolley car, and other tables are designed like four poster beds. In spite of the overwhelming visuals, it's relatively quiet, and Sean and I get to know each other better. He tells me about living with his grandparents after his parents' deaths. His grandmother's reading habit mimics Lando's, and she and Lando are close friends. His taciturn grandfather spends most of his time in their basement building and carving bookcases for his grandmother. I tell Sean about my boring upbringing and why I crawled into the fantasy worlds of television. By the time we're finished with dinner, dessert and discussion, it's nearly ten o'clock.

I don't want the night to end, but I dread Sean suggesting a club or a bar. Alcoholic establishments have never been my scene. Sean puts his arm around me as he leads me to his truck. He opens my door with a flourish and says, "I'd love to spend more time with you, but you've had a stressful day. Plus there's not much to do at this time of night that doesn't focus on drinking."

On the way back to Lando's, we continue our television discussion. We've talked about my favorite medium several times, but after working on Popular Culture throughout undergraduate and a doctoral program, it's my default. My taste remains firmly rooted in the end of the twentieth and beginning of the twenty-first century. I need my heroes to be good. The trend toward morally ambiguous or corrupt protagonists leaves me cold. The few men in my classes loved the anti-heroes, so I expect Sean to sing the praises of drug dealers and mob bosses. Fortunately, he enjoys the same type of characters I do. We debate the decisions made by some of our heroes as if we're discussing mutual friends. The forty-five minute drive to Dormont feels like it takes ten minutes.

We avoid the oppressive discussion about what I discovered this morning. I found another body. Based on my observations this week, there won't be many people who will miss, Gene Johnson because he was a despicable human being. His death will affect people's lives in a variety of ways. Gennifer trying to keep the car lot open for a transition helps. I didn't need my job, but most of my coworkers need theirs.

When Sean and I arrive at Lando's, all of the porch lights remain bright at half past eleven. Sean points to the porch and says, "Lando either wants to see us, or he doesn't want you to trip on the way into the house."

I follow his hand with my eyes, "I think he wants to welcome us back. I bet he's waiting for me, so I can tell him about our evening. On the other hand, he might be reading, and he forgot he left the lights on."

Sean runs his hand through his hair and says, "A single light could be an accident, but I think all of the lights are a beacon for us. I'll walk you to the door which

I planned to do anyway. If he's waiting to talk to us, he'll meet us at the door."

I open my door before Sean can reach me. I like that he opens my doors for me, but it seems so silly to wait for him to circle the car when I can simply throw my door open and exit the vehicle faster. He grasps my hand as we walk up the sidewalk to Lando's side of the house. I want him to kiss me, but it'll be weird if my grandfather's grinning visage appears in the glass as we're embracing. Knocking on Lando's door is also an uncomfortable thought. After a month of living here, it would be like knocking on my own door. Lando solves my internal dilemma. He throws open his front door as our feet hit the first step of the porch.

He gestures us to follow him, "Welcome back. Sean, I'm happy you walked Violet to the door, because I need you for my plan, too."

Lando seems to be way too awake at midnight for a man who's over seventy years old. Sean and I follow him into his favorite room, the receiving library. Lando sits at his oversized desk. Sean pulls me toward the red settee. I slide next to him on the seat.

Lando shows us a notebook, "I've been writing up a plan to help Gennifer keep Genius Used Cars open for at least a month. I'll run the lot taking Gene's place. Lando points his pen at me, "Violet, you can keep selling cars. Sean, you're committed to building my addition. Do you have any jobs scheduled after you finish it?"

Sean glances toward the backyard, "I blocked out my entire summer for the addition from foundation to the finish work on the built-in cases. I've been filming and taking a lot of pictures. I plan to use this job to showcase what my team and I can do. We're a little ahead of schedule."

Lando taps his pen on the desk and interrupts, "So that means no. I'm thrilled you don't have another job waiting for you. The addition's under roof, and your guys are competent. I have a bad feeling about the snake's nest we're going to discover at Genius. I think we're going to need you for protection this month. I don't plan for us to play amateur sleuths again. However, I'm afraid we won't be able to avoid it."

Sean puts his arm around me and says, "I think I can divide my time between the worksite here and Genius Used Cars. I agree trying to run a dysfunctional dealership might not be safe for you or Violet. If I make it a habit to be around for several hours every day, it should discourage bad behavior."

I try to pull away from Sean, but he doesn't release me. I insist, "I'm not planning to try to solve another murder. I don't need a babysitter. I'm neither a child nor a damsel in distress."

Lando shakes his head and says, "This isn't actually about you, Violet. I'm going to be there, and Gennifer will probably have to be at the lot, too. The police aren't going to provide any protection. The other employees are some of the best suspects for Gene's murder. From your descriptions of them, I don't think they worked for him because they have a ton of other options. If you, me, and a vulnerable sixteen year old are going to be with a group of possible murderers, I want them to be aware we have Sean on our side."

Lando's idea makes sense, but it makes me feel like I'm the one who's sixteen. I'm annoyed with him and with Sean for agreeing with Lando so quickly. I pull away from Sean again, leap off the couch and say, "You and Sean can discuss your protect the weak females plan. I'm going upstairs to bed. I'll talk to you both tomorrow. You can tell me where we're going to breakfast before we meet Gennifer and her mother."

I scurry out of the room before either of them can stop me. Luckily, I turn the staircase light on, because my cat, Annika's sprawled across one of the stairs. A stumble on the stairs would not have helped my case that I'm a strong independent woman. I scoop her into my arms and continue to my room. I slam my door which neither of them will be able to hear on the other side of the double. It makes me feel better.

After brushing my teeth and splashing water on my face, I crawl into my bed. The events of the day circle my brain as I fall asleep.

ELEVEN

"You will love connecting with me."

The cloudy Pittsburgh scene echoes my mood when I wake up Sunday morning. Yesterday morning, I was excited about my plan to quit my awful job, but then the dead body. Today, Lando and I need to discuss trying to save Genius Used Cars with an exuberantly needy young girl and her ill mother. I dread this meeting. I drag over to Lando's side of the house before taking a shower. My pajamas are for dormitory living, so they pass for ugly clothing with ironically cute kittens gamboling on a pink heavy cotton background.

I arrive at Lando's kitchen and find Sean and Lando sitting at the table with Lando facing the doorway that I enter. This is my punishment for waking up late and only brushing my teeth before starting my day. Lando smiles and says, "Welcome to the land of the living my girl." His grin makes it seem like he's overjoyed that he thwarts my plan to run back to my side of the house to take a shower before Sean sees me.

Sean turns around in his chair and catches me looking

disheveled and grumpy in my less than elegant nightwear. I don't feel the rising heat warning me of an incoming blush. I'm too annoyed at Lando to show my embarrassment on my face. Sean's face turns the color of my tacky pink pajamas. I'm the one who looks silly. His hair appears darker than usual because it's still wet from a recent shower, and he's wearing a respectable dark green t-shirt and jeans.

I run my hand through my tangled hair and say, "I'm sorry I didn't get ready. I tossed and turned all night. I moved so much that Annika abandoned my room for a quieter one. I wanted to grab a cup of tea and an apple. Sean, why are you here so early?"

"I'm sorry I caught you in your PJs," he says with a shy smile.

I run my hand down my sleeve, "Some people wore this type of attire to class, but I was never comfortable in pajamas as a public fashion statement. I lived in dorms that were gender segregated by floor. However, I never knew who would be visiting, so my nightwear doubled as ugly daywear."

Sean laughs and says, "I live with my grandparents so my sleepwear is basketball shorts and a t-shirt. Some days in high school when I was running late I threw on sneakers and ran to school in the clothes I slept in. I don't understand people who own gorgeous, elegant sleeping clothes."

Lando gestures toward his thick bathrobe, "Before Violet moved in, I slept in the nude. Most mornings I would even wander around the house and make my coffee before I bothered to get dressed. I wouldn't want to spill my first cup of coffee on my professional suit. Now, I have to wear a heavy bathrobe, so I don't scare her."

Sean and I raise our eyebrows at each other. We both turn to look at Lando and burst into simultaneous laughter.

Lando tightens his belt on his robe and defends himself, "I'll have you know before I broke my hip, I was great on my own. I looked good. A lot of women liked me. With that one unfortunate exception, I tended to be picky about my companions, unlike a lot of guys in the car business."

Sean cocks his head to the side and asks, "That brings up something I've been wondering about for years. I've been around you most of my life. I don't remember ever seeing a woman at your house, other than my grandmother. Why didn't you date?"

Lando looks out the back window before he answers, "There're a couple of reasons. My taste alternated between the good and evil sides of the force. The viper left me burned and the good one was taken. Women also didn't tend to like my escape into books. A few said they liked my reading until I failed to notice their new outfit because I didn't glance up from a fabulous scene. I could never be serious about anyone who didn't like to read."

He shakes his head at the idea of dating a nonreader. "No one who met me at the dealership would ever have believed I'm not an extrovert. At home alone with my books, I recharged the energy I expended all day. I didn't want to give up my alone time."

"Do you want more alone time, Lando? Am I in the

way?" I ask. Until this moment, I never considered I might be in Lando's way.

He reaches across the table and pats my hand, "Not at all. Too much alone time left me with an overabundance of energy. This last month with you has been a hoot, even with all of the murder. Hmm, maybe because all of the murder. Anyway, we need to stop talking about me and move on to how we're going to help the girl and her mom."

I rise from the table and pour a glass of iced tea. Lando pulls out his notebook and reviews his plans to revitalize Genius Used Cars until Gennifer and her mom can sell the car lot. He must have worked more after I went to bed. He has spreadsheets, advertising plans, and a list of potential buyers. He asks me, "Do you know if Gene owned or rented the property?"

I take a sip before I answer, "In the week I worked there, he bragged several times that he owned the lot outright. He said he got a great deal when someone died and their heirs had no idea what they had. No bank could interfere with his plans."

Lando waves the notebook at me, "That's fabulous news for the kid as long as she's the heir. I hope the idiot had a will. If he didn't, this might be tied up in probate for a long time."

Mac throws open Lando's back door, "Legal language calls me like an incantation. I couldn't check anything at the courthouse after we talked yesterday because it was a Saturday. On Monday, I'll run down on my lunch hour to do a quick title search on Johnson's properties. Hopefully, the family can show us a Will when we meet with them in a few hours. Violet, I hope you aren't planning to go out in public wearing that."

She flicks her fingers at me and opens a few cupboards. "Lando, where are your mugs? I need coffee. The nearly full pot taunts me with its rich, bitter aroma."

Sean jumps up and opens the right cupboard to hand a mug to Mac.

She fills it with coffee and asks, "How many times have you been in this kitchen, big boy?"

He smirks at her, "Mac, I've known Lando for most of my life. He's close to my grandparents. They were always making me do stuff because I move so much faster than them. I can also reach all of the high shelves."

Mac runs her eyes over my outfit again and says, "Everyone else is ready for the day. Do you need to do something or will you be sporting the college student look for breakfast and our meeting?"

Her makeup's perfect and her hair falls down her back in a gorgeous curtain of black. Her shirt is white with small black polka dots and a keyhole neckline. Her capri pants appear to be pressed. Mac's shoes are black patent leather sandals with small delicate straps and three inch heels. Her manicured fingernails are bright red and match her toenails. My bedhead matches my ugly pajamas and bare feet with unpainted nails.

I take my iced tea glass to the sink and say, "I'm running over to my room to take a shower. I'll be back in about fifteen minutes."

During my quick shower, I wonder what Sean, Lando and Mac are discussing and what I should wear. I can't compete with Mac and I don't have time to paint my nails an attractive color nor do I have any nail polish at Lando's. My makeup stash consists of one tube of mascara, one black eyeliner, and two lip glosses. Nothing I own is elegant and three inch heels would be a recipe for a sprained ankle. We're meeting with a sixteen year old girl. Most of my casual clothes are appropriate for a teenager.

I throw on jeans, sneakers, and a Sunnydale High School t-shirt. Mac is familiar with Buffy based upon her Wolfram and Hart statement yesterday. Gennifer with a G probably has no idea that Sunnydale is on the Hellmouth. However, *Buffy* references make me feel more capable. I pull my wet hair into a high ponytail and don't bother with makeup. I make it back to the kitchen in under fifteen minutes, and I announce my return with a question, "Where are we going for breakfast?"

Sean replies first, "After much discussion, we decided to go for bagels downtown. My favorite bagel place is open on weekends but quiet when the office workers aren't present. According to her whining while you were showering, the idea of so many carbs makes Mac crazy. By the way, I love your t-shirt."

I fiddle with my dressy dangling silver earrings which don't match my casual attire. "How are we getting there? Are we taking multiple vehicles or just Lando's land barge?"

Lando gestures toward the parking pad behind the house and replies, "My car can hold all of us. There's still room in the trunk to store a body or a bunch of weapons."

"Please don't discuss transporting bodies or weapons

in the presence of your lawyer, especially after the joys of watching Detective Andrews interrogate Violet yesterday," Mac interrupts Lando's defense of his vehicle.

As we walk to the parking area, Sean says, "Violet and I can ride in the back seat. Mac you get the front seat with Lando."

I smile and Mac grimaces. I'll take this tiny triumph over Mac. Sean opens the door for her. She looks surprised and says, "Thank you, I appreciate old-fashioned courtesy."

Lando slides into the driver seat and says, "I got out of the habit of opening doors for ladies when I was in the car business. I lost a few sales in the 1970s because I stepped on people's new principles. Sean's grandmother raised him with proper manners."

Sean leans over to me and asks, "Do you want to hold my hand?"

In college, affirmative consent was part of the interpersonal skills talks given at every orientation. Posters in every dorm lounge stated only yes means yes and instructed students they needed to discuss their physical boundaries all the time. However, no one ever asked me such a simple question.

I move closer to him on the seat, place my hand in his, and say, "Yes, I would like to hold hands with you. Thank you for asking and not grabbing my hand. You might've startled me. Then I would have pulled away and possible misunderstandings would have ensued."

In the front seat, Lando and Mac argue over the satellite radio station. Lando prefers instrumental jazz, but Mac wants eighties tunes. I move closer to Sean and rest my head on his shoulder and listen to the disagreement in the front seat. Lando and Mac love to debate, and both back their positions vigorously. I don't care about music. I prefer classical music and scores from television shows.

The Sunday lack of traffic makes the trip to downtown fly by in half the usual time. We park and walk to the bagel place. We're the only customers. Mac says, "I love this place, but I hate it too. I want to order bagels, but I always grab a salad for lunch. At my pocket sized height, every pound I gain seems to be doubled. In my last job, carrying heavy trays of drinks and dodging customers' hands allowed me to eat anything I wanted. Now I'm chained to my desk. My only exercise is walking around downtown at lunch time. Since it's a Sunday and we'll be discussing murder again, I guess I can splurge."

There's no correct response to Mac's statements. So I change the subject, "I brought Lando's notebook and spreadsheets about how we can help Gennifer. I can be the secretary."

The four of us spend the next hour discussing strategies and plans. By the end of the conversation, we're all on the same page. We have two hours before we need to meet them at their house in Lawrenceville. I'm not sure how far we are from it. There are so many neighborhoods in Pittsburgh. Since moving here, I've been more worried about selling cars and finding bodies than exploring Pittsburgh geography.

I spin looking for the right direction, "Where is Lawrenceville? Are we close?"

Lando points to the right with his cane and answers, "It's the neighborhood past the Strip District, so we're nearby. It's been becoming gentrified in the last decade or so. We're less than fifteen minutes away on a Sunday morning with no traffic. That's one of the reasons we picked downtown to eat. The bagels were on our way."

I glance around and ask the group, "What should we do for the next hour and a half?"

Sean pulls out a pack of Big Red gum and offers it to everyone before he answers, "I think we should walk over to Point State Park, so Violet can see where the three rivers meet."

Lando and Mac agree to the plan but not the gum. They lead the way arm in arm. She's adopted Lando as a surrogate grandfather. I like her because she seems to know what both Lando and I need. Her snarky asides to me can be painful but accurate. Sean puts his hand out to me, and we walk behind them together.

Mac chatters to Lando about her daily activities as a junior lawyer at a big downtown firm. I listen, but I'm distracted by how pleasant it is to hold Sean's hand and feel like part of a couple. He's much taller than me so it's like I'm walking in his shadow.

Once we reach the park, Lando and Mac walk toward the reconstructed part of Fort Pitt. Both of them throw pieces of historical trivia at each other to try to gain the upper hand in knowledge. Their impromptu trivia competition must distract them. They don't seem to notice Sean leading me toward the gorgeous fountain.

We stand at the point where the rivers meet with the fountain at our backs. He pulls me into his arms next to the fountain with the faint mist of water traveling on the wind and kisses me. The mist refracts the sunlight with a rainbow effect.

We kiss for a minute. He cradles my face, and I reach up to twine my hands around the back of his neck. There are no festivals this weekend and no photo shoots happening. The park's empty and dominated by the sound of the water splashing in the fountain. I forget about murders, cars, and my grandfather.

My eyes are closed because staring at someone when we're kissing is weird. I realize something is wrong when Sean's knees buckle, and he jerks away from me. Lando is holding his cane behind Sean's knees with a grin on his face.

Lando thumps his cane on the side of the fountain, "I figured I had to do something to capture your attention. Both of you seem distracted. I wasn't sure a tap on the shoulder would inconvenience either of you but a tap to the back of the knees with a cane always works."

Sean spins to face Lando and asks, "Why did you have to interrupt us at all? We're in public. We aren't going to do anything too scandalous in a park in the middle of the day. You and Mac were looking at the historical signs and trying to one up each other."

Lando points to Mac and throws her under the bus, "I saw you two and pointed it out to Mac. She's the one who suggested it'd be funny to interrupt you. Somehow it's far more effective coming from her grandfather and the man who watched you grow up."

The interruption ruins the moment, so the three of us walk back to join Mac near the reconstructed block house. Mac and Lando continue their game of historical trivia, and I listen to them recount some of the history of Pittsburgh. Most of the history I learned focused on the twentieth century and how it related to television. It's enjoyable to learn about Pittsburgh's past from two people treating history knowledge like a competitive sport.

TWELVE

"If you have money down, I have a car for you."

After an hour of listening to the Lando and Mac trivia show, I'm ready to meet Gennifer and her mom. The walk back to Lando's car takes longer than the drive to their row house in Lawrenceville. Their house in the middle of the block is one of the few to retain ugly yellow siding and rusty white metal awnings. Gentrification and rehabilitation mark most of the block with refurbished brick fronts and painted wooden trim work. There's no parking on the street in front of the house.

Lando pulls around to the back and finds the empty parking pad with some weeds shooting through the stones corresponding to their house number. In our brief but wordy phone conversation, Gennifer mentioned they didn't own a car. Gene Johnson sold cars for a living but wouldn't provide a car for his daughter and her sick mother. The overgrown backyard isn't an inviting short-cut, and we don't want to knock on the back door for this meeting. The four of us trek through the alley and around the block toward the front door in silence.

The lack of a car, the overgrown backyard, and the house's neglected façade illustrate this small family needs our help. A teenager, who must be Gennifer with a G, throws open the front door and starts to talk, "I saw you park your car on the parking pad. That's a fabulous idea because like I told you we don't have a car. I don't know if you saw it, but I pulled a bunch of the weeds that were growing in the stones so they wouldn't hurt your car. You probably couldn't tell because I just threw them into the scary backyard. I wasn't going to tackle that mess. I actually barricaded the back door with an old dresser. With just my mom and me, I'm a little worried about possible break-ins. It's not like this house looks like it has a security system."

If we don't stop her from talking, I'm afraid we'll stand outside for hours while every thought that crosses her mind emerges from her mouth. I do a little wave with my hand and start introductions. "I'm Violet Landovic." I point to everyone in turn to introduce them.

"This is Bert otherwise known as Lando Landovic, my grandfather who has over fifty years of experience in the car business." He smiles and nods at her.

I gesture toward Mac, "That's Maxine MacAlister. She's a fabulous lawyer, and she can help us with all of the legal issues that might arise."

Mac gives Gennifer a regal nod to acknowledge the introduction. Then I turn to point to Sean.

"This is Sean." I smack my hand to my forehead as I realize I have no idea what Sean's last name is. It's never come up. I like him, we've kissed and started dating, but I don't know his last name. I'm an idiot.

Lando picks up on my discomfort first and starts to laugh. "All this time you two have spent together, and you don't know his last name, do you?"

I'd deserve it if Sean walks away from me. Instead he walks over to me and gathers me into his arms and starts to laugh. "I've been hearing about you for years from your grandfather and his nickname means everyone remembers his last name. It never occurred to me I only told you my first name. I think it's cute you don't know my last name. It makes me a man of mystery."

Gennifer asks, "What's going on? I don't get it. Why's everyone laughing? Why's the big, cute guy hugging Violet? Why's she acting embarrassed?"

Mac stops the flow of question by putting her hand up, "Stop asking questions or no one can answer them. I can't believe we stumbled onto someone who rambles more than you, Violet. Look kid, Violet realized she's been hanging out with Sean for a few weeks without knowing his last name. There's no rule you need to know someone's last name to kiss them. There were some guys who I never bothered to learn their first names either. I digress, and those aren't stories for young ears."

Sean pats my head and says, "It's Doyle. My last name is Doyle. Gennifer, is your mom waiting for us inside?"

She peers into the darkened house, "Yes, of course. I wanted to be the first to say hello to everyone. I'm nosy like that. It's neat because I got to meet you all and see how you fit together. I can't wait until I'm part of the team. Follow me to my mom. She's in the living room."

Heavy curtains shroud the only window in the room.

Gennifer and her mom sit on a sagging couch on one wall, Lando perches on the reclining chair, Mac is on a kitchen chair. Two mismatched kitchen chairs wait for my butt and Sean's. The walls are covered in dark wooden paneling from the middle of the last century and threadbare avocado green carpeting covers the floor. The room exudes midcentury ugly.

Gennifer's mom wiggles on the couch and says, "Hi, I'm Cynthia Johnson. I know one of you worked for my estranged and now dead husband, Gene. I'd like to offer my apologies for his behavior. Please don't offer us condolences on his passing. His death is the best news I've gotten this year."

Gennifer puts her arm around her mom and interrupts, "Mommm, you can't say you're happy he's dead. I'm pretty sure someone murdered him. We don't want anyone to think we killed him. You cried convincingly when the police came to tell us."

Cynthia rolls her eyes at her daughter, "One of these women worked for your father. So she knows what he was. I'm sure she told her friends. We need to trust somebody. We really need the help." She pats her daughter's leg, "The tears for the police were real, they were tears of joy but I didn't tell them."

This time Lando does the introductions, "I'll get right to it. I'm Bert Landovic but call me Lando. As you might notice I'm the only one in the room who could have over fifty years of experience at anything. Maxine MacAlister's our lawyer, Sean Doyle's our muscle, and Violet Landovic over there is my granddaughter. She's the one who worked at Genius Used Cars for a week."

I observe the two women during introductions. Gennifer is thin and coltish with shoulder length dark hair and brown eyes. In her jeans and faded Pittsburgh Penguins t-shirt, she appears to be the type of teenage girl who isn't distinguishable from most other teenage girls when her mouth is shut. Cynthia's thin frame emphasizes her illness. The heavy sweater, the scarf, and the wool ski cap on her head in June accentuate her fragility. Gennifer, for all of her exuberance, moves carefully around her mother. She tucks the afghan on Cynthia's lap before picking up her mother's hand like it's a porcelain teacup.

Gennifer raises their joined hands toward Lando, "Can you help us? I know I overshare and talk too much. But we need someone to help us. My mom might act too proud and angry, but we don't have that luxury right now."

As she pleads for help, she strokes her mother's hand. It's an unconscious gesture which shows this young girl's heart and her fear. Tears start to well in my eyes. I want to hide my face in Sean's strong shoulder but the chair arrangement places him a foot away from me. These women don't need our tears, they need our help.

Lando clears his throat and breaks the spell, "We talked about your call to Violet for several hours in the past day. We've already agreed to help you to the best of all of our abilities. We certainly didn't bring muscle and a lawyer to protect us from you two."

Gennifer giggles and her mom smiles faintly. Cynthia asks, "So you think we can keep the place open until we can find a buyer?"

Lando pulls the notebook out of his briefcase, "We

have plans and spreadsheets. Between Violet, Sean and I, we could run a car lot. We need to discuss if you want any of the current employees to stay. It would be great if Cynthia would make an appearance when she's able. Since school's out for the summer, Gennifer might be able to help, too. Your involvement could be as much or as little as you can both handle."

Mac stands up and starts to walk around the perimeter of the small room, "The important part of this discussion's the legal side of the equation."

She asks questions as she paces, "Who was Gene's lawyer? Did he have a Will? Do you know where it is? What about life insurance? I'm asking a bunch of questions but these are some of the important ones. You answered one in your introduction, you said you were separated but not divorced from Gene. That's an important detail for you to go to the police and retrieve the lot keys to reopen on Monday."

Cynthia curls her hands in the afghan and says, "Gene and I pretended to be together in our gigantic house in the North Hills for over a decade. I knew he cheated. He knew I hated him. I felt like I deserved to be unhappy because when I was eighteen, I stole him from his first wife with my pregnancy. We both knew a divorce would be expensive, so we stayed together. A few months before he got busted for fraud everything changed."

She stops talking and glances around the ugly room. Her mom's pause allows Gennifer's contribution, "Gene went to one of those buy cheap properties and rent them to poor people seminars. He told me he purchased this awful place in my mom's maiden name. It was one of the last things he bought before he got arrested, because he was afraid he might get caught. The others were all in his name, and I think the bank or the courts took them. We aren't sure. He got super mean and secretive when he found out about the investigation. He made mom sign some papers to buy this place."

Mac holds her hand up to stop Gennifer, "Did your dad have a lawyer?"

Gennifer shudders, "I totally hate it when anyone calls him that. He ignored me when I was little and disappeared to go to jail when I was thirteen. I never thought of him as my dad. Mom and I are super close. She raised me like a single parent. I'm happy he's dead."

I tap my fingers against my leg and say, "Yesterday I spent time being interrogated by the police because I didn't act upset enough that Gene was dead. Let's put it out there that no one mourns his death, but if everyone keeps saying it, it makes it more likely someone will say it to the police."

Cynthia adjusts the afghan covering her legs and interrupts, "Gennifer has no idea about his business dealings or lawyers. I never signed any paperwork except the deed on this house. Gene got a great deal from a confused, sick old lady who was buying a car at the dealership. She didn't have any family and lived in this house for decades. He tricked her into trading it for a cheap used car. He got it outright, no mortgage. He left her live here until she died upstairs a few months later, so she wouldn't be aware he took her house. He bragged he might as well grab it because it'd go for taxes eventually anyway."

During all of these digressions, Mac continues to circle the room like a shark. "Talking to you two is like trying to keep Violet focused, only worse. I'll repeat what we've learned. Gene was a scumbag, which we knew. You own this house free and clear in your name, which is wonderful news. No one knows anything about Gene's other holdings, his lawyer or any Will. Did I miss anything?"

Gennifer crosses her arms and glares at Mac, "You're mean. Violet's been super nice. Why'd she bring you?"

I sigh and say, "I can be comforting and nice. Nice isn't what you two need right now. You need good legal advice. Mac's providing it at no cost to you. At her firm, she has to charge over three hundred dollars an hour. She's brilliant and tough which is better than nice."

Mac stares down at Cynthia from her three inch heels and asks, "The most important question is about the status of your marriage. Were you served with or did you sign divorce papers?"

Cynthia shakes her head, "No. I think he was afraid if he pushed for a divorce, I might make a stink about being disabled. When he got fired and arrested, he told me to move to this house and handed me ten grand in cash. I took my jewelry and my clothes. Between the cash and selling my stuff, we were okay for about a year because we lived cheap and hid."

"I remember Gene got a year in county jail for his shenanigans. By my calculations you should've been running out of money when he got out. Did he help you?" Lando asks.

Cynthia looks toward the covered window, "He got

out and came here once. He told us jail was a crucible. It remade him like a phoenix. He planned to make his own way with his intelligence. He didn't need us holding him down. Then he stomped out the door."

Gennifer puts her arm around her mom and says, "We already thought he was jerk. No one loved him, but it felt like he kicked us in the teeth. He also said everyone forgot us and nobody cared about us. The rest of the week, mom couldn't get out of bed. I got so scared so I called an ambulance. They kept her for a couple of days and found her cancer. We had to apply for medical assistance because no one had a job or health insurance. Gene bragged his business was under the radar so he didn't have to give anyone any insurance. Anyways, I filled out the paperwork and didn't mention Gene at all."

"Why did they let a kid fill out the paperwork?" I ask.

Gennifer shrugs, "They were busy. They didn't ask my age. There wasn't anyone else to do it."

Mac tosses her long dark hair over her shoulder and says, "It's great news that they let Gennifer fill out all the paperwork. The failure to mention Gene could've caused problems if Cynthia did it even if she was sick and delirious. Contracts aren't legally binding if signed by people under the age of eighteen. I have to check the case law, but I'm relatively sure it also applies to legal paperwork and documentation."

Mac stops walking and glares at Gennifer and I before continuing her lecture, "You have all rubbed off on me. Now, I'm becoming distracted by side issues. If she didn't sign divorce papers, and he knew where she was, they were still married. This makes our lives easier. In case of a death with or without a Will, the surviving spouse is presumed to be able to take over the assets. We've determined law enforcement shouldn't be able to question you opening the dealership tomorrow morning if the police are finished. Lando can take it from here."

Lando leans on his cane to stand up and present his master plan.

As he's about to launch, Gennifer interrupts, "We don't care how you plan to do it. We need so much help we'd trust anyone right now. If someone can pick us up tomorrow morning, we can both go to talk to the other employees. I don't think mom'll be able to stay long. Plus she's supposed to have a treatment tomorrow afternoon. I want to be there. This is an awesome chance for me to learn some new stuff. Maybe I can learn to drive. There'll be a bunch of cars for me to try to drive, right? Do you think someone could give my mom a ride to her treatment and maybe stay with her? Riding the bus to treatments has been tough because we have to switch buses, and she gets so tired and sick. She hates taking a special bag for getting sick on the bus. Everyone stares or pretends we don't exist."

Tears fill my eyes as Gennifer describes their predicament getting to the hospital.

I was in my early twenties in graduate school, and my mother had a health scare. When I thought one of my parents might be sick, I never worried about paying for treatment or getting her to appointments. Instead, I offered to watch television with her. This sixteen year old girl who acts like a flighty child has handled stuff I can't imagine. It reminds me how lucky I am to have my parents as safety nets. They may not have paid much attention to me, but they cushioned my life.

Sean runs his hand through his thick red hair and says, "I'll make sure you both have a ride whenever you need one. We want to help you both make it through this. I don't want to insult you, but if it's been hard getting to appointments, how do you buy food?"

Gennifer smiles at him and says, "Sometimes, I buy stuff at the convenience store because it's close. When we got the medical assistance, they asked if I needed help buying food. They told me about a local food pantry but it was too far to walk. At the convenience store, I try to buy the healthiest stuff I can find in cans and boxes."

Gennifer stops and looks at her mom. Cynthia has fallen asleep. It's as if once she heard that someone would help them, she felt safe enough to rest. She might be so ill that nodding off is a regular part of her day.

Gennifer gets off the couch with her mom and leads us into the kitchen. The room between the living room and the kitchen contains grimy blinds and a battered wooden kitchen table. Gennifer must have moved the chairs for our visit. The kitchen's tiny with appliances from the middle of the last century. It looks like someone, probably Gennifer, attempted to clean but some of the dirt appears as old as the appliances.

Gennifer glances toward the room where her mother's sleeping, "I didn't want my mom to hear this because she'd be so disappointed in me. I know it's wrong but you may've noticed that most of the houses on this block don't look like this one. The first time I did it, I thought the people were dumping perfectly good food, but I figured it out. Down the street, on the porch of one of the houses, a farm truck leaves boxes of fresh vegetables once a week. At school I looked up the name on the truck, they do something called a CSA. People buy a share in the farm and get these excellent vegetables every week. It's supposed to be the honor system, so people take their own box they paid for. I steal one of the boxes every week. My mom's supposed to eat healthy. I know it makes me like my father but we need it. I don't deserve your help but she does."

This child's courage and grit astound me. She thinks she's dishonest, but she's learned to survive and help her mom to survive after her formative years were so economically pampered. I'm not sure how to respond to her confession.

I tug on my long silver earrings and say, "Don't feel guilty about taking a box of vegetables. I knew a few people growing up who got one of those CSA boxes, and they threw a bunch of it away every week. At least you're using it. Just tell me name of the farm, and I'll pay for the full season, so you can take the boxes legitimately. Gene's the one who should've felt guilty, not you. This isn't charity. Everyone needs help sometimes."

Lando puts his hand on my shoulder and says to Gennifer, "Violet's made some money selling cars, but I'll take care of buying the vegetables."

I open my mouth to argue but Lando lightly squeezes my shoulder. Gennifer doesn't need to listen to our disagreements, I say, "With your mom sleeping and the details discussed, we should go. We'll pick you up at eight o'clock tomorrow morning. We want to arrive early to present a united front if any of the other employees show up."

She stares down at the battered kitchen counter and traces a pattern on it, "Thank you to whoever pays for the food. Please let me know how I can get it legit. What're the other employees like? I called you first because of your cute name. Can you tell me anything about anyone else?"

I wrinkle my nose, "It's better if you form your own opinions. Your mom should be around for the first couple of hours. We have plenty of cars, someone can bring her home when she gets tired. Try to get a good night's sleep. We'll meet you tomorrow."

Gennifer nods her head. Everyone says goodbye and we file past Cynthia, who continues to sleep, and out the front door into the cloudy afternoon. We walk around the block to return to Lando's car in silence until I can't handle it anymore.

As I pick my way over the broken parking pad, I blurt, "I feel so terrible for Gennifer and Cynthia. We need to help them. I hope we can make enough at Genius Used Cars to save them."

Mac squeezes Sean's bicep when he opens her door and says, "I love a gentleman. I agree they need our help, but you're blinded by Cynthia's illness. They're craftier than you think. Those two lived with Gene Johnson for over a decade, and they learned manipulation skills from a master. I think we should wait and talk about the situation once we're back at Lando's house."

I fume at Mac's cynicism as we pile into Lando's land barge. I'm not starting the conversation again until I calm down or someone else begins. Mac and I see life from different perspectives. After Sean opens my car door, I remain quiet. Sean and Lando don't offer opinions, which is odd for Lando. I rest my head on Sean's shoulder and ignore everyone.

No one speaks during the ride to Lando's. Once we arrive, I don't wait for Sean to open my door. I throw it open and stride to Lando's back door. This conversation should be held in the receiving library, the front room with all of the windows between the bookcases and seating. As usual, it's a cloudy day in Pittsburgh, but some sunlight filters through the sheer curtains.

Mac follows me and the click of her heels makes me want to snap at her. I'm angry, but I need to listen to her perspective. Lando sits at his desk, Sean sits next to me on the settee and Mac paces.

Mac points in the general direction of Lawrenceville, "I know saying anything negative about the woman with cancer makes me look like the villain. Going into this situation, I wasn't even sure Cynthia was ill. My inability to sit still serves a couple of functions. It burns extra energy, but it also allows me to observe people from different angles and investigate their stuff. In the kitchen, there were twenty pill bottles and Cynthia's name was on them. The pill bottles would have been a wonderful prop but getting them in Cynthia's name is probably beyond a baby grifter."

Sean must feel me tense because puts his hand on my arm which stops my explosion. I growl, "Why do you think Gennifer is a con artist?"

Mac stands in front of the windows and puts her

hands on her hips, "Seeing their house, I think she's scared and broke. I thought either one of them might've killed Gene, but if they had, they would have made sure they had their legal ducks in a row."

Lando taps his cane and asks, "Do you think we should help them?"

Mac pauses and says, "I think we should. I didn't really know Gene Johnson, but I'm curious about who might've killed someone who everyone hated."

"If you think we should help them, why are you being so nasty about their motives?" I ask as I tug on my ponytail.

Mac points at me, "I'm a lawyer. I don't trust anyone. It makes dating and making friends nearly impossible. After the fiasco with Tiffany, I can count the number of people who I trust on one hand. You three are part of that small group, and I worry you're all too trusting. I'll try to protect you even if it makes you hate me."

She motions toward Sean, "You want to ride in on your white horse or truck and save everyone."

Sean stands up and walks over to Mac. "We appreciate your trust in us. We need a cynic in the group to balance us."

He throws his arm around her. "We appreciate you trying to protect us, but being a group makes us better at helping people and solving murders."

I interrupt, "I thought we were going to let the police solve this case. Does everyone remember that the last time we played amateur detectives, I almost got killed?"

Sean leaves Mac's side to return to me. "I'm not

saying we should interfere with the police, but we will be at the car lot. It can't hurt if we keep our eyes open."

Lando rummages in a drawer and pulls out his cellphone, "We can start a suspect and clue list. This time we should use a group chat function on our phones. That way we can't misplace the evidence. If we all have it, one of us is less likely to be the target of the killer. I'll keep a hard copy in my notebook, too. Speaking of the investigation, someone needs to call to check if the police will be done with the scene and we can open tomorrow. Should it be Violet or Mac as her lawyer?"

Mac raises her hand to volunteer, "I want to talk to the Detective Andrews again. Before you ask Violet, I promise to ask about the cat that was in Gene's car. If he says we can't open I'll text you. If everything is a go, I won't. I need to go back to my own apartment. I like you all, but I need some alone time to recover before I start my week at the stodgy firm."

Sean walks Mac to her car. Dormont's a safe bedroom community of Pittsburgh. His ingrained manners don't let him send Mac out of the house on her own. Lando and I remain silent in our own worlds until Sean returns.

Sean takes my hand when he gets back and says, "I need to go home to check on my grandparents. Would you like to meet them today or would another less stressful day be better?"

I shake my head, "Another day would be better. It might be nice if I could go a full month without finding another dead body. I'll walk with you to your truck."

We walk into the dark foyer and Sean closes the door to the receiving library. With all of the doors closed, the only light glows from the mullioned windows in the gorgeous oak door. He pulls me into his arms and murmurs, "I've been waiting to do this again all day."

He cradles my face in his gigantic hands and leans in to kiss me tenderly on the lips. I surrender to his embrace. He has to move his hands from my face to my waist because of the difference in our heights. I could kiss him for hours. Within a few minutes, there's an insistent tapping from the closed door to the receiving library.

Lando shouts, "I never heard the front door open which means you two are lurking. I've got to go the bathroom. I don't want to witness whatever you two are doing in my hallway. Break it up."

Sean laughs as he pulls away from me, "This is the joy of living with our grandparents. I have a feeling our relationship is going to have to progress slowly based upon the lack of privacy. You don't need to walk out to the truck. It looks like it's starting to sprinkle outside. I'll meet you at seven tomorrow morning."

I throw open the door to Lando's library and say, "Sean's gone. I feel like Mac because I need some time alone. How about we meet back here in two hours for pizza? We can start watching *Angel* and not talk about the car business or murder."

Lando brushes past me and says, "Sure, sure, get out of my way. I do need to go."

The rest of the night is blissfully uneventful. Lando and I immerse ourselves in the story of the vampire with a soul. Annika, my hero cat, joins us. We don't discuss anything about murders or car sales.

THIRTEEN

"No one is better at selling cars than me."

Annika walking on my chest wakes me up at six o'clock. As tough as Tiffany appeared, her cat's behavior illustrates she spoiled this fluffy beige beast. The sun should be up, but it's Pittsburgh in June so it's raining. Hopefully this isn't a bad omen for today's endeavor.

After a quick shower, I decide to wear a long sleeveless emerald sundress dotted with tiny blue flowers and a hem that skims my ankles. I put on my comfortable black shoes which can be almost dressy under a long skirt. I don't own any jackets or sweaters that look right with this ensemble. The lack of sleeves makes this outfit appear too carefree for today's tasks. There also aren't any pockets for my phone, and I hate carrying a purse.

When I reach Lando's side of the house and his kitchen, I ask a man in his seventies for fashion advice. "Do you think a big scarf I fold into a shawl would make this outfit be more professional?"

He waves toward the stairs to the second floor, "I have just the thing for you to wear. Remember all those suits I wore to work? I still have a bunch of the suit jackets. I think I have one that matches the blue flowers on your dress. I remember women wearing dresses with blazers. It'll dress it up a little. Plus it'll help to protect you from the rain. The news says this'll keep up all day."

Sean comes to the back door while Lando's fetching a jacket for me. He walks in without knocking and shakes the rain off his head. His hair looks like mahogany when it's wet. I like it better when it's auburn with glittering strands that pick up the sunlight. When he notices Lando isn't in the room, he comes to me and gathers me into his arms. When I wrap my arms around his neck, I shiver.

I run my fingers through his hair, "Your hair is still so wet and your neck's cold."

He laughs and tugs on my ponytail, "Your hair's always still damp in the morning. Do you own a hair dryer?"

I shake my head, "Nope, I hate spending time in the morning getting ready, so I always shower and go."

He cups my cheek, "That's one of the many things I like about you, your lack of pretense. Now let's stop talking and take advantage of your grandfather's absence."

When Sean kisses me, I lose all sense of time and place. Unfortunately, my grandfather doesn't.

He knocks his cane against the doorway, "Aww, can't you two hear me coming down the hall with my cane? I sound like a herd of elephants in tap shoes. I get you two are dating, but I don't want to witness it. My granddaughter and the little boy who I watched grow up is weird. Listen for the cane and separate for the sake of my old eyeballs. I swear my eyes are the only things that work good on me. Don't make me want to wash them out with bleach. I better never catch any clothing moved or removed."

We stop kissing and turn but we keep holding hands. Sean says, "Lando we'll try to respect your wishes."

Lando points out the backdoor toward the parking pad and says, "I think we should take two cars in case anyone needs to run errands."

I sigh, "My car's still at Genius Used Cars. I didn't want to move it, because of the active police investigation. If we take your Lincoln, we'll still have two cars."

Lando taps his forehead, "That's right. Let's go. Sean can sit in the front. I'm not your chauffeur. I don't like sitting in the front with you two canoodling in the back seat."

On the ride, we discuss who and what we think we might find today. None of us called the other employees. I don't know any of their numbers. Genius Used Cars wasn't the type of place that pretended to have a family atmosphere.

I pull out my cellphone, "I was thinking I don't know anyone's number from Genius, I wonder how Gennifer found mine. I was only working there for a week."

Sean swivels to face me, "That's an excellent question. I'm sure Mac would have some theories."

I put both hands on the seat divider between the front and back seats and say, "I thought of something else. How are we going to get into the office trailer?"

Lando taps the steering wheel and interrupts, "I hate it when people talk between the front seat and the back seat when I'm driving. I can't follow the conversation and focus on the road. Hush up you two. We'll figure it out when we get there."

I ruffle Sean's hair which is nearly dry and settle back into the deep, comfortable leather seat. I accepted Gennifer and her mother as Gene's victims during our phone conversations and meeting at their house. In retrospect, some issues are arising.

"Where are you going?" I ask as Lando drives into the tunnel toward downtown Pittsburgh. "Genius Used Cars is in Whitehall, we don't drive into the city to get there, do we?"

Sean turns around in the seat to answer me as Lando focuses on exiting the tunnel and picking the correct lane on the bridge. "We have to take Gennifer and her mom, Cynthia to the lot today. We're detouring to Lawrenceville to pick them up."

I pause to appreciate the view of downtown Pittsburgh and then say, "I totally forgot. I've been focusing on returning to the scene of the crime."

Everyone in the car remains quiet until we reach Lawrenceville. Lando pulls in front of Cynthia and Gennifer's house. On a Monday morning, there's street parking available in front of the house. Sean hops out of the car and goes to get them. We're five minutes early, but Gennifer's waiting at the door. She's wearing a business suit from the twentieth century. It's black with pinstripes, shoulder pads and a knee length straight skirt. It almost fits her, but she looks like a teenager playing the part of an eighties anchorwoman in a sitcom. Her hair, in a severe French braid, doesn't make her appear older but enhances her youth.

When Sean brings Cynthia out of the house, she's wearing a lovely, expensive suit from this century. She must've looked lovely in it at the country club years ago. The weight loss from her illness causes it to hang on her in odd places.

Gennifer runs to the car, and stumbles in her high heels. She grabs the door and slides in next to me. She's wearing pantyhose and a slip which emerges from the bottom of her skirt as she moves across the seat. "Hi, I'm excited and nervous. How do you think this'll go today?"

She seems genuine, excited and pleasant. I'm more cynical about her motives after one day of interaction. Sean and Cynthia are still walking to the car. Sean's supporting her and letting her set the pace. Gennifer ignores that I haven't answered her question and launches into more, "So what's up with you and Sean? Is he your boyfriend? He seems super awesome. He's really big though. I bet he could pick my mom up with one arm as thin as she is now. He could probably even pick you up. It must be cool to have a boyfriend. I haven't had one yet because of all of the changes."

I'm not sure if I want to answer Gennifer. I want to find out how she got my number if she wasn't in much contact with her father. We need to discover if she has a key, so I change the subject, "Gennifer, do you or your mom have a key to the office trailer at the car lot? I was also wondering how you got my cellphone number since I only worked at Genius for a week."

She points toward her mother, "We do have a key. We

got it when the police came to notify us of Gene's death. They gave us his phone, too."

Lando interrupts, "That seems odd. I thought the police kept the personal items during a murder investigation."

Sean's opening the back door and assisting Cynthia into the car as Lando questions Gennifer. He winks at me over Gennifer's head. I slide to the seat behind Lando, leaving Gennifer in the middle and Cynthia in the seat behind Sean.

Gennifer looks at her mom and then at her lap, "I might not have been completely truthful about how often we saw Gene. He came over to the house every couple of days. I'm not sure where he was when he wasn't at our house. The house has three bedrooms, and he stayed in one. He didn't help us, that part was true but he had a key and let himself in whenever he felt like it. He ignored both of us, but sometimes he brought food or paid the light bill. Sometimes he was drunk when he showed up. I went through his stuff when he was passed out. Depending on how much cash he had, I'd take some."

Sean gets into his seat, turns around and asks, "So you basically robbed your own father?"

Gennifer runs her hand over her French braid and replies, "I hated him and I was afraid of him, but we needed the money. I never stole from anyone else."

I say, "Other than the CSA."

She glances at her mother and then glares at me. "Okay, I'm a terrible person, but I can explain where I got your number and the key if you let me finish. I watched a video on the Internet on how to copy keys. It's easy. You need modeling clay, baby powder, a spoon and some lead weights. Hopefully, it works to open the door."

I bite my lip and ask, "Why'd you copy his office key? Were you planning to get rid of him?"

She squares her shoulders and answers me, "No, he made us weak. I wanted to have secret power over him. So I copied all of his keys. I always scrolled through his phone when he was passed out, too. He used his birthday as his pass code not my birthday or my mom's or his wedding day. It was always all about him. Anyways I wrote down all of the telephone numbers and checked to see how many new ones were in there. He hardly ever added phone numbers for men, mostly just women. In the contacts, he added an extra field but it was numbers like a code. I worked to crack the code, but I'm not sure if I succeeded. You were the only new one, when I snooped last Tuesday."

Sean turns around to face the back seat. "This is the weirdest, out of nowhere reveal, I've ever heard. So Gennifer's a budding spy and thief, and since Cynthia hasn't said a word, you must not be surprised."

Cynthia lifts her head and grabs her daughter's hand, "My life's been so messed up. I was afraid of my husband. A part of me's a little scared of my own daughter's deviousness. I'm sure yinz are wondering if I'm even sick."

Whipping the bandana off her head, she says, "I wouldn't shave my head for a con job. I wish my illness was fake because then I wouldn't be facing leaving my sixteen year old alone."

Cynthia's defiant attitude makes me like her more than I did yesterday when she was acting like a victim of her circumstances. Gennifer's slyness she learned from her father, but it seems like her toughness came from Cynthia.

Gennifer pipes up to deflect our attention from her mother who's putting the bandana back on her head. "Besides, in the only pictures of you in his phone you were wearing clothes and your clothes weren't sexy at all. Plus you seemed clueless about his photography hobby."

"Eww, he was taking pictures of me." I shake my head in disgust, but then the rest of her statement hits me. "Wait, what do you mean the ones of me were wearing clothes? Does that mean he had were pictures of women who weren't dressed in his phone?"

She focuses on me and seems to avoid looking in Sean's direction, "Yep, that pig who's my sperm donor had tons of pictures of naked women in his phone. So many of them looked sad or super mad if you looked at them close. Most of them had makeup and tears smeared on their faces. You didn't look sad. You looked like you had no idea he was taking your picture. I figured you were safe to call. We do need your help, a lot. No one listens to a sixteen year old and a sick woman."

Gennifer finishes her speech, crosses her arms and glares at me. She isn't pleading, she's insisting on our sense of decency to compel us to help her.

Lando hasn't said a word during this entire conversation. He could be focusing on driving because the morning traffic through downtown Pittsburgh is terrible. There are many traffic lights and pedestrians and bridges and tunnels between Lawrenceville and Whitehall.

He doesn't turn around or participate in the

confrontation in any way. He announces, "We said we will help you, and we will. Mac texted me this morning that the police officer in charge of the case will meet us at Genius Used Cars. Don't produce your copied key unless he doesn't bring one. For God's sake, don't share anything you told us with him unless he asks you pointblank with your mother and a lawyer present. I hope Gene's unprotected phone gave them evidence on a long list of other possible suspects. No one talk the rest of the trip. I'm old, and you people in this car are stressful when I'm driving."

Gennifer's mouth opens, and she's probably not planning to agree, so I jab her in the side and put my hand over my own mouth. She narrows her eyes at me but doesn't say anything. Cynthia's pallor and dark circles under her eyes make her exhaustion clear as she slumps against the window. During the rest of the ride, everyone remains silent.

FOURTEEN

"Genius Used Cars ia all about me...helping you."

The moment we pull into Genius Used Cars, Gennifer opens her mouth, "There's a whole bunch of stuff I want to say and none of you are my parents. I have the right to free speech. This is important. We need to solve Gene's murder while we're running his dealership."

I put my hand on Gennifer's shoulder since even in the gigantic back seat of Lando's Town Car, she's touching me. "That's it. That's the real reason you called me. It was my whole name in his phone wasn't it? You looked me up and discovered I was involved with the murders at Roar Motors. You figured I'd be happy to play amateur detective again, didn't you?"

She nods, "Yep, no one said you helped solve the case, but I figured at least you've seen a dead body before."

Sean glances over his shoulder and says, "This line of conversation should end now because a huge man who carries himself like he has authority is coming this way."

Pointing to the man walking in our direction, I say, "That's Detective Andrews. He was the first detective on the scene when I found Gene's body. He's also the guy who interviewed me. Mac didn't like him at all."

I slide out the car and walk over to Detective Andrews, "Good morning. Thanks so much for meeting us here. I hope the case's going well. My lawyer promised to ask you about the cat, but she didn't tell me what you said."

He looks down at me and smiles. "You and your focus on the cat are weird. An alley cat isn't more important than a murdered guy. After your adventures at Roar Motors, I guess you're comfortable around murder. I talked more to Detective Rousch, and he told me about your amateur investigation."

I lift my shoulders and reply, "That's good because I can't kill an eight legged ladybug much less a person."

He quirks his lip, "Ladybugs have six legs. Spiders have eight legs."

I stop smiling and say, "I don't say the "s" word, they scare me. I have arachnophobia. On a serious note, I also discovered what happens to the people who are left behind when someone's murdered. I'm not sure if you knew that my attorney Ms. MacAlister was best friends with Tiffany King, the first victim. She's still grieving. Please don't tell her I mentioned this to you."

The detective cocks his head to the side, "Following your conversations reminds me of navigating a maze. Back to the cat, he's fine. We kept him at the station over the weekend in a cage to make sure he didn't produce any evidence he may have consumed in the car. We swabbed his claws for DNA, too, and that's at the lab."

I look up at Detective Andrews because everyone's

taller than I am, "Can I adopt him directly from the police station? I feel a certain kinship to him since we were the first two on the scene of Gene's unfortunate demise."

He crosses his arms, "First of all, who says unfortunate demise? I just finished my law degree and I don't talk like that. I don't know anyone who talks like that. I remember you babbling something about wanting the cat. Someone at the station called a few shelters and found out they were all full. You getting him saves me from strong arming an animal rescue. If you want the cat, you can pick him at the station today."

I grin at him, "Awesome. As soon as we get everyone set up, I'll go to the closest pet store to buy another carrier. It'll take too long to run home, obtain a carrier and come back. I don't want to make him stay at the police station too long. Speaking of driving home, is it okay if I take my car?"

Detective Andrews tilts his head and asks, "Why wouldn't you be able to take your car?"

I wave toward the block service building, "It was part of the crime scene because I parked behind the building. I didn't want to mess anything up by taking it."

He glances in the direction I'm waving toward, "We've cleared the crime scene or I wouldn't have let all of you show up this morning. Do you know which other employees will be coming to work today?"

I shake my head, "Nope, we have no idea. I only worked here for a week, and none of the other employees were people who I wanted to add to my contacts."

He gestures toward Lando's car, "What about Gene

Johnson's wife and daughter? How did they find your number but not the numbers of employees of longer standing?"

Detective Andrews has been charming this morning but it feels like he's interviewing me. I'm not sure if I should tell him about Gennifer's snooping. It's not my information to share. I shake my head, "That's an excellent question. You should talk to Gennifer Johnson."

Evading a question from a police officer isn't lying. It's creative avoidance. I need to distract him by changing the subject but make it seem natural.

I pat my ears, I'm back to wearing my diamond earrings which my parents gave me for graduation. "During the Roar Motors case, the diamond earrings I usually wear ended up as part of evidence. Once the killer confessed, and the earrings had nothing to do with the murder, Detective Rousch allowed me to get them back. How long do you keep things in evidence like the cat?"

Detective Andrews laughs proving my distraction works, "Okay, that's completely out of left field. However, it's a question I can try to answer as a police officer and a future lawyer. Most of the time, you'll get your property back after the case is over including appeals. It depends on the item and its relationship to the case. Unless the animal was the murder weapon, we don't tend to want to deal with them."

I sigh, "I know I keep returning my attention to the orange and white cat I saw in the car, but something about him tugged at my heart strings. Sorry, sometimes my train of thought stops at weird stations. What were we discussing?"

Detective Andrews looks me in the eye and says, "We were discussing the other employees at this lot and if you thought any of them would show up this morning."

I glance over my shoulder at the car where Lando, Sean, Gennifer and Cynthia remain seated, "Lando, my grandfather, told me we would play today by ear. After over fifty years in the car business, he can handle the sales and the financing. He paid the ninety dollars to renew his sales license because it's one of the lowest numbers still active in the state. I can help with sales because I got a sales license when I was working at Roar Motors. Sean is here for detailing and running errands. Cynthia was a title clerk when she met Gene, so in a pinch she could do that."

He asks, "What do you mean sales license? Don't car salesmen just have to have drivers' licenses?"

Lando must have been listening to the conversation from the car, because when he hears his name, he hauls himself out it. I don't understand the reason behind sales licenses for car salesmen or the purpose. I gesture toward my grandfather and wait for him to answer Detective Andrews.

When he reaches us, he shakes hands with the detective, "I'm Bert Landovic, Violet's grandfather. Everyone calls me Lando. In Pennsylvania, car salesmen need licenses which need to be renewed every two years. When someone applies for a sales license, they're supposed to self-report any felony convictions. Some like Driving Under the Influence aren't a big deal. If car lots fired every fool who got busted for drunk driving, there would a lot less salespeople. However, people who commit odometer tampering, auto theft or title forgery aren't supposed to be able to get licenses."

Detective Andrews looks toward the sales trailer and back at Lando, "Thanks for the info. I'll check out the sales license thing when I return to the station. The whole license thing puts a wrench in my plan. This case has too many suspects because it sounds like Gene Johnson left a lot of unhappy customers, and I thought about staying here for a few days going through the paperwork to understand what happened to Gene Johnson."

Lando taps his cane on the cracked parking lot, "Did you get permission from your bosses? If they said okay, I think you should be fine as long as you don't finish the deals. You can talk to people, but you can't negotiate prices. One of the things I'm going to change about this used car lot is putting window stickers with prices on every single car. For used cars, there doesn't have to be a window sticker, but it helps sell cars if you're honest."

I interrupt, "I don't think honesty was one of Gene's goals or attributes." I throw my hand over my mouth when I realize I'm insulting the victim again.

Detective Andrews looks at me and smiles his gorgeous smile, "Violet, I know you didn't like the victim. If you two think I can handle being an undercover car salesman, we can do this."

A thought pops into my mind and out of my mouth, "Wait, we obviously know you're a police officer, and you said I'm still a suspect. Aren't the other employees and Gene's family suspects too? How will this be undercover?"

He puts his arms across his impressive chest and says, "This is more like a hybrid undercover assignment. The customers won't be aware I'm a detective. My supervisors hope if one of the employees who actually shows up is the killer, they'll forget themselves around me."

I shrug my shoulders. This plan seems to be a gigantic waste of police resources, but it isn't my call. Detective Rousch never tried to pretend to be anything other than a police officer during my last murder investigation.

While I'm talking to Detective Andrews, Sean helps Cynthia out of the car and guides her over to where I'm standing with the cop. She smiles up at Detective Andrews. "I feel so tiny compared to all of you big men. My dearly departed husband wasn't such a big guy even though he always wanted to be. I'm Cynthia Johnson, Gene's wife. Thank you so much for investigating. Anything you need from me or my daughter, Gennifer, just let us know."

Gennifer doesn't join the rest of us. She skips to the office door and yanks on it to open it. I hope she doesn't try her copied key, because it might raise the detective's suspicions. When it doesn't pop open, she darts behind the office trailer toward the small service garage where I found her father's body.

I stand on my toes and aim up to his ear and whisper, "Detective Andrews, did anyone clean up the blood from Gene's murder?" It feels indelicate to talk about blood and murder in front of the wife of the victim, even if she hated him, especially since she called him dearly departed to a police officer.

He shakes his head, "No, that isn't the job of the

police. A couple of cleaning companies specialize in crime scene cleanup. It's the property owner's responsibility to take care of it. This murder happened outside, and it's Pittsburgh, I assume the rain will wash most of it away. Why?"

I point to the service building, "Umm, the victim's daughter just dashed toward the crime scene."

He grabs my hand and pulls me after him at a brisk clip. "Can you come with me to talk to her? This might be awkward."

When we reach Gennifer, she's leaning against the building staring at the blood stain, and she's still. This child talks and darts and moves constantly but focusing on the spot where I found her father's body, she stands utterly motionless.

She throws her hand toward the spot, and it trembles, "So I guess that was his final resting place. Could it have been an accident? Maybe someone didn't realize he was next to the building and ran into it."

I look up at Detective Andrews, raise my eyebrows, and shrug my shoulders. He takes the question, "I'm so sorry but our investigation points toward murder. Someone ran over your father four times. I talked to you Saturday, but you may have forgotten my name. I'm Detective Andrews, and I'm assigned to find your dad's killer."

Gennifer starts to sob. I'm surprised based upon her callous attitude about Gene's death during our conversations. She throws herself at the detective and he catches her. The look on his face is priceless. It appears he doesn't have any idea what to do with a sobbing, clinging teenager.

I hesitate for a minute as I remember his attitude toward me at this crime scene. He was also rude to Mac in the interrogation room. Maybe, I'll walk back to the group and let him deal with a girl bordering on hysteria. I turn to leave, and he pulls one arm away from cradling Gennifer to wave me to a stop.

He transfers Gennifer to my arms and says, "I'll leave you two here. I'm going to open the office. I have a key. I'll wait to see if any other employees show up."

Gennifer's sobbing trickles into sniffles as I hold her. Once the door to the office slams shut, she lifts her head, winks at me with a sly smile and asks, "So how'd I do? Do you think he bought it?"

I pull her to the other side of the service bay, the farthest point from everyone. I don't want to keep looking at the blood stain that used to be Gene Johnson. I don't want anyone to notice Gennifer's sudden recovery or my imminent conversation with her. This child learned manipulation and deviousness at her father's knee. If she doesn't repair her moral compass, she could become a monster.

The only reason she's not on my internal suspect list is logistics. It would be too difficult for her to get to Genius Used Cars late at night, grab his car keys, run over him, and return to her house with her mom with no car. The two of them might be lying about their lack of a car. The overgrown parking pad supports their story, but Gene must have parked his beloved car somewhere when he visited them.

I glance toward the sales trailer, "Your performance could have won you an Emmy award. You've told me how much you disliked your father, and I totally bought it." I shake my head, "I'll admit you scare me a little."

She giggles at me, "Well, I got us new information. Someone ran over Gene four times."

FIFTEEN

"I have cars for any budget."

I grasp Gennifer's hand to pull her toward the office. From this angle, it looks like a car's pulling into the lot. It is quarter to eleven. Some of the other employees could be showing up for work. The motley employee crew makes a fabulous group of suspects. I'll wait to discuss Gennifer's duplicity with the people I trust tonight at Lando's.

Walter, the old salesman, parks his car next Lando and the others. He rolls down his window and asks, "Hey, I know you. You're that girl's grandfather. So is we working today? Who's in charge? I don't care as long as I get paid. I still have pay left from the last two weeks, so I thought dat I'd come in to see how to gets my money. I'll keep working. I ain't got nothin' better to do."

Lando answers Walter, "I'm running the car lot with the permission of Gene's widow." He gestures toward Cynthia but doesn't introduce her. "We'll see if anyone else shows up. There'll be a staff meeting in the trailer at nine o'clock. I'll see you there."

Another car enters the lot as Walter drives away to park. Dalton, the young salesman, drives this car. He idles next to Lando and rolls down his window. "I'm sorry sir. I saw you talking to Walter up there. I worked here before the tragedy. I came in to check if anyone would be here. I'm still owed two weeks of back pay. I wasn't sure who to talk to about that. Can you help me?"

Lando leans toward Dalton's window, "We're reopening the car lot today. If you want a job, we can keep you. If not, you can come into the trailer and leave an address so we can send you your pay check. We haven't had a chance to investigate the books. There might be a delay."

Dalton looks Lando in the eye and says, "Well, sir, I'm not sure what I plan to do. I'll need to hunt for another job, but I don't have one yet. If it's okay with you, I'll work this week while we figure out my pay. It's not like I have anything lined up."

Lando surveys the lot as Dalton moves his car. "So now we have three actual salespeople, an undercover detective fake salesman, a prep guy, and me as the manager. We need a title clerk and a technician. I know some retired service guys who might help us." He looks at Cynthia who's being held upright by Sean. "I know you have the experience but I don't think you have the stamina. In fact, we need to put you in the trailer and get you off your feet."

As we walk toward the trailer, a car speeds into the lot and blocks our progress. Phoebe, the title clerk, throws open her car door and slithers into the parking lot. She leans against her car, "What're yinz doing here together?

It's the worthless sales girl, the abandoned wife and the bratty kid. Is this a convention of Gene's rejects? Are you here to celebrate his death? Maybe yinz are returning to the scene of the crime."

Her venom surprises me. She ignored me last week when Gene introduced me to her. She muttered under her breath I wouldn't last a week. She glared at me throughout the week and sighed with disgust whenever I asked her anything. Her level of nastiness must be directed at the three of us.

She puts her hands on her hips and glares at us, "Look at the three of you there in your expensive clothes, thinking you're better than other girls. After all yinz are the type of girls men marry and don't just fool around with."

I have nothing in common with this woman so I abandon all manners and ask, "Were you involved with Gene?"

She rolls her eyes at me and glares at me like I'm an idiot. "Well duh, he fired the last title clerk cause she stopped putting out. He said my car would be free and he'd pay me under the table. I need under the table because my mom took my kid and got the court to say I had to pay child support. Who heard of a mom having to pay child support?"

No polite response occurs to me. I'm sure her child will have a better life with Phoebe's mother. Of course her mother raised her into the upstanding citizen before me. This conversation is the longest I've had with her. I should keep her talking to ascertain if she's Gene's killer.

This time, I'll tell Detective Andrews everything I discover. Solving murders is his job, not mine.

Out of the corner of my eye, I notice the rest of the group watch this exchange with varying degrees of horror and confusion. Cynthia interrupts Phoebe's diatribe and says, "I need to go into the trailer to sit down. Standing in this heat is tiring me out."

Cynthia peers up at Sean, "I hate to ask this but I've noticed how strong you are. Could you carry me?"

Sean lifts her into his arms and carries her to the trailer rather than bothering to reply. I doubt he wants to engage with the classy Phoebe.

Phoebe points to Sean and says, "Men never carry me like dat. She got Gene to marry her and now caught a man who carries her around without saying a word. He lifted her like a man carrying his bride. Do you see those arms? How do some girls get lucky, and I get scummy? Gene said she was a cold fish, but she hooked him and now a hottie."

I bite my lip so I don't proclaim Sean isn't Cynthia's, he's mine. Claiming Sean as my boyfriend won't help solve Gene's murder. Gennifer glances at me and opens her mouth possibly to contradict Phoebe's assumption about Sean. I look at her and shake my head. She shrugs and follows Sean to the trailer. This conversation has illustrated subtlety isn't Phoebe forte, so I should question her.

Lando comes to the rescue by introducing himself to Phoebe, "I'm Lando, and I've been in the car business for many years. I've always believed title clerks are the heart of dealerships, but they never get the appreciation they deserve."

For the first time since I've met her, I witness Phoebe smiling at someone. Her entire demeanor changes. "Hey, didn't you buy your granddaughter the snazzy Fiat? When you did dat for her, I thought what a class act. Well, once Gene told me you were her granddad and not her old sugar daddy, I thought you was the real deal. I saw lots of old guys buying cars for girls, but not ones with da same last name."

The sun glints off his diamond pinkie ring. This is the first time I've noticed him wearing it since I moved to Pittsburgh. He always wore it when I visited as a child. It must be part of his salesman persona, like the custom made suit he's wearing today.

He smiles at her and pats his suit jacket, "As a matter of a fact, I did buy her the lovely Mocha Latte Fiat. I believe a gentleman should take care of the ladies in his life."

She reaches toward him, "Wow, no one never thought they should take care of me. Would you like to try?"

Lando looks at the ground like he's bashful. It'll be fun to observe the old codger try to wiggle out of this inquiry without offending her with his refusal.

He runs his hand through his thick silver and white hair, "Well, when I was a younger more energetic man if you catch my drift, I would've loved to have taken care of a lady like you. To my great chagrin, now I'm too old for you by decades. Plus my son, Violet's father, is so worried about me meeting a lovely lady he sent Violet here to keep me away from temptations like you."

Phoebe giggles, walks over to him and puts her hand

on his chest. "Aren't you just the cutest? I love a man with some experience but if you got a minder, I get it."

Lando puts his hand on her shoulder but backs away from her, "You mentioned Gene treated you badly. Do you want to talk to an old man about it?"

This question opens a floodgate in Phoebe. She wraps her arms around her middle, "I hated him, but I'm so mad someone killed him. I ain't never goin a find another job that pays me this good under the table. He trained me, but I don't got a high school diploma so no one else'll hire me as a title clerk. I wish I knew who run him over. I'd kick them where the sun don't shine."

The interaction between Phoebe and Lando fascinates me. A little flattery and Lando charms her. He looks her in the eye and pays attention to everything she says. Sometimes all people want someone else to see them and be engaged with what they have to say. I stay silent so I don't break the spell. I could've tried to compliment her, and she might've ignored me or kicked me.

Lando tilts his head to the side, "Who do you think killed him?"

She shrugs her shoulders with her arms crossed under her breasts, "So many people hated him. Seemed to me to know Gene was to hate him. There had to be something in it for them. I think runnin' over someone a couple of times takes a lotta mad. He fired a lotta people and conned a bunch more with bad cars. The cat is the weird thing. If someone had just hit him and run over him a few times that'd be one thing but putting a cat in the car, it's like they was making a point."

She glances around the lot and her eyes shift, "I

heard them cops talking about what happened. Blood makes me puke so I'm happy I didn't have to see nothing."

Dalton and Walter must have been talking to each other behind the building because it took them a long time to park their cars. They've been missing during Lando's questioning of Phoebe. The two salesmen walk up together and Dalton interrupts us, "Hey Phoebe, we should go in the trailer and see what's going on today."

The interruption seems to break Lando's spell over Phoebe. She reaches out to pat him on his hand holding his cane. I follow the trio toward the office trailer. I don't think Phoebe killed Gene. She might be lying to us about being upset for losing a job which pays her under the table. However, she has no idea I'm looking into Gene's death. She doesn't have to convince me she didn't kill him. She has to convince the police she's not the murderer.

She overshared about not paying child support, making her guilty of fraud. Being trained by Gene as a title clerk also doesn't point to her ability or her honesty. I doubt Lando's planning to pay her under the table because it isn't worth the potential trouble. Maybe Cynthia can train Detective Andrews to be the title clerk. I've never seen or heard about a male title clerk. The picture of the masculine Detective Andrews sitting at Phoebe's desk filing his nails makes me giggle.

My giggle makes Lando raises his eyebrows at me but I wave at him. The other three either didn't hear me or are ignoring me. Phoebe opens the door and yells, "What's the cop doing in my office?"

Detective Andrews motions all of us into the sales trailer rather than answering her rude question.

He addresses everyone in the room, "I'm here undercover to investigate Gene Johnson's death. I want to see how things work at this car lot and narrow down the extensive suspect list. No one is allowed to tell anyone I'm a police officer. I'm another salesperson who can't sell cars. From what I've heard about this car lot, poor sales skills won't make me unusual. If anyone wants to leave, there's the door. Leaving doesn't make you less of a suspect."

Phoebe turns around and grabs the door handle. "I'm out of here. I didn't kill the jerk. I ain't working with no cop."

After the door slams behind her, Detective Andrews asks, "So is anyone else leaving?"

I say, "No sir." Everyone else shakes their heads no.

I raise my hand.

Detective Andrews turns to me and says, "This isn't the military with the sirs and it isn't school, you don't have to raise your hand to speak."

I bite my lip, "Well, I didn't want to be rude. Phoebe used all the rude for the day with her dramatic exit. Her departure leaves the lot without a title clerk. Cynthia knows how to do the job, but she doesn't have the energy to stay all day. Since you're going to be here, and you don't have a sales license, I thought maybe you could be the title clerk. Phoebe spent most of the day filing her nails so it would give you time to check out all of the paperwork."

Lando points to Phoebe's desk and says, "I've never

worked with a male title clerk but I think it might be a good idea."

Cynthia chimes in, "I can teach you what you need to know, and Lando should be able to keep an eye on you."

Detective Andrews sits on top of the desk and says, "I'm going to have to do my real job. This isn't a hobby for me. I doubt many people will be trying to buy a car from a used car lot connected to a murder. Cynthia can we set up a comfortable chair for you to rest in Gene's office so you can stay during the day?"

Cynthia nods, "I'll try my best."

Detective Andrews's gaze sweeps around the room, "Sounds good. Lando's in charge of the operations. Are there any questions?"

Walter asks Detective Andrews, "Dalton and I want to know if we're goin be getting paid. That's why we came back to this pit. Gene owed us for two weeks of pay. Plus I don't got another job to go to."

Lando sweeps his eyes toward Dalton and Walter to take this question. "I'm spending the day looking through all of Gene's paperwork. It'll be helpful to have Detective Andrews's eyes on it too. We'll make sure everyone gets what they deserve. As salespeople your jobs are to sell cars with as much honesty as you can. It's after eleven o'clock on a Monday morning, let's turn on the open signs."

Lando moves to the window and flips on the neon open sign. Lando's dramatic pronouncement should have led to a rush of customers. However, Genius Used Cars serves customers who work long, odd hours. The busy times for this lot are late afternoon to evening rather than mornings.

Dalton told me my first day if Gene caught a salesperson alone, the salesperson could try to avoid Gene's explosion. He explained the best way to distract Gene was to ask Gene to talk about his accomplishments. When Gene discovered two salespeople together, he would feed on the audience. Gene would pick one of the salespeople and harangue them until something distracted him. If no customers arrived to distract Gene's tirade, it often ended in one fewer salesperson. He'd fire them or they'd quit because of his rude behavior.

For the first five minutes after the lighting of the open signs, everyone stays in the sales trailer in uncomfortable silence. The old rules of behavior at Genius Used Cars no longer apply. No one is sure about the replacement rules.

Gennifer breaks the hush with a roll of her eyes and a stamp of her foot, "I can't take it anymore. No one ever accused me of being too quiet in my life. I'll talk about the weather if I have to. This feels super creepy."

Lando taps his cane to grab everyone's attention, "Gennifer's right but the weather isn't the topic we should be discussing. We need to talk about the type of sales training you've received."

Before anyone answers Lando, Cynthia moans. "I wasn't sure how long I'd be able to be here before the pain became too bad. Apparently it isn't very long. Can Sean drive me home? I have my doctor's appointment at one. Based on the commute, I think he should stay with me. Do you need him here?"

Sean spending the day with Cynthia isn't okay with me. I don't trust anyone who stayed married to Gene Johnson for over a decade after she stole him from his first wife. Cynthia's illness makes her beauty appear delicate and ephemeral like a dying fairy. Compared to her, I feel sturdy. Sean's feelings for me started during the most needy time of my life last month. At the time, I was a combination of damsel in distress and amateur investigator. He might be attracted to wounded women. Cynthia beats me in the disadvantaged Olympics. If I object, I'm a monster who's being callous to a sick lady.

As I contemplate an acceptable response, Gennifer bounds over to her mother and gently hugs her. "I think Sean will be an awesome aide for you. He should totally stay. Maybe he could make you lunch or vacuum or do laundry. I hate doing those things, so he could be a big help."

Cynthia shakes her head at her daughter, "Everyone here is helping us so much. Sean didn't volunteer to be my personal caregiver. He offered me a ride. We can't expect a busy man like him to do our laundry."

Sean shrugs, "I'd love to help you two in any way I can. I started helping around the house and doing my own laundry when I was ten. My grandmother who raised me always said she wasn't raising a lazy boy. If we pick something healthy to eat on the way to your house, I'll have more time to take care of you."

While Sean proves he's truly a kind guy with his earnest reply, I watch Cynthia. The subtle smile on her face illustrates this conversation may not have been Gennifer's idea. As soon as she notices my interest, she winces and says, "The pain washes over me sometimes. I so appreciate everything you do. If you could support me on the walk to the car it should be enough."

Sean smiles down at her and says, "You should lean on me in the close quarters, but I'll carry you from the trailer to the car. It's no trouble at all. You're lighter than most of the loads I lift on the job site."

He's so focused on supporting Cynthia he nods and says a blanket goodbye to everyone in the room. He doesn't acknowledge me.

As soon as they're gone, Gennifer turns to Dalton and asks, "So how old are you? You don't look that much older than me. Sometimes looks can be deceiving. You might be really old like twenty-seven."

My sigh and eye roll at my age being considered old doesn't slow Gennifer's interrogation of Dalton. "Do you like selling cars? Obviously you didn't like working for my dad, no one ever liked working for my dad. Do you have a wife or a girlfriend? Do you live with your parents?"

He laughs and tucks a stray piece of hair into his man bun, "Didn't anyone ever teach you no one can answer your questions if you don't pause to let them talk?"

"Actually everyone tells me that." She bats her eyelashes and giggles at him.

He leans against the wall and grins at her, "I'm eighteen, so I bet I'm pretty close to your age which you didn't mention in your questions. After my sister bought her car here, I got a job selling cars. Like I said, I'm only eighteen, so I'm not married. I live with my mom and sisters."

I wish I could take notes on Dalton's answers to Gennifer's questions. Her interrogation seems cute rather than nosy because of her delivery method. She's either investigating or flirting but everyone else in the room sees a cute teenage girl trying to charm a teenage boy.

Gennifer leans agains the wall opposite Dalton and mirrors his stance. She starts again, "I have so many questions. I'm always afraid if I don't say everything in my head, it'll just leave my brain. I know I talk fast, but hopefully you can follow me. How long have you worked here? Do you live nearby? You didn't answer if you liked selling cars. I noticed because I'm super curious about that one. I might want to sell cars after I graduate from high school. It depends on my mom. Gene used to say people need cars, so selling them is like shooting fish in a barrel."

Lando puts his cane between the two young people as if he can't stay quiet at this statement, "People do need cars, but it's bad sales practice to think of your customers as fish in a barrel. You have to see your customers as people. Gennifer's correct that we should talk while we wait for customers to arrive. I suspect Gene never did any sales training. This is a great time for me to tell you how car sales should work so it benefits the customer as well as the salesperson and the dealership."

Detective Andrews and I make eye contact. He shrugs. We've both been observing Gennifer's skillful interrogation, but all Lando must have heard was the insult to his lifelong career.

Lando launches into a defense of the professional way to help people buy the cars they need. For the next hour, he shares his view of car sales. In the time I've lived with him, he's shared some of his advice and stories mixed into conversations. In front of an audience of people with varying degrees of sales experience, he's amazing.

He addresses Walter and tries to make Walter feel included because of his liquor sales experience. He encourages him to make connections between the different types of sales. Lando discovers Dalton's sales training consisted of a five minute speech from Gene that was basically reel in the suckers and hand them over to him. This hour teaches me more than I learned in my three weeks at a substantial family owned Ford dealership. He manages to entertain and inform even Detective Andrews who has no desire to sell cars.

When the trailer door bangs open, I realize while learning about selling cars, no one's been watching the lot to actually sell cars. It's not a real customer. It's Butch, the repo guy.

He's the opposite of a customer. He epitomizes conflict which he demonstrates with his loud tone. "Who's in charge here? I need to be paid right now or I'm going to bust some heads. Gene owed me like ten grand, so someone needs to pay up."

I'm so proud of my brave grandfather who walks over to the bully and replies, "We are unraveling Gene Johnson's business dealings at this time and keeping the dealership open. Any outstanding debts will be investigated by me and the attorney representing Mr. Johnson's widow and daughter. Everything will be done legally and documented."

Butch pounds on his own chest. His chest is huge but hitting it makes it jiggle. He insists, "You're going to give me my money now. I ain't waiting for no lawyer to investigate any papers. Me and Gene had an understanding. He sold the cars and I snatched them when the deadbeats didn't pay. I'm not goin' be out of my money cause he got himself run over."

As Butch presents his demands he invades Lando's personal space. Lando never moves. Butch remains focused on Lando, and he doesn't seem to be aware Phoebe's desk isn't inhabited by a bottle blond title clerk but by an intimidating police detective. Butch isn't the sharpest person in the room.

Detective Andrews observes Butch and his mannerisms. Part of me wishes Sean was here to protect Lando. He'd probably have stopped this altercation before Butch's ire reached this point. I found out during my last murder investigation, angry people occasionally say things that help to solve cases.

Lando doesn't raise his voice. He glares at the bully and crosses his arms over his chest, "As I said, whoever you are, Gene Johnson isn't running this dealership. People with legitimate claims backed by documentary evidence will receive the money they are owed. Threats and blustering will not change the situation."

Lando makes me proud he's my grandfather when he continues, "Did you understand all of those words I used or do you need fewer syllables?"

Gennifer giggles. Butch pulls his fish back telegraphing his aim to punch a man in his seventies. Detective Andrews glides to the rescue and grabs Butch's arm on the back swing.

He twists the bully's arm behind his back and says, "As entertaining as it would be to arrest you for assault after you hit Mr. Landovic, I don't want you to hurt him. Besides, I think your threatening attitude and demands for compensation without any paperwork to back up your claims rise to the level of extortion and terroristic threats."

Detective Andrews keeps Butch's wrist anchored behind his back and doesn't allow the jerk to move. Butch begins to moan, "Ow, ow, you're hurting my shoulder. Let me go. I was just tryin' to scare the old man. It's my money. If you help me get it, I'll cut you in. I'll pay you more than the old man."

Detective Andrews makes eye contact with me, "Everyone heard his offer, so now I can add bribery of a police officer to your list of charges. Feel free to keep talking Butch, we'll keep adding charges."

Butch wiggles and moans, but fails to escape Detective Andrews's grasp, "You're a cop. How was I supposed to know you was a cop? I thought you were just muscle for the old man. I was Gene's muscle. I figured the old man got his own protection."

Detective Andrews raises a single eyebrow at Butch, "This argument you are attempting will not hold up in court. I sat in the office in plain sight when you entered, and I interviewed you on Saturday about Gene's death. We can keep going with charges if you attempt to resist arrest when I cuff you."

Detective Andrews pulls out his cuffs but drops them on the floor because he's focusing on Butch. He looks over at me, "Can you grab my cuffs?"

I have to get on my knees to retrieve them because they bounced under the desk.

Butch starts to laugh, "Gene bet me a hundred bucks he'd have you on your knees in this trailer by the end of this week. He had a lotta girls in that position in this trailer. I guess I can't add the bet to the money that jerk owed me."

He winces as Detective Andrews tightens his hold. "You need to learn to show some respect."

I jump off the floor with the cuffs and hand them to Detective Andrews. I look at the floor and feel the heat in my face from rage and embarrassment. I worked for Gene Johnson for a week. He treated me like a valued employee, but I guess he must've been thinking of me as a different type of professional.

Detective Andrews cuffs Butch and hustles him to his car. He promises to return after processing Butch.

SIXTEEN

"I can get you in a car!"

Lando looks at the four of us remaining in the trailer, and he returns to instructor mode, "Now you are all going to learn the proper way to do a lot walk."

During the lot walk, a few customers arrive at the dealership. Lando employs a management style that's the complete opposite of Gene's. Lando keeps the four of us with him on the lot. No one gets to hide inside the trailer in the air conditioning. The service guy never comes to work, and there aren't any cars in the service building. Lando pulls up the single garage door on the service building and uses it as his command center. He makes Gennifer his gopher, and she brings him paperwork on every vehicle.

He points toward the trailer and complains, "I don't know how anyone could run a successful car dealership from inside a trailer. There aren't any windows so no one could watch the lot. It's warmer in here, but we can all see everything. That's the reason real car dealerships have so many windows. I remember guys fighting in the old days for the best view of the lot."

Dalton, Walter and I work with two customers each. The lack of financing ability by many of our potential customers continues to be a problem. Only two of the customers are able to buy cars and Lando does all the paperwork himself. His years of experience and friendship with the women in the office at Roar Motors make him a fantastic manager, salesman, and an adequate title clerk.

Detective Andrews returns at four o'clock and chooses to stay inside the trailer. The trailer contains reams of paperwork that may point to Gene's killer. Cynthia, the widow and presumptive heir gave him permission to peruse all the paperwork without a warrant. After the Butch incident, I'm happy he's on site. Especially considering the muscle Lando planned to bring with us is too busy chauffeuring Cynthia to doctor's appointments.

Sean must have been in communication with Lando. After his long day helping Cynthia, he finally returns to the dealership at five o'clock, he brings sandwiches from Primanti Brothers. Lando loves these amazing sandwiches with the fries and coleslaw on them from the original location in the Strip District. Lando raves about them often, but this will be my first experience.

Gene never fed anyone at the car lot. Dalton and Walter reach for their wallets to pay for sandwiches they didn't order. Lando assures everyone the meal's on him. Everyone except Detective Andrews grabs a sandwich.

Detective Andrews shakes his head and explains, "I'm a police officer, and it's against department policy for me to accept food from any member of the community or business. I understand the rule, but there are times like now where it bites because I can't."

I pat my sandwich and say, "Why don't you give the money to Lando for your sandwich, because the jealous expression on your face is making me feel guilty and ruining my appetite. Then Lando can forget the money on the desk and Gennifer can find it. That way you follow the rules, Lando doesn't have to take your money and the sixteen year old gets a little money for her day of watching what happens at a car dealership."

Everyone follows my suggestion without acknowledging my idea, but I accept it with quiet grace. Dalton and Walter go outside to eat their sandwiches in the service building without any prompting so they can watch the lot. As we're eating, Mac breezes into the trailer bringing with her a rush of expensive perfume.

She leaves the door open and points toward the block building, "Those two guys in the service building both ran over to greet me as soon as I stopped my car. The young one beat the limping, older one. Both of them looked so disappointed when I explained I was here to meet with Violet."

She notices Detective Andrews and stops. She puts her hands on her hips and glares at him, "What are you doing here, shouldn't you be at the station harassing people's attorneys?"

Before he can answer her, she turns to me and asks, "Did you pick up the cat? I meant to let you know he's yours if you want him. Someone at the station told me you could have him today."

I drop my sandwich, "I totally forgot about the cat in the excitement of coming back to reopen the car lot. Detective Andrews told me I could pick him up this morning, but it slipped right out of my head. I hope he's ok. I'll take my Fiat to save him right now."

I pivot toward Detective Andrews and ask, "Do you think they would have gotten rid of him because I forgot to pick him up this morning? Can you call someone to check before I leave? If I get there and he's gone, I might cry which would be embarrassing."

He smiles down at me, "Sure, I forgot about him too. It's been an exciting day with sales, paperwork, and arresting a bully."

He whips out his cell phone and turns his back on the room to make the call. The rest of us sit in awkward silence eating our sandwiches and pretending not to listen. Lando hands Mac a sandwich. The bag of sandwiches seems to be a magical neverending source of food.

Detective Andrews turns around and waves his phone at me. "The cat's been hanging out in an interrogation room all day. Apparently, he's sweet and eats anything. My coworkers have been feeding him leftovers from the fridge and made an old cardboard box with shredded reports into a litter tray. If you didn't show up by tomorrow morning, several of them were discussing making him the office mascot."

I rush to the door, and say over my shoulder, "Tell them I'll be there within the hour. I'm sorry I forgot him. He deserves to live inside a house, not back in a police station."

I drop the door and rather than the typical loud slam,

I hear footsteps behind me. Sean follows me to my car. "Are you sure getting another cat's a good idea? You didn't even remember it existed. If you want to adopt it, I'll come with you to get the cat. It'll give us some time to talk without any interruptions."

I want to retrieve the cat alone. I'm working on taking responsibility for my choices. I ask, "Are you sure you want to come with me? I don't want to inconvenience you. If you stay here, you can give Gennifer a ride home. Then you can see Cynthia again."

As the words leave my mouth, I bite my lip. Somehow Cynthia's illness makes saying anything vaguely sarcastic about her feels like speaking ill of the dead. I'm afraid Sean's got a hero complex, and Cynthia makes a better ethereal princess than I do. I don't wait for a response, I keep walking to my car and digging in my bag for my keys.

Sean clutches my arm to stop me, and I stumble. He catches me and turns me to face him. He keeps his hands on my shoulders as I sigh. "I need to drive to the police station to liberate the poor orange alley cat. I don't have time to talk to you right now."

He holds me immobile in his strong hands, "I'm not sure what I did to offend you, but now I can see we need to spend some time together. I can't believe you're arguing with me about a stray cat. I like animals, and I missed you today."

His words make me melt a little. Maybe I'm blowing things out of proportion. He's such a sweet guy. He ruins my warm feelings as the next words emerge from his mouth.

"Cynthia needed me." He continues to hold onto me and look down so he can watch my face. "She's so strong in the face of the adversity she's been fighting. She's only thirty-four, a few years older than us. She's had so many awful things happen to her. I just want to help her."

I hate hearing her name on his lips. It's possible he gravitated to me in the last month because I seemed like a damsel in distress which I'm trying not to be. Sean might have a savior complex, and Cynthia acts more comfortable accepting help than I am. She doesn't appear to have anyone who's helped her other than Gennifer during her illness.

I wiggle to encourage him to release his grip. He doesn't let me go. Detective Andrews must have been watching our discussion from the doorway of the trailer. When Sean keeps holding onto me in spite of my attempt to leave, the detective shouts, "Violet do you need my assistance?"

Pulling away from Sean, I say, "No, I'm fine."

Andrews must not think I'm fine because he lets the door slam and approaches us. I doubt Sean would be confrontational with a police officer, but to defuse any possible situation, I put my hand on Detective Andrews's forearm and smile at him. "Do you mind coming with me to your police station to get the cat? I would feel much better going with you because everyone at the station knows you."

He pulls himself straighter and replies, "I'd be delighted to go with you. Protect and serve is my motto."

Sean rolls his eyes behind the detective's back. "You know what, I'll go into the trailer and talk to your lawyer friend, Mac. I'll have a chance to talk and catch up on the events of the day with Lando. After all, I'm here to keep an eye on him and Gennifer."

Detective Andrews and I walk in silence. I wave at my car and ask, "Do you want to drive my car?"

He cocks his head, "As a police detective, we should take my car, but I need to get it detailed because Butch behaved disgustingly in it. Are you sure you're okay with me driving your car?"

I pat the hood, "I'm not the most comfortable driver on earth at the best of times. This is my first car and I've only owned it for about a week. At home, I used my parents' car when necessary. Then in college and graduate school, I walked everywhere. I walked to my last job most days. Anyway, driving with a police officer in the passenger seat will make me a nervous wreck."

He laughs with a deep rumble and puts his hand out for my keys, "Even though I'm a detective not a traffic officer, I get it. I bet you'll be afraid of breaking a single traffic law."

He unlocks the doors from the key fob, but doesn't run around to open my door. His size shrinks the interior of my car. This wouldn't have been a good plan if I had anything to hide. Luckily, I don't.

As soon as we leave the lot, we both try to talk at the same time. He nods and gestures at me to go first. "This is going to sound like a weird question, but what is your first name? I'll call you Detective Andrews, which is better than the Detective with no name. I thought of you as that when I found Gene's body. I'm curious unless you don't want to tell me."

He watches the road and replies, "Hmm, the Detective with no name. I don't often tell people my first name because it's a little embarrassing but you have a trustworthy face. It's Andrew."

I raise my eyebrows, "So your parents named you Andrew Andrews. That must've been fun in school. At least everyone could pronounce your name."

He glances away from the road for a second, "It's a family thing. Everyone's called me Drew for as long as I can remember. I guess some people stumble over your name."

"My first name's easy. Although in elementary school, some purple crayons ended up dropped on my desk. However, Landovic is a long last name and some teachers overemphasized syllables."

He waves toward the car window and changes the subject, "I know I've passed a pet store in one of the plazas on this road. I don't have the time for a pet. I never got called to this strip mall so I'm not sure exactly where it is. I assume you need to buy a carrier since I don't see one in your tiny backseat."

I'm not sure if it's appropriate to laugh at crime jokes with a detective, so I swallow my giggle and hunt for the address and direction on my phone. "It's about halfway between here and the police station. My phone should alert us when we're close. What were you planning to ask me?"

He glances at me out of the corner of his eye, "I was going to ask you about your relationship with the big redhead at the car lot. It looked like it was getting tense.

Are you two together? If you are together, do you feel safe? He's much larger than you are."

I sigh, "I thought you were going to ask me more questions about Gene's death. I was prepared to defend myself from a murder accusation not explain my complicated personal life."

He interrupts me, "I talked to Detective Rousch since he was around when you found Johnson's body. He assured me you might be a trouble magnet but not a killer. He explained your role in the Roar Motors case. Technically, everyone remains a suspect. I give you extra credit because you were at the center of several murders a month ago and assisted the police without taking any credit."

"I'll start by answering your most important question. I feel safe with Sean. His biggest problem is overprotectiveness. I'm not sure if I know the answer to your other question. We've only known each other for about a month and a half. We just agreed to try dating. Life's a little awkward because we both live with our grandparents, who've been friends for decades."

I pause and look out my window as I fidget with my earrings, "Anyway, Sean has been exceptionally attentive to Gene Johnson's widow, Cynthia. She seems like the type of woman who wants a man to take care of her. I want the type of man who respects me. Back to Gene Johnson, I think he might've been trying to take advantage of my desire for respect. If I were younger, I might call his behavior grooming."

He nods but doesn't ask any more questions about Gene or Sean. We drive the rest of the way to the pet store in silence. Mac's voice plays in my brain as I focus on ways to avoid oversharing with a police detective, no matter how nice he acts. Tension rises in the car with each passing mile, but I don't know how I feel about Andrew Andrews. I disliked him at the crime scene when he treated me like the main suspect. During his interrogation at the police station he played good cop. Today, he appeared to change his personality again into a polite and interested observer. I don't trust these various personas he changes like some men change socks.

At the pet store, Detective Andrews waits in the car. I buy another litter box, food bowls, more food, more litter, some toys, and the carrier. I need to take two trips to bring everything to the car. He starts the car when I come out with the carrier and litter box. "I need to run back in for the rest of my stuff."

When I slide into the passenger seat, he asks, "Why all the stuff? Don't you already have a cat?"

I wave toward my purchases covering the back seat, "I've been reading up on cats. It's better if they each have their own litter box and different food dishes. The cats also have to be separated and introduced to each other gradually. The orange and white boy needs to visit the vet before he gets anywhere near my pampered Annika. The stray might have fleas or other diseases. We have more than enough space at Lando's house. I could even keep them in different houses."

He raises a single eyebrow, "I thought you mentioned living with your grandfather. What do you mean different houses?"

I tug on my ponytail, "Lando owns two half doubles

that he merged into a single house years ago. Technically, I live in one and he lives in the other. That isn't how it's worked out. It would bother him to be away from any of his books and his kitchen is stocked."

He keeps his eyes on the road but tilts his head in confusion. "Okay, okay. None of this makes sense and as a detective, I want everything to make sense. Lando gives the impression that before you came he lived alone. How big are these two half doubles?"

"Each side has four bedrooms plus full attics and basements. You should visit the house sometime. Most of the rooms in the houses are libraries devoted to different types of books. Lando's been collecting books for as long as he sold cars. Television is more my thing. Lando had to buy a television, because he hadn't owned one in this century." I make a gesture like a television set with my hands.

"Let me get this straight. Your grandfather's lived in the city with the best sports teams in the country for most if not all of his life and never watched games on television?" His eyebrows rise.

I nod, "Lando was born and raised in Pittsburgh. He doesn't follow sports but when he sold cars, he talked about the teams all the time. He reads the newspaper to obtain his sports knowledge. Lando loves to read anything. His home serve as his oasis of books. Upstairs between the two houses, there's even a sliding bookcase like a secret entrance. It's the coolest place."

Our arrival at the police station interrupts the conversation. I'm excited about getting the cat. It's almost seven o'clock and the lot contains a few cars. We park close to the building and walk in with me swinging the carrier. I fail to judge my increased mass with the carrier so I bang the carrier into the glass doors. All conversations stop and everyone in the station stares at me.

I brazen my way through my embarrassment and hold up the carrier. "I'm here to pick up the cat who was found in the car that crushed Gene Johnson. Who should I talk to about him?"

I glance behind me, and Detective Andrews grins at me rather than bailing me out of my awkwardness. So I start to talk faster and gesture at him, "Detective Andrews told me I could adopt the cat because most of the shelters are full and even though he seems to be socialized, he needs medical attention and a home."

As I talk a few smiles emerge from the taciturn faces at the desks in the room. Andrews finally pushes himself off the wall and saves me, "I wanted to see the affect that making you uncomfortable would have on your speech patterns. It further reinforces that you have no control over your mouth when you're nervous. The acceleration of your word vomit amuses me. Follow me to the interrogation room."

As we walk down the hall and stop at the room, I realize the cat is staying in the same room Andrews interrogated me on Saturday. "Did the cat do something wrong to end up in the official room where you talk to suspects in Gene's murder? I guess the cat's the only real witness. Too bad he can't talk."

He pats the wall, "No, that's a coincidence. You don't need to enter if the room gives you flashbacks."

I shrug, "I'm fine going into this room to retrieve a

poor cat. After all, I got to watch the fireworks explode between you and Mac in this room. You also realized I'm not a murderer here."

Detective Andrews looks down at me and says, "You're still officially a suspect. Everyone who knew and despised Gene Johnson continues to be a suspect in this case." He escorts me into the room, "That's the official police line. However, if you killed Gene, you should move to Hollywood immediately."

I cock my head to the side, "Why Hollywood? I'm pretty sure California would send me back for a trial."

He looks me up and down and says, "If you can continue the innocent act for this long to fool me and Rousch, you could be an award winning actress."

"Okay, thanks I guess. My face conveys too many of my feelings. Have I told you what my college and graduate school major was?'

He says, "If you say acting, I'm going to be disappointed in my instincts."

I shake my head and say, "I studied other people's acting skills. I graduated with degrees in Popular Culture."

I glance down when a warm furry body rubs against my leg. He peers up at me with a devilish twinkle in his clear eye. His other eye's obscured by a milky film. The cat reminds me why I came to the police station today.

I lift the cat and cuddle him. It may be a dangerous decision to hold a stray cat near my face. Instead of scratching, he climbs onto my shoulder and starts to purr like a broken lawnmower.

Detective Andrews crosses his arms and says, "I might

not snuggle him if I were you. He's probably covered in fleas."

I rub the cat's head, "I don't care. I'll give him a bath as soon as I get him home. I bought a pill which kills everything on his fur in twenty-four hours. My awesome bathroom contains only tile and porcelain. He can quarantine in there. I'll remove all the towels so no evil little beasties jump onto fabric."

Detective Andrews walks toward the front door of the police station, "If you aren't worried about your car, your plan sounds okay."

"He'll be in a carrier. The seats are leather, so it should be fine. I'm heading back to Genius Used Cars now. Isn't your car still there?" I say as I follow him.

We leave the police station. I'm more careful on departure since the cat's in the carrier. I load him into the back seat. During the ride, I don't want to talk to Detective Andrew Andrews. The cat helps me by crying unless I'm turned toward the carrier telling him he's safe now with me. If I stop looking at him, the cat starts to make scratchy yowling sounds.

Detective Andrews says, "He must be part Siamese, my grandmother owns one. If you pay attention to him, he's sweet. If you ignore him, he walks around the house making awful noises."

My current cat, Annika, doesn't make any noise other than quiet purring. A loud cat might be an adjustment, especially for Lando. I hope good care and security will quiet the vocalizations. Based on the missing patches of fur and scratches on his body, this boy's a survivor.

We get back to the car lot after closing time, so Dalton

and Walter are gone. Lando, Sean, and Gennifer are waiting for us at the trailer. Mac hurries up to the car and opens my door, "Did you answer any of the detective's questions without counsel present? I didn't realize you were going with him. I wouldn't have allowed you to go if I'd known."

"Thanks for your concern and getting my door. I'm fine. The cat's fine. Detective Andrews is fine. Everyone's fine. We can talk about this when Detective Andrews isn't here." I walk past her toward the trailer.

She starts on him as I walk away from the car, "If you didn't read Violet her rights again, a case could be made that since she has counsel who wasn't present, anything she said would be inadmissible."

"Calm down. Our discussion of her college major and the probable fleas on a stray cat aren't going to move the case forward. As much fun as it is to be attacked by a tiny attorney, I've been working for twelve hours, and I'll be back tomorrow. I'm heading home." He turns his back on Mac and waves to me, "Bye Violet, it's been nice getting to know you better as a person. I look forward to seeing you tomorrow."

When I join the group at the trailer, Sean asks, "What does he mean he looks forward to seeing you?"

This hint of jealousy from Sean annoys me. He spent most of the day at the beck and call of Cynthia and his first words to me are about Detective Andrews. I might not be ready for an exclusive relationship.

I point at him, "I'm not dating Detective Andrews. I'm not dating Quentin. In fact, right now it doesn't feel like I'm dating you. I want to go home to Lando's and bathe my cat. I've had enough of drama and murder investigations for today."

I pivot and stumble on the turn ruining my dramatic exit. I don't glance around or acknowledge anyone. I'm done for the night. Everyone can discuss the case and the day without me. I don't care if they spend the rest of the evening discussing me and my rude behavior.

In my rush to get to my car and leave without engaging with another human, I left the cat in the back seat rather than moving him to the front seat. It's impossible for me to face the cat and talk to him while I'm driving. I tried talking to him from the front seat but it didn't calm him. During the half hour ride home, the cat and I sing duets to my CD of "Once More With Feeling." My awful voice and his screeching match in quality. The *Buffy* singalong allows me to express aggression.

When I get into the house with the cat carrier, Annika appears to investigate. Annika follows me with her tail in the air conveying indignation. I ignore her attitude. I climb to the second floor and push the bookcase on its track so I can access my side of the house. My side has its own front door, but Lando only gave me a key to his door which is the main entrance. Having a key to my own side of the house might make me feel more independent but it's not worth hurting Lando's feelings.

I shut the bathroom door in Annika's face. I don't want her to possibly acquire any of the fleas I'll be removing from the cat who needs a name. While singing with him, I thought about possible names for the cat. I tested a few during breaks between songs.

I place the carrier on the tile floor, and run back to

the car to grab the flea medication and shampoo. Annika waits at the door. I ignore her on my quest. I change out of my work clothes and into a well-loved college t-shirt and black leggings. While arranging the washing materials and filling the tub with warm water, it occurs to me this project would've been easier with assistance.

Washing a potentially feral cat with which I've shared a car ride as a new pet owner proves only slightly more daunting than facing a killer. I carefully open the door to the carrier and the cat sniffs and jumps into my arms. With the first hurdle cleared, I face the worst part, a cat and a bathtub. I gingerly place him in the water expecting a mess with claws. With his legs and belly submerged, he looks up at me and meows. There's no thrashing, no hysteria, just a meow. I lean over the tub to wet and scrub him. He wanders around the tub in the water that covers him to his chin and investigates. The shampoo works as advertised on the bottle. Flea carcasses and flea dirt drift away from him. The water turns pink from the blood that feeds the nasty parasites.

The cat treats the experience like a harried housewife at a spa day. His behavior delights me. At the end of his treatment and rinse cycle, I cuddle him in an old towel. He purrs, wiggles and steals my heart. Once he's dry and clean, his orange and white swirls are like a creamsicle so I ask him if he likes the name. He keeps purring and butts his head into my chin.

Introducing Creamsicle to Annika worries me. I'm able to procrastinate. I can't do it until after Creamsicle visits the veterinarian. He's clean of fleas and dirt, but I'm not sure about possible diseases. Annika's former owner took meticulous care of her and left all of her vet records in a file. I'll call her vet for a Creamsicle appointment tomorrow. The two cats can learn each other's scents under the bathroom door. Spending time in this gorgeous bathroom snuggling my new cat won't be a hardship.

When the cat's dry, I leave the bathroom. The sun has set, but no one's called me or come to the house. I'll deal with the drama tomorrow. I wish solving murders was as easy as getting rid of dirt and fleas. I turn off my phone and curl up in bed. Annika joins me in my bedroom and stations herself at the top of my pillow. I fall asleep to the sound of a purring cat.

SEVENTEEN

"If you're not first, you're last."

The sun shines onto my face as it rises and I'm awake before six o'clock in the morning. I check on Creamsicle in the bathroom, and he's curled on his new cat bed. He rises and stretches to greet me. After rubbing against my leg, he looks at his empty food bowl and yowls. He ate more last night than Annika eats in three days, it must be his prior food insecurity.

I use my laptop to check if the vet has any openings today. There's a nine o'clock appointment. I need to let Lando know I'll be late to work. I run over to his kitchen, and it's empty. I don't want to bother Lando in his bedroom. So I dash back to my side of the house to get ready for my day.

Lando never mentioned a dress code under his management of Genius Used Cars, so I dress in khaki pants and a light blue polo shirt to highlight my grey eyes with sensible black shoes. Yesterday's cat hair demonstrated the difficulty of wearing black clothing with light colored cats. It's easier to carry a cat carrier when I'm not worried about moving a long skirt out of the way.

I'm surprised when I return to Lando's side of the house at seven o'clock, and Lando's kitchen remains empty. I check my phone for texts or messages. I make iced tea and oatmeal in silence as I flip through yesterday's newspaper. Lando becomes annoyed when anyone else gets the newspaper off the lawn. It's easier to read yesterday's news than argue with my grandfather because getting the newspaper is something he's done since he bought this house.

At half past seven, my worry reaches crisis levels. Since I moved into Lando's house, he's always been in the kitchen by seven o'clock. He told me after retirement but before my arrival, he ate at nine or ten, but hated it. It made him feel old and useless. Based upon the excitement of the new challenge of running a used car lot, I'm not sure what's to blame for his absence.

As I'm getting ready to knock on the door to his bedroom, the back door opens. I turn expecting it to be Sean, but it's Sean and Lando. I ask, "What were you two doing at this hour of the morning?"

Sean lifts a brown bag and Lando shows me a cup carrier with three cups, "We didn't see you when Sean arrived around six thirty so we went to grab bagels for breakfast."

I show Lando my phone, "Since I didn't know where you were and didn't see a text message, I made breakfast. I got a vet appointment this morning. I want to make sure I'm on time. Can I be late to work today?"

Smiling broadly, Lando says, "That's right. I'm your

boss. Sure, I can be magnanimous and let you be late today. After all, it's not like Genius car customers show up til later in the afternoon."

I ignore Sean as I leave the kitchen. I don't need the angst of discussing my jealousy. I have ninety minutes to get to an appointment that's fifteen minutes away from Lando's. Sean doesn't follow me to my car to ask me why I'm upset with him. He's a jerk.

I drive to the vet's office in a strip mall. It's in the opposite direction from downtown. I'm over an hour early with a cat trapped in a cat carrier in my car. Creamsicle hates being in the carrier. He experienced the freedom of the bathroom last night. He cries during the trip and while sitting in the parking lot. I don't have a book to distract me.

A closed car with a screeching cat isn't the best atmosphere for maintaining my sanity. I don't put the carrier on top of the car hood because scratches won't enhance the beauty of my Fiat. I lug the carrier over to a tree at the far end of the strip mall. The fresh air lessens the cat's vocalizations to an occasional yowl.

I sit next to the carrier under the tree. Khaki pants and dirt aren't a professional combination but I'll pull my long shirt down while in the vet's office and stop at home to change before going to work. I make a list on my phone of possible suspects in Gene Johnson's death. I'm not investigating. This is an intellectual exercise.

Cynthia Johnson owns the top of the suspect list. She needed the money and hated her husband. She also might have been protecting her daughter from him. She's ill but running someone over with a car doesn't require physical strength. She's got motive but means and opportunity are a little harder to pin on her.

Butch, the car repo guy, dwells in second place on my list. I never bothered to learn his last name but it's not important. He's a jerk whose motives are also money or possibly jealousy. He and Gene were both involved with Phoebe, the title clerk. Anyone who's able to threaten an old man and steal people's cars for a living is capable of murder. I'm not sure about his criminal history, but I don't think repo guys need a criminal background check. He knows how to start cars without the keys. He checks off means, motive, and opportunity.

Phoebe, the title clerk, is another suspect. She admitted to having an affair with Gene and with Butch. She wanted Gene to divorce Cynthia, and he didn't. She's also mean and hateful. Running someone over with a car wouldn't chip her nails. She also has means, motive, and opportunity.

Dalton, the eighteen year old car salesman, hated Gene. He warned me about Gene's treatment of women. During my week working with him, he presented a kind and friendly face. However, he glared at Gene with contempt and revulsion if he thought no one was looking. His attempt to throw me under the bus when Detective Andrews interviewed him strengthens his position on my list. He also has means, motive, and opportunity.

Walter, the former liquor salesman turned car salesman, feared for his job. He might've snapped because he didn't want to lose another job. Gene treated him like dirt. Gene's death has improved his life.

Most of the rest of the people who interacted with

Gene Johnson in recent years should also be on the list. This suspect list includes many of the people who purchased cars from him and the ones who worked with him at his last dealership or the salespeople he fired from Genius Used Cars. I don't know any of them.

This time I'm not investigating a murder, I'm thinking about possibilities.

"Isn't he an interesting looking cat. Haven't I met him somewhere before like at a crime scene?" Quentin asks as he peers into the carrier.

I yelp with surprise and my body makes an odd jerking motion. Sitting with my legs crossed on the ground limits my movements but also keeps me from falling. "Hi, Quentin. I didn't expect to see you today."

He shrugs, "Today's my day off. I was on my way to meet my uncle, Detective Rousch, for breakfast. I saw the prettiest tan Fiat in the parking lot. There aren't many of those on Pittsburgh's streets. I pulled over to check if you were in it. When I noticed you over here with a cat carrier, I thought I'd come say hello."

I wave at my beautiful car, "It's Moche Latte not tan, but that's not the point. It's great to see you. I'm super early for my vet appointment, so I've been sitting here and thinking."

He motions toward my phone, "It looks like you've been texting. Is it with the Jolly Red Giant?"

"I'm not texting. I'm jotting some notes into my phone." I ignore his dig about Sean. I don't want to talk about Sean to anyone much less Quentin who Sean told me I had to avoid. In all of the excitement over helping Gennifer and Cynthia Johnson, I forgot to call Quentin and tell him about Sean wanting to be exclusive with me.

I gaze up at Quentin. "I'm happy to see you. It's been busy with trying to keep Genius Used Car lot open for business and help Gene's widow and daughter cope. Plus as you can see, I got another cat." I gesture toward the carrier. "I named him Creamsicle. He needs me."

The beige cat carrier with blue accents has a door at the front and one on top to make it easier to get animals in and out. The openings are meshed with thick bars to help the animals breathe. Quentin gestures at the top opening, "I figure you can't let him out of the cage but will he bite me if I put a finger in to pet him?"

I shrug, "I don't think so, but I can't make any guarantees. He behaved for me last night when I gave him a flea bath." I laugh at the memory. "I should have asked someone for help but as soon as I got him from the police station, I wanted to wash the funk of jail and fleas off him."

Quentin turns away from the carrier to glance at me. "It seems to be a habit for you to leap before you look. You gave a cat you hadn't taken to the vet yet to have checked for diseases a bath alone. What if he bit you and has rabies? Although I'll admit to being a little distracted by the idea of you wearing a wet t-shirt after washing the cat."

I smile and ignore the innuendo of the flirtatious statement about wet t-shirts. Quentin flirts. It doesn't mean anything, especially if I ignore it. "It was only an old, bedraggled t-shirt and yoga pants. I agree about not weighing the risks, but there are shots for rabies, right?"

He nods his head. "Yep, twenty-one shots into your stomach will clear rabies right up if you come into any contact with an infected animal."

I grab his calf because I'm still seated, "Really? I don't ever remember Buffy getting rabies, not even when she tangled with werewolves."

He pats my hand and laughs, "Sorry, sorry. I was joking. Back in the twentieth century, the twenty-one shots thing was real. However, you have to be bitten to contract rabies, not just handle an animal that has it. Based on the purring from the cage and the fact he allowed you to give him a bath, this animal's not rabid. I did want to scare you for a minute because it sometimes seems like you take too many risks by trying to solve murders."

The blush overtakes my face. "Very funny. This sweet boy is clearly not rabid." I throw my hands up for emphasis, "I'm not really investigating Gene's murder, just making a list of suspects."

Quentin crouches down to lock eyes with me, "Didn't you promise my uncle, no more murders?"

I nod my head, "I totally promised him. I never wanted to find another body. This time, I'm helping Lando run Gene's car lot. There are so many suspects in this case because to know Gene was to hate him. Speaking of your uncle, aren't you supposed to meet him for breakfast?"

He stares into my eyes, "Do you want to get rid of me because my questions are making you uncomfortable or maybe calling you out for nosiness?"

I can't hold his gaze and look at the grass beneath me, "Yes, Detective Andrews is working half undercover at the car lot, and all of the clues seem to revolve around that trailer where I worked yesterday. Plus, I don't trust Gene's widow or his daughter, Gennifer with a G."

He shakes his head, "Back up, what does half under-cover mean?"

I pull up a piece of grass and twirl it between my fingers, "So, Detective Andrew Andrews is the detective from Gene's crime scene. He's big and built like Sean, but he's bald, and Black with amazing cheekbones and gorgeous eyes. He's young like us not old like your uncle. Anyway, my babbling during my interview with him and Mac as my lawyer seemed to have charmed him and made him realize I'm not a killer. I'm still on his suspect list but closer to the bottom than the top."

Quentin sits down in the patchy grass facing me, "I know when you start a story crouching will become uncomfortable because it's going to take a while."

I forgot how easy it is to talk to Quentin. Meeting him and Sean within days of each other confused me. Sean's longstanding relationship with my grandfather gives him an unfair advantage. Quentin hiding his relationship with Detective Rousch while pumping me for any information on the last case doesn't help me to trust him.

I glance up at him and ask, "Are you saying I talk too much?"

He shakes his head, "No, not at all. Since I've met you, you've been involved in several murders and you solved two of them. Your stories are so much more inter-esting than other girls who tell me about the person who stole their favorite treadmill at the gym." He reaches over and takes my hand, "Back to my original question, I've never heard anyone described as half undercover. Through my uncle and my job as an EMT, I've met a lot of people in law enforcement."

I move my hand from Quentin's and explain, "Detective Andrews interviewed everyone at the car lot on the day I found Gene's body. All the employees are aware he's a police officer. He thinks Gene's murder is connected to the business and he doesn't have a way to find out which customers wanted Gene dead. This case has too many suspects."

"Let me get this straight, he's hanging out at the car lot in the hopes a suspect will magically appear?"

"When you put it that way, it does sound a little weird. He's also keeping an eye on some of the suspects, and he's looking through all of the paperwork at the dealership. Gene's widow's allowing him to do it without a warrant." I jerk at the sound of a blaring horn.

I sense before I turn to look at the parking lot there's going to be a white Ford F-350. I don't turn my head until the car door slams. Quentin stands and offers me his hand to help me to my feet.

Sean approaches us. He reaches out to shake Quentin's hand. When they glare at each other and grip hands, I want to hide in the cat carrier with the cat. Creamsicle begins to yowl as if he senses the tension swirling in the air. I throw my shoulders back and face the situation.

Sean glances down at me and says, "I guess this is why you left the house so early without uttering a word to me. You must've already made plans with Quentin. Two guys in one morning is impressive."

My eyes widen with shock and my jaw drops. He's making it sound like I spent the night with him, and I'm cheating on him with Quentin. "After you met my grandfather at my house for breakfast, I told you both I had an appointment for the cat. We're outside the vet's office. Quentin and I didn't arrange to meet, not that I owe either of you an explanation."

Quentin laughs and breaks the tension, "Violet, it's like after our first date when I saw you pull into the parking lot and jump out of Sean's truck. I know you studied Buffy, but sometimes your life seems to channel sitcoms. Of course, funny misunderstandings are easier to deal with than murderous demons. I watched a few episodes while you were avoiding my calls. "

I don't care if the vet's waiting room is full of gigantic dogs. The cat is safe in the carrier. I'd rather get between big dogs and my cat than between these two guys. Quentin's cracking jokes. He doesn't deserve to be pulled into this drama.

I turn my back on Sean and talk to Quentin, "I know you're supposed to meet your uncle for breakfast. Thanks for hanging out with me while I waited for my appointment. I'll text you later today once I go to work."

He waves toward Sean and asks, "Are you sure you're going to be okay with him?"

I peek over my shoulder to catch Sean staring at me. "I'll be fine, but I don't want to cause a scene. I'm afraid if the three of us try to have a conversation it'll become awkward."

Quentin strolls toward his car as I turn to face Sean. I start to talk before he can say a single word, "I get you told me I had to pick between you and Quentin if I wanted to try to have a relationship with you. I agreed to give dating a try, but that doesn't mean I can't talk to a guy who's been there during some of my worst experiences."

He opens his mouth and I hold my hand up to stop him. "I'm not experienced at this whole dating thing, but I thought if you wanted to be with me, you would have tried to spend more time with me than with Cynthia. I suspect you have a thing for damsels in distress. I've recently been in situations that might make me look like one, but I'm not. By the way, trying to make Quentin think we spent the night together was a jerk move. The only ginger who I spent time with last night was my new cat."

The clapping starts before Sean says a single word. Quentin walked toward his car but didn't get into it. Quentin returns to join us and interjects, "I think becoming exclusive is a lovely idea. However, it isn't a requirement to get know someone. I didn't realize you'd been told to stop talking to me. I figured you were busy and not ghosting me."

"I wasn't avoiding you. I've been busy trying to help save Genius Used Cars for Cynthia and Gennifer. I planned to text you and meet with you to give you the friend speech. I heard about it enough on *Buffy the Vampire Slayer* to know the drill. I like talking to you and don't want you to disappear from my life."

I grab the cat carrier and stomp toward the door to the vet's office. I glare over my shoulder and say to both of them. "I'll text you both after I make sure my new cat is healthy."

The cat's cries drown out any possible responses from either of them. Dating or even trying to date frustrates me. Avoiding it throughout high school, college and graduate school made my life much easier. Real life men don't always respond like the characters on television shows. Sam and Dean, my favorites, from *Supernatural* rarely stayed in one place long enough to develop healthy relationships. Most of Buffy's romantic relationships were toxic and sometimes deadly.

The vet gives the cat a clean bill of health and offers to neuter him if I can leave him until five o'clock this evening. She explains neutering him might cut down on his incessant vocalizations along with keeping him from spraying or running away in search of females. I agree with relief.

When I arrive at my car, there's a peach rose with a note attached to it under my windshield wiper. Either one of the two guys wants to keep trying with me or I've got a weird stalker.

The words on the note are

"I think trying with you is worth it. I hope I'm still an option. I don't need to be exclusive, I want to get to know you better. My uncle will totally understand you're worth being an hour late for breakfast. Q"

On the way back to Genius Used Cars, I'm trapped in the car with my own thoughts and no chorus of kitty cries. On Saturday I found a body under a car and picked Sean. I didn't weigh my options or consult anyone. At the time, I felt insecure and was happy Sean wanted to save me. I agreed to Sean's ultimatum that at the age of twenty-seven within a month of meeting him and Quentin to rush into an exclusive relationship. I've never dated, and I don't know what I want. My rash decision could lead to both guys disappearing. I text a quick thank you to Quentin for the rose.

I arrive at the car lot and see Walter and Dalton surveying the empty lot from the service building.

"Where's everyone else?" I ask from the doorway of the trailer.

Detective Andrews examines paperwork as the sole occupant of the trailer.

He replies, "The Medical Examiner released Gene's remains to the family. Sean and your grandfather are helping Gennifer and Cynthia make funeral arrangements. Your grandfather said you should text him when anyone starts working with a customer so he can make it back to do the paperwork. They took two cars."

I nod and say, "Thanks," as I turn to leave to walk around the lot. The cars haven't changed since yesterday but it looks like I'm busy while I think. Walter and Dalton won't try to talk to me. No one texted me to let me know their plans for the day. It feels like I'm not part of the inner circle.

A car appears within five minutes and distracts me from my worries. As soon as the occupants tell me they need another car because the one they're driving won't pass inspection, I text Lando. By the time he arrives, Dalton's working with a customer too.

The four of us remain busy for the rest of the day, so I don't have time to comment on the fact that Sean and the

Johnsons never returned. Detective Andrews continues to peruse paperwork in the trailer, and he's more than capable of providing security. There's no need because there's no excitement.

By four o'clock, I've sold a car and talked to a few other people. Rather than interrupting Lando's work with customers, I get into my car and text Lando I need to pick up the cat from his surgery. I never asked about Sean or the funeral arrangements. I also failed to tell Lando about the confrontation this morning. He didn't ask which either means he was too busy to talk or Sean didn't mention anything.

EIGHTEEN

"If you're not smart, I am."

After fighting Pittsburgh evening traffic, I arrive at the veterinarian and pay the bill with my credit card. Living with Lando is like living with my parents without the guilt trips. He won't let me pay for food or give him any money for utilities or rent. I don't have to worry about student loans because as I recently found out Lando paid for all my college and graduate school expenses. He tells me my company provides more than enough payment. I appreciate Lando for his generosity. His love and support are his best gift to me.

I'm not returning to the car lot. I'm going back to Lando's to think or maybe watch *Supernatural* so I don't have to think. My advisor didn't approve of my interest in *Supernatural* because she thought they displayed traits of toxic masculinity. I disagreed, but I never argued with her, because I followed her authority as my professor and mentor.

When I arrive at Lando's, there are several text messages on my phone. The one from Lando states I don't need to go back to the car lot. That message is convenient because I wasn't planning to.

Quentin wrote.

> If you're not busy, do you want to go out
> tonight?

I feel guilty about not talking to him and jumping into a relationship with Sean. Sean's jealous response to my innocent meeting with Quentin makes me uncomfortable.

I reply

> I can be ready in an hour to go out as
> friends. How does seven o'clock sound?

He texts back immediately.

> Sounds great. Being friends works
> for me.

He uses punctuation in his text messages, there aren't any odd abbreviations or emojis. I'm impressed. I take Creamsicle to the bathroom with me because he's still dopey from his surgery. He and Annika need to meet as equals. A day on the humid car lot means I need another shower for my meeting with Quentin.

After my shower, I peruse my closet which doesn't contain enough cute clothes to make this a hard decision. I grab a flowered sundress with a teal background and yellow flowers. The asymmetrical hem skims my lower calves in the back and my knees in the front. I match it with brown closed toed clogs because I haven't ever had a pedicure. The sundress is perfect for a warm humid day, but I'm not sure about the evening temperatures or if we'll be inside an air conditioned building.

I'm ready for our meeting fifteen minutes before I told Quentin to arrive, so I wait on the front porch. He pulls up to the house ten minutes early in the practical blue sedan I sold him during my first foray as a car salesperson at Roar Motors. As I walk to his car, he gets out to open my door. Sean always rushes to do this courtesy but this is the first time for Quentin. He pulls me into his arms before I get in the car and says, "Let's try this before we start the date or kissing you is all I'll think about tonight."

I move away from him and he lets me go. "I want to try to be friends with you. In the text, you agreed."

He shrugs and ushers me into the car. He smiles, "I think you're adorable. I'm here to be your friend or more, but I respect your boundaries. I've got a secret. I'll still be thinking about a kiss during dinner. Is there anything special you'd like to do tonight?"

I run my hand through my damp hair which I wore down for the not date and say, "I haven't seen much of Pittsburgh and you've lived here most of your life. Next time, we'll make plans more than a day in advance, and it'll be my turn."

"So, you're thinking there'll be another time. I'll hold you to that. Hopefully, you won't find any more bodies so we can plan something," he replies with a quick smile flashing his white teeth. "How does dinner and a movie sound? If you pick the movie, I'll find our dinner location."

There're no movies I'm dying to see. Movies tend to be too limited in their storytelling scope for me. I prefer television shows because I get to know the characters. Two hours isn't enough time for me to develop a relationship with the protagonist. For a date, I don't want to pick an animated movie or a romantic comedy because I don't know how he'll feel. Given his time in the military, I'm not sure if he enjoys or hates movies with explosions and car chases. I choose a recently released superhero blockbuster.

He agrees and adds he wants to see it because he missed the opening weekend and has seen all of the others in the series. We make the early movie and have dinner after the show.

At dinner he delights in telling me all about the series. I haven't seen the others so he explains the various back-stories of the characters and plots from the prior movies. He's also a fan of the comic books, so he expounds on the differences and similarities.

My degrees come in handy because I'm able to listen and respond to him without sounding clueless. He tells me about his love of comics, an art form I appreciate. We don't finish dinner until ten o'clock. Quentin invites me back to his place where he lives with his mom to show me some of the comic books we discussed.

I wrinkle my nose, "I don't want to meet your mom for the first time late at night. I'll feel awkward."

He reaches out and squeezes my shoulder, "I promise she isn't scary. Well, not most of the time. But I get it. I haven't dated anyone seriously for years. I want to keep getting to know you better. I had fun talking to you tonight. I'd be happy to be one of your friends in Pittsburgh. I want to show you the joys of Pittsburgh teams."

I put my hand up to stop him, "I like your idea of seeing where this goes. I didn't date in school because doctoral study took so much of my time. I'm getting to know who I am as an adult. I don't plan on rushing into anything. I have no idea what's going on with Sean. I think dating more than one person casually is fine. As long as everyone's honest, my life won't feel like a bad sitcom. On that note, I need to talk to Sean to see if he is okay with casual since I agreed to try to be exclusive with him."

He winks. "I have a good time with you. I get it, but I think kissing can be fun."

I smile. "On the honesty note, I've alluded to my lack of dating experience. I also didn't hook up in college, so when I'm ready to be with someone, I want it to mean something. I'm not necessarily holding out for a ring but I want to be in love."

His eyebrows raise in surprise, "I respect that. The first person I was with was my serious high school girl-friend. By the way, I'm not seeing anyone else right now. I'll let you know if I do go on other dates."

I reach out my hand to shake on it. It's easy to talk to him about inconsequential things. We spend the drive back to Lando's talking about television shows based on comic books. Most of my research focused on turn of the millennium television, so I'm not familiar with many of his favorite shows from the DC Universe.

When we arrive at Lando's every single light in the front of the house blazes. Quentin parks and turns to me, "Violet, did you let anyone know that you were going out with me tonight?"

I put my hand to my forehead and rub my eyes as guilt rushes through me. I've tried to be so careful of Lando's feelings. I feel terrible and now Quentin might also think I'm a jerk. "Oops, when I was in college and graduate school, I got out of the habit of letting people know about my comings and goings."

I pull my phone out of my pocket and grimace. I silenced it for the movie and forgot about it. I have six missed calls and ten texts.

I bite my lip and say, "I'm so sorry Quentin. I need to go in there and face my grandfather to apologize. Thank you so much for the lovely evening."

He takes my hand as I'm fumbling with the door, "I think I should go into the house with you. I haven't talked to your grandfather yet and I know this isn't the best circumstance. How bad can it be?"

I'm fairly sure it's going to be awful, but I'm a little bit of a coward about confrontations. I nod, "I'm not sure who if anyone will be with Lando."

Quentin releases my hand and stays next to his car.

The front door opens as soon as my foot hits the squeaky step to the expansive front porch. Lando rushes out as fast as his limping gait and cane allow him. He pulls me into a hug and says, "We were so worried about you."

Before I can apologize, he continues, "There's a murderer on the loose. You've already tangled with one killer. How was I supposed to know you were okay? You didn't leave a note or send a text. You failed to answer my texts and calls."

Lando and I stand on the porch for this conversation.

Quentin remains on the sidewalk. Mac stands inside the house with Sean behind her blocking the light from the hallway. Lando's quick transition from hugging to scolding and the addition of Sean and Mac illustrate this isn't going to be a fun or short conversation.

I suggest to Lando, "Why don't we discuss this inside the house. There's no need to bother the neighbors."

"Quentin, I'm safely home. Why don't you leave?" I say over my shoulder.

Quentin walks up the sidewalk to move behind me. He puts his hand on my shoulder and asks Lando, "Is it okay if I come into the house, sir?"

Lando sighs and says, "Come on in. The more, the merrier."

The five of us gather in the receiving library before saying a word. I start, "I don't think you and Quentin have officially met. You've encountered each other a few times. Lando this is Quentin Stevens, the EMT who's come to my rescue several times."

"Quentin, this is Bert Landovic, my grandfather, everyone calls him Lando. I've told you about him."

The two men shake hands and nod at each other.

Lando turns to me and crosses his arms over his chest, "Introductions and a new face aren't going to distract me from this discussion. Violet, what were you thinking?"

I stare at the floor. I deserve this reprimand. All I can do is apologize. "I'm so sorry. I was completely inconsiderate. When I ran into Quentin this morning, it was nice to see someone who wasn't involved in the 'save Genius Used Cars' drama. When he asked me out tonight as friends, I agreed. I should've left a note or sent a text. It didn't occur to me people would worry about me. I'm not used to anyone noticing my movements."

Lando shakes his head and says, "The last I heard from you, you were picking up the cat. I knew you got that done because he's making so much noise. I can hear him on my side of the second floor. If you weren't back here by midnight, I was going to call Detective Andrews. He gave me his personal number. I know the police wouldn't respond officially to a young woman missing only a few hours."

Lando's disappointment makes me feel guiltier than when I entered the house. I'm afraid to even look at Mac or Sean, especially Sean.

I babble, "I'll run upstairs to check on Creamsicle. Maybe he's in pain. Quentin can come with me. He can check out the cat. I know he's an EMT and not a vet tech, but a feline is a mammal."

I scurry out of the receiving library. Quentin follows me up the staircase. He must notice the open doorways to rooms filled with bookcases. He remains silent until I pull the lever which moves the bookcase to access my side of the house.

Quentin runs his hand over the bookcase, "That's so cool. I'm not a big reader of books. I prefer comics. When you told me about your grandfather's house of books, I thought you were exaggerating. You weren't. I only saw a few rooms last time I was here with so much going on. By the way, thanks for pulling me out of the uncomfortable room. I was getting sick of the glares from your friend, Sean."

I ignore his comment about Sean and respond,

"Growing up, I always preferred television to novels. I'm acquiring a greater appreciation for books living in a house full of them."

Annika twines around our feet as we enter the hall on my side of the house. I point at the cat, "That's Annika. She was Tiffany's cat. I adopted her after the murder. I need to toss her in my room for a few minutes. I don't want Creamsicle to get out and rush into their first meeting."

"Maybe I can see your room more closely in the future," Quentin smiles and winks.

A voice from Lando's side of the house interjects, "Or maybe not."

Creamsicle's vocalizations drowned out Sean's footsteps on the stairs. I wish he wouldn't have followed us.

I shout back, "I need to check on the cat and make sure his incision looks okay."

Quentin puts his hand on my shoulder, "I'll help her because I have medical training to take care of humans, not cats, but stitches are stitches. I agree we should all talk in a few minutes."

I risk a glance at Sean over my shoulder to see him standing in front of the open passageway between the two sides of the house, and he's clenching his jaw. I ignore him because I want to make sure Creamsicle's not hurt.

Creamsicle rests on the pile of old towels I left on the floor of the bathroom. He's ignoring his new cat bed. We walk over to him and roll him onto his back. There's no sign of infection, and he purrs as soon as I touch him. With the cat taken care of, I sigh because I need to address Quentin and Sean.

Quentin and I leave the bathroom and face Sean in the foyer. I move away from both of them to collect my thoughts. "Sean, I'm sorry we haven't been talking much since Sunday. I thought I was ready to try a relationship. I'm not. I barely dated in my years of high school, college or graduate school. I'm not sure how to communicate in a relationship type of way. I'm also sorry I worried everyone by not letting anyone know where I was going tonight. Based on Buffy's dating history, she might not be the best role model."

Sean's response surprises me, "I'm sorry too. On Saturday, I got worried. All I could think about was making sure I didn't lose my chance with you. I know a good thing when I see it but I'm okay with not rushing into anything. I just didn't want to be your Riley, over-shadowed by Angel and Spike."

Before I respond, Sean spins around and leaves.

I look at Quentin and he shrugs. "It sounds like Sean said you can do whatever you want. I don't know any of the people Sean mentioned other than Buffy and Angel. I'm still watching the first season. We should go back downstairs and face the wrath of your grandfather and your scary friend, Mac."

I sigh, "Sean and his grandmother watched every episode of *Buffy the Vampire Slayer*, the subject of my doctoral work. He was speaking in code to me. During the seven seasons of the television show, she dated two vampires and a human super soldier. Riley was the human guy who broke up with her because she couldn't get over the first vampire."

Quentin shrugs, "I just started watching the show.

Will bingeing a turn of the century teen show help me understand you better?"

I shake my head, "I spent years immersed in television. I worked with my advisor from my freshman year of college until I finished my Ph.D. She directed my research. I didn't make many friends or date. All I talked about was the stuff my mentor studied. It's refreshing to hear about other things. Please don't feel like you have to watch *Buffy* for me."

When we return, Mac and Lando sit with their heads together whispering in the receiving library. Their heads pop up in unison when they notice us. Mac starts, "You need to watch yourself. I thought you would've learned your lesson almost getting murdered less than a month ago. Don't scare us. There are so few people in this world I care about. I don't want to lose another one."

Lando nods with enthusiasm throughout Mac's short speech. "What she said. Plus if anything happens to you while you're in Pittsburgh, your father will toss me in a nursing home. What would happen to my books?"

With the lecture part of the evening over, Quentin says goodnight to everyone and leaves. I don't ask about Sean. I leave Lando and Mac to their machinations in the library and go upstairs to bed. Creamsicle rubs against my hand in the bathroom but doesn't seem to be in a hurry to leave the enclosed, safe space. I take one of his towels with his scent and wrap it around Annika who sleeps at the foot of my bed.

NINETEEN

"After all, I am a genius!"

The next morning Lando has oatmeal and tea waiting for me. There's no sign of Sean. I'm relieved, because I'm sick of the relationship drama he brings with him.

Lando explains, "Sean's going to meet us at Genius. He left early this morning to pick up Gennifer and Cynthia. While you were taking care of cat stuff yesterday, I found out there's a morning meeting at the funeral home. One of us needs to open the dealership. Would you rather help with funeral planning or the car lot?"

There's only one possible answer to this question. I have no desire to see any of the Johnsons or the inside of a funeral home sooner than I have to. "I've got the car lot. I should be fine with Walter and Dalton. It's never busy in the morning. We'll delay anyone who wants to buy until you get there."

I'm the first to arrive and the trailer feels empty and dangerous without Detective Andrews's oversized presence. I check my phone to find a text from him stating he needs to be at the station today.

A pile of deal jackets sit on the title clerk's desk. I page through them and notice some of them have numbers written in black ink on the bottom right corner of the first page. Some of the other jackets have red X's in the bottom right corner. Others have nothing in the corner. At the last dealership, I never dealt with deal jackets. I have no idea what Gene's notes mean.

The trailer door bangs open as Dalton and Walter walk into the building together. They nod at me and turn to go to their lawn chairs in the service bay. Rather than sit in the vacant trailer, I join them in the service building with the garage door open.

Dalton tells us about his life growing up as the youngest in a family with three older sisters in a tiny three bedroom house with one bathroom. He mentions they were jealous because he had his own tiny room, and he could pee off the back porch when the bathroom was full. His humorous stories illustrate that while he complains about having all those sisters, he loves them.

I ask, "Do you have a favorite sister?"

Dalton taps his teeth, "My sister Felicia's only eighteen months older than I am. She and I are the closest. She always covered for me. My other sisters are older like almost your age. Those two act like a team, but Felicia's my buddy."

I never think of being an adult. Most of the time I feel like the youngest person in the room, but I'm almost a decade older than Dalton. I tilt my head back to look at the grimy ceiling of the service building, "Do you all still live at home?"

Dalton tilts his chair back and the front legs lift off the floor, "Yep and now it's even more packed."

I open my mouth to ask why his house is more crowded. Then Walter interrupts, "It's just me in my little one bedroom apartment. I never needed much space since I never found the right lady. I lived in a nicer place before the booze wholesaler let me go."

Walter launches into stories about his formative years with an older brother. He's more animated than I've ever seen him. I ask if he and his brother are still close. Tears glisten in his eyes. He shares that his brother died in the war in Vietnam during his first week of active duty. Walter tried to volunteer with the aim of avenging his brother but childhood asthma disqualified him.

Sibling stories fascinate me. As the only child in a comfortable middle class home, I missed out on funny stories about brothers and sisters. Our four bedroom house contained an office and a guest room no one ever used. My mom's allergies meant I never even had a pet. No wonder I developed a deep and abiding love of the only place I witnessed drama and relationships, the television.

When customers arrive, we alternate which one of us approaches them. For the ones who seem like real prospects, we ask them to return after four o'clock to talk to Lando. Most people understand that the owner of the dealership died and they need to make accommodations. Lando returns alone at three o'clock.

He tells me they made all of the funeral arrangements and scheduled it for Friday. The car lot will be closed so everyone can attend.

Without Detective Andrews, Sean or the Johnsons the day flows comfortably. With Lando as a manager, we three salespeople start to learn to work as a team. We deliver four cars over the course of the afternoon and evening.

Lando tosses me the keys to the trailer and tells me to lock the door. He sits in his car to watch me because no one travels alone with a killer on the loose.

Before I leave for the evening, I run into the ladies room in the trailer. Most of the time, I use the unisex one in the service building. The restroom's dark when I enter it. It smells like hairspray and cheap, acrid patchouli-based perfume. A chill races down my spine when I turn on the light. Red lipstick streaks the mirror. It say, "Stop Just Stop."

I don't touch the glass. I freeze and wonder who the message is for and what it means. I haven't used this restroom since before Gene's murder. Phoebe glared and pouted when I used it my first few days before I discovered the grimy service building one. I dash from the room and run to Lando's car. He doesn't look up from his book as I approach.

I tap on his window. He rolls it down and the sound of jazz spills out of the car. "Violet, what's wrong?"

Taking a deep breath, I ask, "Have you gone in the women's room in the trailer?"

He shakes his head at me, "Why would I use the women's room? The only decent amenities the old trailer contains are two closet sized bathrooms and air-conditioning."

Swiveling toward the building, I say over my shoulder, "You should follow me to it, now."

Lando follows me into the stuffy trailer and I move so he can open the door. "You might want to use your handkerchief to open the door. I know my prints are on it, but there's no reason to add yours."

"Please tell me you didn't find another body."

I swallow and reply. "It's not a body. Please take a look."

He opens the door, turns on the light and gapes at the mirror. He runs his shaking hand through his hair, leans on his cane and says, "I got nothing. I haven't watched who has used the ladies room. I don't know who the message is directed at. We need to call Detective Andrews."

I nod once, "I agree. This is a police problem. He can take care of it. I don't have a handy fingerprint kit or any type of forensics lab. Let's go home."

Lando and I drive our separate cars to his house. I leave first while he calls the police. He still beats me home. It's sad when my seventy-two year old grandfather in the Lincoln Town Car drives faster than I do in my Fiat.

The vision of the mirror dripping lipstick haunts me during my ride. To clear my brain of the image, I think about my cats.

As soon as I arrive at Lando's, I run upstairs and cross to my side of the house. It's time to introduce the cats to each other. According to the book I found in Lando's small nonfiction library, cats should learn each other's scents before meeting in real life. Annika and Creamsicle spent the day with items infused with each other's scents. I bring Creamsicle into my bedroom for their first meeting. The large, airy space allows them to smell each other without trapping them. Creamsicle investigates the room and Annika watches him from the superior height position of my bed. When Creamsicle jumps on the bed to face Annika directly, I move closer with the piece of cardboard, prepared to separate them if necessary.

Neither cat hisses, growls, or swats. They stare at each other from either end of the bed. They resemble Quentin and Sean in their unwillingness to engage with each other. As with Quentin and Sean, I'm happy they aren't actively fighting. I'll take guarded staring contests.

The red lipstick message haunts me, but I'll deal with it tomorrow. I hope it wasn't directed at me. That would be awful, but I never even used the trailer restroom. I'm sure there's a logical explanation.

I wake up Thursday morning with Creamsicle above my head and Annika at my feet. At least, my body occupied neutral territory all night. I'm not sure if I should separate them for the day or let them figure out their own dominance issues.

I leave the two cats alone in my room during my shower. There's no blood or piles of fur. They're two adult cats who are about the same size, they can decide how to get along with each other. Lando's house is over six thousand square feet, they're free to avoid each other all day or develop a friendship.

Gene's dress code of a skirt for women selling cars doesn't apply with Lando as the manager. Gene suggested short skirts. Phoebe acquiesced, but I didn't. I wear black pants and a comfortable blue polo shirt. The blue matches Sean's eyes. Contemplating his eyes must have made him appear in Lando's kitchen. When I get downstairs, Sean's sitting at the table with three cups from Giant Eagle.

He doesn't look up when I enter the room but waves at the cups, "I got you a chai. I figured I'd replicate our first time together but skip the finding you wandering around lost in my neighborhood part."

Dropping into the chair across from him, I say, "Thank you. I'll jump right into this. I've got no idea what's going on between us. I hate drama in my personal life and it feels like Pittsburgh is a drama vortex for me. If you want to date Cynthia, she needs someone, please don't worry about me."

I'm prepared to keep filling the uncomfortable silence with words, but he puts his hand on my arm to stop me.

He moves his hand from my arm to grasp my hand, "Sorry, I didn't realize some of your distance from me was based on your worries about Cynthia. I like being needed. After my parents died, I needed my grandparents so much. As I grew up and they grew older, I returned the favor and helped them. When people lean on me, I'm used to handling it and accepting more. It seems like you should want my assistance. You've found three bodies after being sheltered for most of your life. It frustrates me you keep jumping into danger."

I'd rather run away from him and this conversation. I stand up, pull away from him, and cross the room to lean on the counter. His size overwhelms the room and my attraction to him bothers me. I cross my arms over my chest as if it will protect me from this unwelcome discussion. He doesn't know about the threat on the mirror, but he's in protective mode.

"My heroes are women like Buffy, Wonder Woman, and Scarlet O'Hara. If you want someone who's going to gaze at you like a Bond girl and say save me, it's good we've discovered this before anything started between us. I may stumble across bodies, but I want to solve the murders, not wait for someone else." As I talk, I inch toward the back door. I'd rather face a murderer than face my feelings of inadequacy and his psychoanalysis of my failings.

He must realize my plan because he vaults out of his chair and stands in front of me, blocking my departure, "You're so busy trying to escape from me that you're not listening to what I'm saying. I don't want Cynthia. I admit to being flattered by her flirting, but I'm not attracted to her. I'm interested in you. I want to give this thing between us a try. I won't push you into an exclusive relationship until you are ready."

I've been so busy anticipating Sean's thoughts I haven't been listening to his words. Apparently jumping to conclusions based upon my own fears isn't a good idea. I'm not sure what to say to his declaration.

Lando walks into his kitchen, looks at Sean standing close to me at the counter and then at the three drinks on the table, "Oh, good, you brought me coffee. Which one's mine?"

He breaks the tension, but Sean doesn't move away from me. I put my hands on his chest to push him. It's hard to think when I can't see anything other than the wall of his torso in front of me and his gorgeous blue eyes if I look up at his face. Rather than moving away from me, he moves an inch closer into my personal space.

"I can't talk about this right now. Shouldn't your crew be here soon to ask for directions on building the addition? Why don't you give me a ride to Genius Used Cars today? We can talk in the car." I wiggle away from him as I push on his chest.

He turns to walk toward the door. "I'll accept the pause in this conversation as long as you promise to talk to me in the car."

Lando doesn't say a word for two minutes. He drinks his coffee. My anticipation of his comments annoys me. I don't want to share confidences and boy talk with my grandfather. It's weird and uncomfortable.

"You seem to be embroiled in a love triangle with Quentin and Sean. Do you think this is a good idea?" he asks as he raises his bushy white eyebrows.

I haven't got an answer and since I'm done with my chai, I toss the empty cup in the trashcan and leave. I forget about Annika who's appeared in the hopes of getting a can of wet cat food for breakfast. I trip over her as Sean opens the door to come back into the kitchen.

Falling into his arms to prevent a full-fledged accident with bruises and other dire physical consequences isn't the best way to prove my independence. In his regular hero capacity he rushes into the room, catches me, and holds me a few seconds longer than necessary. He receives nice guy points for not pointing out my clumsiness. Stumbling makes me feel like a bumbling character in a sitcom rather than a strong woman like Buffy or Beckett from *Castle*.

I pivot and grab a can of cat food. As soon as I pull on the can tab, Creamsicle joins Annika in the kitchen. As the cats devour the wet cat food, a blanket of silence overwhelms the room.

Pointing out my dilemma in front of Sean isn't fair. I'm sure Lando has an opinion and he's letting the drama rise so he can drop it on me. Lando taps his cane and opens his mouth. Sean looks between us from the doorway, "I'm going to check on my guys again. It seems like this is a conversation no one needs me for."

I drop into one of the kitchen chairs across from my grandfather and toss my ponytail, "Yep, I seem to be involved in an uncomfortable situation. Sort of like having a conversation about dating with my grandfather. They both seem like nice guys. I want to get to know them better. I've never dated much. It's bad timing that I met them both within a day of each other. Now hit me with your sage advice."

Lando shakes his head, "I think you've got this covered. I've known Sean since he was a little boy. I think of him like an honorary grandchild. It'd be wonderful to make it official. On the other hand, I've got nothing against Quentin." He shrugs and continues, "Violet, this is your decision. You could get hurt or you might hurt one or both of these nice boys. However, in your twenties is the time for these type of situations. Good luck, kid, you're going to need it."

Sean opens the door and asks if I'm ready to go so I don't need to respond to Lando's lack of guidance. I know trying to date two guys at the same time is far more complicated than dating one. As long as I'm honest with both of them, and they both agree, it should be okay.

Sean reaches his vehicle first and lifts me into the truck after opening my door. I watch his face for signs of exertion but don't see any. He starts his seemingly rehearsed speech as soon as he turns on the ignition.

"I want to say this before I forget the words," he pauses until I nod, "Violet, I'm sorry I pressured you into committing to dating me. The only other time I dated someone we drifted into a more serious relationship the longer we dated. This time, I thought about you before you even met me based on Lando's stories and the pictures of you growing up. Then I watched for the two weeks I worked on the addition and you didn't seem to know I existed. I wasn't trying to be creepy or a stalker, I was just afraid to approach you."

I interrupt him, "I watched you for that two weeks, and never thought you'd notice me. You seemed like such a great catch with your steady job, air of authority, and looks. From television, I learned the good guys were already taken in their late twenties. I was sure you were in a committed relationship."

He puts his hand up to stop me and continues, "You make me nervous. You don't recognize your own attractiveness. You're confident about your intellect, but oblivious about your other strengths. Then we talked and had so much in common. When I found out about Quentin, I didn't want him to sweep you off your feet. Can we pretend the last week never happened? Let's get to know each other better and see where this goes?"

Glancing out the passenger window, I reply, "That's okay with me. I'm not rushing into anything with anyone. At this point, you and Quentin seem to rub each other the wrong way. I won't plan any group outings with both of you. We can hang out alone or with Lando or with Mac. You have a bit of an edge because you are with me at Genius Used Cars."

He smiles, "You're right. I'm done with my speech. Why don't you tell me about your cats?"

We talk about pets for the rest of the half hour ride. Sean loves animals. His grandparents always made sure at least one furry pet lived in their house at all times and occasionally more. Multiple pets at a time produces the best stories. One of Sean's cats used to put his head in the golden retriever's mouth. One of his friends became hysterical when he saw red ringing the white fur around the cat's neck. Sean's grandmother laughed at him because he didn't realize the dog's food stained his teeth and transferred to the cat's fur.

When we reach the car lot, I wait for Sean to open my door. Whenever I jump out of the car before he opens the door for me, he looks disappointed. In the time I've known him, I've become accustomed to his gentlemanly behavior.

He opens my door and when he gives me a hand to help me out of the truck, he remains in my personal space. His incredible blue eyes seem to darken as he traps my gaze with his intense stare. He leans down and captures my mouth with his. I wrap my arms around his neck and pull him closer to me. As I feel his tongue probing my lips, two car alarms start to blare in a cacophony. I disentangle from Sean and hunt for the source of the noise.

Dalton and Walter are sitting in the service building. Something makes them laugh so hard Dalton falls off his lawn chair. As soon as I spot them, blessed silence returns. I march over to the two howling salesmen, "What are you two laughing about?" As the words leave my mouth, I realize how silly the question is. They're amused by interrupting my kiss with Sean.

Dalton grabs Walter's leg to pull himself off the ground. "Ya know, it's good we caught yinz before Cynthia showed up. She would've given the big guy a piece a her mind. She expects him to dance to her tune."

I look at Sean over my shoulder and wave, "Thanks for the assist but Sean's not dating Cynthia. He's just being kind to her because she needs help right now."

"Whatever, if she catches you with someone she wants, it's your funeral. That woman stole Gene and stayed married to him for over ten years. She can't be right," Dalton insists.

Sean appears behind me during Dalton's speech, "I think you're judging Cynthia unfairly. However, she may act differently with me. Did she ever come here when Gene was alive?"

Walter answers, "I never seen her until after he kicked. He didn't talk about her. Course, he only yelled at us or did the deals. We wasn't friends."

Lando's car glides into the lot containing Cynthia and Gennifer so I change the subject. Discussing her behind her back is one thing, but I don't want to get caught. Dalton's probably right about the potential increase in tension when she sees Sean and I together. "Are you guys going to the funeral tomorrow?"

Walter brays with laughter. "I want to see what type of turnout he gets. So many people hated him. I bet he gets just the people who work here. We can split up so dat the room don't look too empty. It's sad when no one shows up for a funeral."

I shrug, "Lando told me he and Cynthia put it in today's paper. A few more people than us should be there."

"Maybe some of em'll be there to dance on his grave. That'd be a sight." Dalton says with a gigantic smile on his face as if he's picturing a graveside party.

Walter adds, "Or piss on his grave."

Sean rushes over to help Cynthia out of the car. She must've gotten into it with only her daughter's help but she seems to become extremely helpless when there's a big strong man in the vicinity. Sean assists her into the trailer and deposits her with Lando. No one mentions the message on the mirror. I guess Detective Andrews removed the evidence last night.

Sean joins me and the salesmen in the service building so we can watch the lot from our lawn chairs. Walter regales us with stories from his days as a liquor salesman. Some of his stories are hysterical and others are frightening. I see the man he was a decade ago before he lost his job and his sense of self. He reminds me of Willie Loman from *Death of a Salesman*. This man had a sense of himself and his place in the world, but without his job, his self-definition evaporated like whiskey spilled on a bar.

The three of us take turns approaching customers.

We decide it needs to be fair. We don't judge the customers on the cars they arrive in or the number of people with them or their clothing. It's a cloudy, humid day in June but not unbearably hot. Lando comes out to check on us. Gennifer flutters around Dalton and he tries to avoid her.

Detective Andrews arrives about an hour before closing time. Dalton runs up to him and asks, "So, have you solved the murder?"

When I hear the question, I try to move toward them stealthily but I might look like more like an eager puppy than a graceful, disinterested cat. Detective Andrews says, "Violet, I can see you're interested as well. Feel free to come closer to hear my answer, so I don't have to repeat anything. No, I haven't solved Gene's murder. Tomorrow, I'll attend the funeral in a suit. I don't want any of you to blow my cover by addressing me as Detective Andrews. In fact, everyone should ignore me."

I think in television tropes. It would be fascinating if the murderer is so overcome with guilt they confess at the funeral. On the other hand, the villain could use the opportunity to bring his minions and disrupt the funeral to kill all of the other people who he blames for his failures. I zone out of the conversation as I picture an army of demons invading Gene's funeral and Buffy's the only one that can defeat them. This vision turns awful because without Buffy's presence, Sean and Detective Andrews would feel compelled to be heroes. They're both huge and strong but not demon strong.

Everyone stares at me and no one speaks. Someone must have addressed a question to me and now they all know I'm not paying attention. I shrug and ask, "Was someone talking to me? Sorry, I zoned out."

Detective Andrews sighs, "I simply asked you to promise you wouldn't act like you know me at the funeral. Can you do that, Violet?"

I nod, "Sure, no problem. I won't blow your sort of undercover cover."

I start to walk toward the trailer and toss a question over my shoulder, "Do you want me to tell everyone inside or should I let you do it? I should let you do it, because if they don't listen, I don't want to get the blame." When he fails to answer within five seconds, I continue as if he said yes, "Ok, I'll see you inside. Thanks."

The occupants of the trailer include Lando, Walter, Gennifer, and Sean. Sometime this afternoon, Sean gave Cynthia a ride to her house. He and I haven't talked since the car ride. He didn't linger with her for as long as he has the rest of the week which feels like progress.

After Detective Andrews tells everyone to pretend they don't know him, Gennifer asks Sean for a ride home. Lando answers her, "I'll give you a ride home, kid. It'll give me a chance to stop in and talk to your mom. We can arrange a meeting time so I can drive you guys to the funeral home."

Gennifer looks at me and whispers, "I think my mom was kind of hoping Sean would give me a ride. She mentioned she was going to ask him if he could stay overnight because tomorrow's going to be such an awful day."

Apparently, Sean and I talked at the right time.

Cynthia is tightening her web. I'm surprised Gennifer's volunteering this information. Her statement makes everyone in the room quiet. Gennifer breaks the silence and asks, "Violet can I talk to you outside for a minute?'

Once the door closes, she explains, "I know I wasn't supposed to tell everyone my mom's plan. I'm a flake not an idiot. Her sudden obsession with Sean makes me super uncomfortable. She won't listen to me about backing off him. Between Lando and I, we should be able to distract her tonight. Please be careful at the funeral tomorrow. My mom's temper can be super out of control."

I nod. I'm not sure how to respond to Gennifer's statement. I stick my head back into the trailer and motion Sean to follow me to his truck. Gennifer's confidences about her mother move Cynthia to the top of my suspect list. Running someone over with his own car doesn't require any physical strength, just ruthlessness or desperation.

TWENTY

"I'm the credit genius, and I can get you into a car."

When we get in the car, Sean asks me about my conversation with Gennifer. I'm afraid I'll sound like I'm jealous of Cynthia if I tell him about Gennifer's warnings. It isn't like I'm going to hang all over him at the funeral tomorrow anyway. That would be tacky. I ignore his question and change the subject to Detective Andrews's strange behavior on the case. This leads to a discussion of detective techniques on my favorite television shows. My favorite procedurals are *Law & Order*, *Bones*, and *Castle*. Sean prefers sitcoms and science fiction. We talk the whole ride home. I never tell Sean I think Cynthia might have killed her husband.

At Lando's house I invite Sean to watch television with me. Lando didn't have a television set for over twenty years until I moved in with him. He created a media room in one of the libraries for me. The bookshelves still line the walls but a state of the art television blocks one of the bookshelves. He told me he put the books he didn't enjoy on the case behind the television.

He wasn't ready to get rid of them, but he didn't need to see them.

A comfortable dark brown couch dominates the center of the room with the best viewing position. It's long enough for two people to watch television with a three foot couch cushion between them. Sean doesn't let me have my own side of the couch. He sits on the left corner of the sofa and snuggles me against his chest. There's no kissing, just his strong embrace and the *Buffy* episode with no dialogue. As I fall asleep in his arms, he says, "I've always believed Riley didn't get a fair shake."

I awaken sometime in the middle of the night. The disc of *Buffy* continues to play but somehow it's the episode before the one I fell asleep watching. Sean whispers, "I watched the whole disc and started over. You need the sleep."

I disentangle my arm and tap my fitness tracker to check the time. It's one o'clock in the morning. "Will your grandparents worry because you aren't home?"

"That's sweet of you to think of my grandparents, but no. I texted my grandmother when you passed out." He reaches his arms up to stretch. "I've enjoyed watching you nap, but I should get going now that you're awake. We need to go to the funeral tomorrow. Please remember how safe you felt tonight, because tomorrow I might have to coddle Cynthia. She may be particularly needy."

I hate that he's nice to Cynthia. I don't trust her, but Sean hasn't seen through her act. If I tell him I think she might have murdered her husband, he'll blame my jealousy. I nod and say, "I understand, but we aren't going to hide our relationship to make her feel better, are we?"

He holds my hand and walks toward the front door, "Tomorrow we can be discrete, but I promise I'll make it very clear to her next week that you and I are dating. I won't even mention Quentin."

I gloss right over the dig about Quentin. It's late, and I don't want to start this disagreement again. He leans down to kiss me before he opens the door. If we kiss in the open doorway, the cats could slip past us and we'd never notice. I close my eyes and wrap my arms around his neck. I feel safe in his arms and forget about the world. After a few minutes, he pulls away, drops a kiss on my nose, and says, "We have an early morning and a full day. I need to go."

I lock the door after him and walk up the stairs in a haze. When I crawl into my bed, Annika joins me on the other pillow. The next thing I hear is my alarm blaring. Most mornings, I wake up before the alarm, but even sleeping until it shrieks gives me plenty of time to get ready.

The last funeral I attended my mom picked out my outfit. It was an elderly relative when I was in elementary school. Mac didn't have any service for Tiffany because she said the only people who would attend would be us and some ghouls. I didn't respect Gene at all, but I like Gennifer. Given Gene's reputation and personality, I don't want Gennifer to feel alone. I'm also curious to see who attends the funeral.

I pick a long black broomstick skirt which reaches my ankles. I wore it once to work at Genius Used Cars. Phoebe pointed at me and told me Gene would hate it. He ignored it. I pair it with a long dark purple tunic. My comfortable black shoes complete the outfit. The humid, overcast day means the ensemble feels a little too warm, but funeral homes should have excellent air conditioning systems.

When I arrive Sean and Lando are eating bagels and drinking coffee in the kitchen. They're both dressed in dark suits with white shirts and somber ties. When he was selling cars, Lando wore ties with cartoon characters or other decorations with his custom tailored suits. He told me interesting ties were an easy conversation starter for customers. Funerals aren't the appropriate setting for eye catching ties. Lando looks dapper in his suit, but Sean appears breathtaking. When he turns around as I enter the room, the suit coat strains at the breadth of his shoulders.

As I appreciate the view of Sean in a suit, Mac throws open the back door. Her clothes shout responsible, dignified lawyer. Her opening statement contradicts her look. "I'm wearing racy underwear. Don't I look boring? I always wear expensive lingerie when I have to wear these terrible suits. So, pretty much every single day, I wear lovely underwear."

Sean and Lando look at the ground which raises them both in my estimation. I answer for the three of us. "Mac, do you ever feel like sometimes too much information isn't helpful?"

She throws back her head and laughs, "From me nope, I'm establishing trust with you guys. We've all been friends a while. I don't have many, or okay, any other friends. It was a little test which you cuties passed brilliantly."

She points at me, "Violet shares too much information when she talks to the police. Cops like arrogant Detective Andrews don't deserve any extra words about my underthings."

I shake my head. "On a different note, which cars are we taking?"

Lando answers, "My Town Car and Mac's sedan are the best choices. Violet, your car doesn't have enough passenger capacity and Sean's truck looks like a construction vehicle. We need to pick up Cynthia and Gennifer. For the ride to their place, we can split the vehicles based on gender."

I smother my pout. I want to ride with Sean, but Lando's decision sounds logical. Once I'm in Mac's passenger seat, I ask her, "How awful do you think this funeral will be?"

She grins and says, "I think it'll be fascinating. We'll get to watch Detective Andrews chase his own tail a little as he tries to find the killer in the mourners. Cynthia will sob all over Sean's big, brawny shoulders. Gennifer will babble and the few other people who show up will look uncomfortable. I'm looking forward to this one almost as much as when the old, should've retired years ago partners kick it at the law firm."

I ask, "Have you attended many other funerals?"

She pulls her long, dark hair over one shoulder, "When I was a teen, various members of my extended family kept passing away. I got dragged to their funerals where the surviving women asked me when I was getting married. I'd stare down and pretend to be demure and bite my tongue so I didn't say maybe after high school. I developed a funeral face. An old law partner dies on average every six months, so I attend a bunch of those, too."

This worries me. I don't have a funeral face. This is the first time I've heard of a funeral face. I'll get it wrong. I start trying to make sad faces, but not too sad. I couldn't stand the victim. Gennifer's in a better place with her father dead. He's in a far worse place, one with flames and pitchforks.

Mac glances away from the road and asks, "What are you doing with your face? Do you have gas? I can roll down the window."

"You told me about a funeral face. I haven't been to a funeral since I was in elementary school. I'm working on a funeral face." I continue to try to look sad, but I turn to face the window.

Mac grabs my arm. "Stop doing that. You're going to scare the people in the lane next to us. I meant that I don't smile or make wisecracks. You spend most of your time trying to blend into the background so just act like yourself. It's a little harder for me to be subdued because I'm so fabulous."

I burst into laughter because she's right. When Mac turns on the charm, she compels the room to watch her. I've always been an observer rather than a participant. I love television because I can watch without ever being called upon to interact.

Mac waves at me and says, "As long as you keep from laughing like a demented clown, you should be fine. Besides, I suspect this is going to be the Cynthia and Gennifer show."

Mac spends the rest of the trip telling me stories about the various funerals she's attended. Some of her stories are so hysterical that I lose my breath from laughing and tears stream from my eyes. Her deadpan delivery of tales like the wrong person being in the coffin deserve a greater audience. I'm proud of my decision to forego makeup as I usually do. It would've been a smeared, ugly mess because of Mac. Her makeup remains perfect.

As we drive on to Cynthia's block, I ask, "Have you ever seen a deal jacket for a car deal? I meant to ask Lando about it but forgot."

She shakes her head. We park behind the house and walk around the block. From half a block away, I appreciate Cynthia's presentation. She stands on the front step of her house, staring into the distance. Cynthia's makeup and ensemble make Mac look like a frumpy housewife. Cynthia wears an immaculate black two-piece suit which fits her perfectly. Her makeup makes her skin porcelain. A pillbox hat with a flirty half veil perches on her head to complete her costume.

Lando and Sean pull in front of Cynthia's house as Mac and I walk toward her. Lando idles the car in front of her on the street. Sean approaches her. I witness her perfection for a few moments before she throws herself into Sean's arms. She keeps her head turned to the side, presumably to protect her fabulous makeup. He pats her on the back awkwardly and looks at me over the top of her head with pleading eyes. I shrug. Today she can act the grieving widow and lean on him. I'll let him deal with her histrionics.

Mac rolls her eyes at me, but she also manages to keep her mouth shut. Gennifer runs over to us, ignoring her mother clinging to Sean. "She looks beautiful, doesn't she? She whined to your grandfather that none of her clothes fit her. She couldn't be expected to attend her husband's funeral in oversized rags. Your grandfather paid for her outfit from a local boutique. She picked out several from their website. They delivered them last night because of her tragedy." Gesturing to her own outfit, "I guess thrift store apparel work for me."

Gennifer's black dress with a square boat neck line fits her. However, it's a grandmother dress and not in the cool way. Gennifer continues, "I'm not sure if I'll even be walking by the end of this fiasco. These shoes are from two years ago when my feet were not this size. I saw your grandfather give her cash. I assume her pretty hat cost more than my whole outfit."

Gennifer must feel betrayed. She doesn't usually snark about her mother. Painful feet might encourage more honesty, so I suggest, "Why don't Mac and I drive Gennifer. Cynthia can ride with Sean and Lando."

Cynthia delicately sniffles and nods at my suggestion, "That's a lovely idea. Sean can sit in the backseat with me for support."

Her ready agreement annoys but doesn't surprise me. I open my mouth to reply to her treatment of my grandfather like a chauffeur or Sean like her personal servant. Lando shakes his head at me and calls to Sean, "Please bring Cynthia to my car, so we can stop blocking the road."

Mac laughs and addresses Gennifer, "Kid, it's more

realistic to get accustomed to uncomfortable shoes than it is to think people are regularly going to drive around the block to pick you up. Come on."

Gennifer follows us to the back to the overgrown parking pad. "Wow, I never get back here. This backyard looks terrible. So, Sean's awesome and all, but I don't want a stepfather, especially one who is as close to my age as he is to my mom's. I hope he's not falling for her act. She is really sick, but she's acting like she used to when she and my father were still together. I've liked her better when it was just the two of us."

Gennifer continues to talk as she opens the door, gets into the car and closes the door. Once the girl's on a roll, it's hard to stop her or direct her. I interrupt her flow once the car's in motion, "Do you think your mom could've killed Gene?"

My question shocks her into silence, and she surprises me with her response. "Gosh, I hope not. If she did kill him, what'll happen to me? Do you think I can come live with you and Lando?"

Mac interjects at this point, "I think we're putting the car before the train with that response." I tilt my head at her odd idiom but I'd rather hear Gennifer's reasoning. The girl learned to be self-sufficient to the point of self-absorption from her parents.

As Mac backs out of the parking space, I turn around to the back seat to look at Gennifer. "Do you think your mom had motive, means and opportunity to kill your father?"

"Wow, that's a cool way to ask the question. How did you learn so much about legal stuff? Isn't Mac the lawyer and not you? I thought you majored in television."

I hate it when people denigrate my doctorate. I tap my hand on the seat rest between us, "I majored in Popular Culture focused on television. I watched over one thousand episodes of *Law and Order* and its spinoffs. In your gut, do you think she killed him?"

Mac snorts and interjects, "Yes, viewing of *Law and Order* gives Violet all the legal lingo and knowledge. It's like a law degree but not."

Gennifer runs her hand through her blonde hair, "My mom had motive but so did most of the people who knew him. I avoided him to the best of my ability but I think if I spent more time with him, I would've had motive."

She holds one finger up for motive. "Second means, that's an easy one for her too. He left his keys around all the time. She could have copies of the keys."

She holds another finger up. "The opportunity's the reason I can clear her. He was killed at the car lot. She would have needed someone with a car to take her there to kill him. It's not like you take an Uber to commit a murder. There's no one in her life she could trust to help her kill him."

Gennifer smiles and makes a fist. "I think I'd like living with you and Lando, but I'll be okay with my mom. By the way, I know I have the motive and means, too. I'm not one of those teenage crime queens who can bend guys to my will. Just sayin, I didn't kill him either. In case I'm a suspect. Ohh, am I suspect?"

"You're on the list but not near the top. You would've needed an accomplice. You were too eager to bring us into this situation to have killed him." I say with a smile. "On a different note, is there anything we can do to make today easier for you?"

She shakes her head so the tips of hair hit the car window, "No, I figure it'll be us from the last car lot and possibly a few people who worked with him other places. I'll try looking sad and being quiet."

TWENTY-ONE

"I want to work with you and get you into a car."

We pull into the small parking lot of the funeral home to find it full. Funeral homes have multiple rooms and several funerals might be happening at the same time. Friday mornings in the summer must be popular. I'm not sure about the agenda for today because I wasn't at the planning. This funeral should be short because not even his widow or daughter are upset about his death.

Sean, Lando and Cynthia arrive within a minute. Mac puts on the flashers on her car and idles it. There's got to be an additional parking area for family members. The funeral director rushes over to Cynthia's window. I jump out of Mac's car and dash over to listen.

He's wringing his hands as he talks to Cynthia, "When we met this week, you didn't mention your husband was so popular. I must admit we were unprepared for the onslaught of mourners. Luckily no other funerals are scheduled until three o'clock this afternoon. We'll move him to the largest room. I'm calling in help for parking now."

I want to ask if they switched the body or if every-one's confused. Lando taps his cane and asks, "What do you mean Gene Johnson is famous?"

The flustered funeral director points toward the funeral home, "We already have forty people here and the funeral doesn't start for an hour."

I say, "Did anyone check for a misprint in the obitu-ary? Maybe the wrong time or the wrong person?"

My question is so insensitive. If Cynthia were in mourning for her husband, it'd be awful. Since she's playing the part of the grieving wife, we look callous to the staff of the funeral home. He lowers his prodigious eyebrows at me and then peers at Cynthia to see her reaction.

She turns in her seat to stare at Sean, "I'm so devas-tated by everything, I need someone to hold me and comfort me."

"I'll go get your daughter Gennifer, you can cling to each other in your time of need." I turn toward Mac's idling car to get Gennifer.

"No, I don't want my poor child subjected to this discussion." She turns back to the funeral director, "Sir, I thought this would be a small event. My husband's circumstances have changed in recent years. I didn't think the people who knew him before his difficulties would attend."

He nods at her and reaches into the car to pat her hand. Sean looks up from his phone in the back seat and says, "I may have solved some of the mystery. The news-paper and the television morning news covered Gene's murder today. Several of the stories identified today as the day of the funeral. The stories didn't give the address of the funeral home but the obituary did."

The funeral director covers his mouth with his hands and says, "Ghoulish attention seekers have invaded my funeral home. Miss, I thought your husband was involved in an accident. You never mentioned someone murdered him."

His shock seems disingenuous. The funeral home retrieved the body at the coroner's, and it was run over by a vehicle numerous times. These people have seen thousands of bodies, and they didn't suspect murder. I've only seen three and I knew it was murder.

The cars are idling on a narrow Pittsburgh street. Our vehicles in front of the funeral home affect the traffic flow. The other drivers have been patient for several minutes because it's a funeral home, but one yells out his window, "Can yinz move? I got to get to work."

The interruption pulls the director out of his daze and he says, "Pull into the parking lot. You are the family. I don't give a darn if you park in some ghouls. My staff will take care of you if you give them your keys."

Lando grumbles and pats the dashboard, "Not one scratch on my baby, she's irreplaceable. They don't make Lincoln Town Cars anymore."

It's wonderful my grandfather's priorities remain consistent. His car is more important than Gene. While true, it's a little rude to articulate at the man's funeral. When Cynthia exits, one the employees tries to assist her, but she pulls her arm away from the skinny young man. "Sean's the only one who I trust to help me during this trying time."

With the cars taken care of and Cynthia's tantrum momentarily averted by Sean, the six of us assemble in the funeral home. The director leads us into his private office. "We reserve the half hour before the beginning of the viewing for family. However, many of the unexpected number of mourners appear to know each other, and they're becoming restless. Would those closest to Gene be devastated if we begin the viewing early? I hope some people will pay their respects and leave."

"Anything that will make this circus pass more quickly is fine with me," Cynthia adjusts her veil and bats her eyes at the funeral director.

He leads us into the viewing room with Gene's corpse. They did a professional job preparing his body. As I saw last Saturday morning, his head and shoulders looked unmarred. The drape covers his body from below the armpits to mask all of the trauma from his fatal encounter with the car. The makeup artist removed the gray from his face. Without an arrogant expression, Gene appears more pleasant in death than he ever did in life.

Gennifer gasps and clutches my arm. This reminds me she's still a child and Gene was her father. I pat her hand to offer a modicum of comfort. Cynthia collapses into Sean's arms. Those closest to him have to face the reality of his death.

One glance at the body's enough for me. Bodies look much better prepared for funerals than they do when found at car dealerships by unsuspecting me. However, even at a funeral I hate looking at a corpse. I don't know what to say. I'm not sure where I'm supposed to sit. I've been roped into an unnatural role. I knew Gene for about a week while he was alive. If he hadn't been murdered, this week he would've been a cautionary tale about not taking jobs which are offered too quickly.

The funeral director asks Cynthia if she's ready to begin. She doesn't release Sean from her grip. Gennifer looks at me pleadingly, but I move toward the front row of seats with Lando and Mac. Sean's chivalry makes him a part of the receiving line for this fiasco.

When the largely male crowd begins to pour into the room, several of them see Lando in the front row and approach him. Over fifty years in the car business makes him the familiar face, not Cynthia, the widow. He sighs and joins the widow, the daughter and my boyfriend in the receiving line.

I recognize a single person in the early wave. Jeff Hastings, the salesman from Roar Motors whose wife owns a flower shop, stands on the other side of the room. He always wears a flower in his lapel as a memory device for customers.

By the official starting time of the funeral, mourners fill the room past capacity. The funeral employees attempt to direct the flow, but the mourners linger and stand in the aisles between the chairs talking to each other in loud, boisterous tones.

At half past ten, I see a familiar face. Walter enters and waits in line to view the body. He tries to hug Cynthia, and she freezes him with a look. For the last hour, the only men that she allowed to touch her have been under forty and attractive. Her look stops most attempts at contact and the more persistent, she stops by grabbing Sean and hiding behind him. Seans moves to the side for Walter who hugs her and whispers in her ear. Then Walter pats Gennifer on the head.

He approaches me and points at the crowd, "Can you believe this turn out? I guess being murdered makes a guy a lot more popular in death than he was in life."

I nod at him. The noise level makes conversation difficult, and I'm not sure what to say. Walter almost sounds like he admires the size of Gene's funeral. The crowd makes me nervous and unsettled. I'm able to talk to people in small groups, but this mass of humanity bothers me.

I sit in the front row of seats in the corner. No one from the funeral home tries to move me out of the room. I've watched over one hundred men look at Gene's body with various degrees of disinterest and occasional loathing. The few female attendees' faces reflect a continuum of disgust. No one spits on the body or dances next to the coffin. Although several try to move the drape to peek at the injuries. The funeral home must've attached the drape to the coffin with surgical wire because no one's able to dislodge it. Some ghouls whip out their smart phones and snap pictures of Gene.

Detective Andrews lurks at the back of the room. He never walks through the receiving line. He watches everything with an impassive roving stare. He probably hopes someone will solve the case for him by dancing around the coffin singing I did it, I did it. A case with too many suspects must be as frustrating as a case with no suspects.

Gennifer's facial expression alerts me to the appearance of someone interesting. Animation appears on her face for the first time at the funeral when she catches sight of Dalton. Despair replaces it at the sight of the girl. A lovely girl who appears to be about my age clings to his arm. She's ethereal with light brown hair and enormous cornflower blue eyes. However, she's incredibly thin and wearing a long sleeved dark blue dress on a ninety degree day.

She cries when she peers into the coffin and leans on Dalton the way Cynthia's been attached to Sean all morning. After viewing the body, Dalton and the young woman veer to avoid the receiving line. Dalton never looks at Gene's body. His eyes remain on the girl. He ignores Lando, me and even Walter who has continued to hover near me in spite of my silence.

Walter waves at Dalton. When Dalton fails to respond, Walter chases after him. I want to hear the conversation when Walter catches him but not enough to brave moving through the crowd and losing my protected space.

I look over my shoulder at Detective Andrews and motion toward the two salespeople. He won't tell me if he learns anything. I'm trying to reform my snooping ways. If he learns anything based upon my observation, it's his job. He's the police detective, and I'm not supposed to be involved.

The viewing was supposed to end at eleven, but even with the half hour head start, I'm afraid that won't happen. At eleven fifteen, the funeral director enters the raucous room and announces, "The funeral will begin promptly at eleven thirty. We have cameras and will simulcast it in the other rooms in the funeral home. When the funeral begins, please be respectful and keep the noise down. Also, please no filming of the funeral and no photographs in the funeral home."

Half an hour late isn't the definition of beginning promptly. It didn't occur to me people would take photographs at a funeral. As weird as it seems, the funeral home should have a sign about no photographs at the entrance to the building. Third, he told people not to film when the staff will be filming.

At eleven twenty-five, Phoebe arrives and the fireworks begin. She's wearing a black bandage dress that reaches the middle of her thighs when she's standing. Her black four inch heels have soles that are painted red. The attendees see the bottom of her shoes when she throws her body across the coffin and lifts both feet from the floor. The dress also rides up displaying her lack of undergarments.

She wails, "How could anyone do this to you? You were the love of my life. We were getting hitched." Cynthia glares at her. Gennifer breaks the tension and possibly averts an attack upon Phoebe by her enraged mother. Gennifer begins to laugh with a shrill hint of hysteria.

She talks through her laughter, "Seriously woman, those cheap shoes just have paint smeared on the bottoms. That doesn't make them Louboutins. Anyway, Gene was never going to marry you. He didn't even bother to file divorce papers from my mom. You were one of many in his phone. Your ratings were even on the low side."

Phoebe climbs off the coffin and spins to face

Gennifer. "Little girl, you'd better shut that smart mouth or I'm goin shut if for you."

Phones start appearing in people's hands to film the confrontation. Lando moves Cynthia closer to my seat in the corner to protect her, and Sean moves into a defensive position in front of Gennifer. Mac and I move to flank Sean and get between Phoebe and Gennifer.

Phoebe pulls her dress down so that more of her prodigious chest is on display for the crowd. "What do ya mean my rating?"

Gennifer pushes herself between Mac and me to face Phoebe. She's brave but savvy enough to keep Sean close in case the woman attacks her. "Gene was such a scumbag that he kept a digital version of the old-fashioned black book. He kept dirty photographs of the women he banged with notes and number ratings. You were only a five out of ten."

At the description of herself as a five, Phoebe bursts into real tears and crumples to the floor. The circus acquires additional monkeys when her other special man friend, Butch, the repo guy muscles his way onto the scene. "What do ya mean a five? Phoebe is at least a six in the sack. She'll do anything."

He lifts her up off the ground and throws her over his shoulder which again exposes her backend and cheap, painted shoes to the crowd. "We're not standin for this."

He pushes through the crowd of filming men. He flees through the back entrance of the viewing room. The room becomes quiet at their departure for approximately thirty seconds. Then the crowd begins to discuss the scene. Some of the men play the video to check on their version of the details or to double check the amount of skin Phoebe displayed.

The funeral director pushes into the room and attempts to silence the unruly crowd by clearing his throat into his discrete microphone. Everyone ignores him. Cynthia sobs into Lando's lapels. If she were doing her usual act, she would've made sure Sean was the one comforting her. Sean's holding onto Gennifer who's trying to wiggle free and head in the direction of Butch and Phoebe's departure.

I turn around and nod at Detective Andrews. He taps his phone and gestures at me. I put my phone on silent out of respect for the customs of a funeral. He must have texted me. The rudeness level of this room with the filming and video sharing means checking a text is one of the most polite things to occur.

The text states.

> There are police outside too. I'm sure they're in custody. Please let the girl know.

I push my way over to Gennifer. "You need to calm down. The police have those two in custody. After this fiasco, we need to get the phone you have to the police. It might crack the case."

She flips her hair and rolls her eyes. She pulls out her own pink, sparkly phone and starts to play the song, *Highway to Hell*, on full volume.

Gennifer shouts, "Whatever, I don't care who killed him. He deserved to die."

The ineffective funeral director must have turned the

volume on his microphone to the maximum level and moved directly behind Gennifer. As she says, Gene deserved to die, the words blast to the entire room.

A sixteen year old stating her father deserved to die shocks the room into silence. Then Dalton starts to clap and Walter joins him. I hug her to try to calm her. Two people clapping turns the tenor of the room and most of the people add their applause to the cacophony.

The funeral director shoves Gennifer to the side and screams, "Everyone stop right this instant. Clapping isn't allowed at funerals. You're all animals. People are supposed to pretend they care someone died. It's sad. People have behaved much better than all of you when the dead person is a murderer and not the victim. This is my business. I reserve the right to refuse service. Everyone get out. You're all refused."

A few of the guys must be drunk on the adrenaline in the room or the alcohol from the flasks which have been appearing from pockets. They start to mutter that this little twit can't tell them what to do. There's only one of him. Sean, in his typical hero mode, moves in front of the funeral director and pulls off the man's headset to use it for his own microphone.

The men in the crowd feel comfortable threatening a skinny, pale middle-aged funeral director but when a six and half foot red haired giant protects him, the energy changes. Sean says, "Everyone needs to calm down and leave. The show is over. When he refused service that made all of us trespassers so just go."

Mac, Sean, Lando, and I move Gennifer and Cynthia into a corner and form a protective wall. The room looks like a cyclone moved through when the last man exits. The funeral director glares at us, and says, "You all caused this. You need to get out, too."

Mac wraps herself in her super lawyer persona and faces the man. "I haven't identified myself until this point. I'm Mrs. Johnson's legal counsel. You had better apologize to us right now or we can wait and you can apologize in court. It isn't the responsibility of the bereaved to control a situation at a funeral. It's your job. Clearly, you didn't schedule enough staff or institute any type of crowd control. The travesty of this circus falls at your feet. Of course, with the amount of cell phone video evidence, suing you will be fun."

She sweeps past him after her pronouncement and the rest of us file behind her, leaving Gene's body sitting alone in the mangled viewing room. If this had been the funeral for someone anyone loved, this travesty would've been a tragedy. Gene's terrible life contributed to his awful funeral.

When we reach the parking lot, Detective Andrews waves at us. I'm not sure if that means we should leave or join him. Mac marches over to him and pokes him in the chest. "You and your police people should've prevented this riot."

After a few seconds of shocked silence, he laughs down at her, "Look, lawyer girl, this isn't my jurisdiction. I came to this fiasco to see if anyone did something crazy like confess to the dead body. I brought a few guys but not proper backup for a mess like this."

She puts her hands on her hips and asks, "Why didn't you pull your gun?"

"I'm not going to pull my gun in a crowded room when no one else had a gun or threatened violence. This isn't a television show. Now you should all go away because I need to get the tapes of the event from the funeral home cameras. I doubt anyone connected with this facility is thrilled with any of you right now." He points toward our vehicles.

I raise my hand because I sometimes still feel like I'm in a classroom around authority figures, "What about Gene's body? How is he going to be interred if no one drives him to the cemetery?"

I look around at everyone's face and shock is the only expression. I guess no one else considered burial.

Detective Andrews rubs his forehead. "I think I need to reclaim the body to see if it contains any additional evidence. I saw some people spitting on him in the chaos." He turns to Cynthia, "Would you mind if I have my coroner come get the body again?"

She glares at him, "I'm done with him. I don't care what happens to his body. He can be thrown in a pauper's grave for all I care."

Mac grabs Detective Andrews's arm, "My client paid this funeral home for the entire package. In fact, Mr. Landovic paid for it until Genius Used Cars is sold at which time Cynthia will reimburse him. Please inform the staff we expect the body to be buried by them when the authorities are done with it. We will save them the cost of a graveside service, but they better fulfill their end of the contract."

I walk toward the cars in the hopes that someone follows me and we can escape from this drama. At the cars, Lando asks, "Should we all get together for lunch or does everyone want to go their respective homes and rest?"

I say, "I vote for rest. This has been incredibly stressful. We can reflect and talk tomorrow at Genius Used Car Lot."

Gennifer tosses her hair and opens her mouth but Mac stops her by agreeing with me, "I need to take notes on today's events for a possible lawsuit. If we rehash everything at lunch, it will taint my recollections. In fact, I encourage everybody to go home and reflect and write notes about their perceptions."

Sean nods and opens Lando's passenger door. Cynthia gets into the car, and Mac says, "As your lawyer, I don't trust you two to stay quiet about today if you're with Sean and Lando. I'll drive you home and give you legal pads for the car. I have some in the trunk."

As she escorts the Johnsons past me, Mac winks at me. Sean holds the door for me to get into the car so he can close it after me. His innate courtesy makes him seem like a man from another time.

As much as I appreciate his gestures, my legs are so much shorter than his. "I'll sit in the back seat, so you can stretch out your legs. You were on your feet all morning. Before the exciting bits, I was able to sit."

"Okay, this time. I'll take the front seat." He turns around as soon as Lando starts the car, "I want to make reservations for tomorrow night. Would you please go out to a nice dinner with me at the Grand Concourse?"

I hesitate for a moment to think about what to wear.

Lando interrupts, "Answer the boy already so we can rehash the funeral."

I smile at Sean, "Of course, I'd love to go out to dinner with you. My wardrobe issues distracted me. I think I need to go to the mall this afternoon."

TWENTY-TWO

"Remember be smart and buy a Genius used car!"

After the funeral catastrophe, the three of us ignore Mac's instructions and discuss our perceptions of the scene. No one expected the gigantic turnout or Phoebe acting like she cared about Gene. Gennifer's announcement of the cell phone pictures and ratings also shocked everyone in the audience. The numbers on the deal jackets were from one to ten. I can't remember if any of the deals with men's names contained numbers in the corner. When we get back to Genius Used Cars, I need to check those deal jackets with Lando and Detective Andrews.

Sean offers to go clothing shopping with me, so I don't have to drag Lando. I want to surprise him with a lovely outfit and his presence on the shopping trip would ruin the surprise. He also needs to check on Lando's addition and put in an appearance on the site.

I call Mac and she informs me she needs to stay with Cynthia and Gennifer because Detective Andrews is on his way. He needs the cell phone for evidence and wants to know why it wasn't given to him sooner. She says, "I'd much rather go shopping with you than deal with him."

I spend a lonely but blessedly silent afternoon shopping at the closest mall. I buy a gorgeous green sheath dress with a lace overlay. It's a little shorter than my comfort level but walking on car lots have shaped my legs. My current small shoe collection won't do justice to the dress, so I purchase a pair of dark green heels to match.

A salon at the mall provides a trim and deep conditioning treatment. Then I approach the most frightening part of the mall, the makeup counter. I've never been good at makeup. I show the woman at the counter the dress and purchase a makeup and skin care set to compliment it. She shows me how to apply the makeup and tells me about several places on the Internet with tutorials. My relationship with the Internet has always seemed more like my heroine Buffy than someone in my generation. My graduate school mentor called social media the ultimate time waster and discouraged me from exploring it. I avoid the web whenever possible.

I return to Lando's several hundred dollars poorer but with exciting new purchases. The cats appear to be the only occupants of the house. Between the funeral and the shopping expedition, I'm exhausted so I take a nap with the cats and my phone on silent.

I wake up in the dark and have no idea of the time. My phone's missing from the bedside table. I suspect a cat. My eyes are glued to the inside of my eyelids because I didn't remove my contact lenses before the nap. I'm still wearing my funeral clothes.

When I finally get my bearings, I search under my bed and find my phone. It's four o'clock in the morning, and I'm starving. I slept for ten hours, so I'm not tired. No one else is awake at this ludicrous hour. After my shower, I get dressed for my upcoming day. It's Saturday, and after yesterday's potential publicity, Genius Used Cars might be busy with gawkers and some possible buyers.

Between the four of us, we sold about fifteen cars last week. Lando didn't buy more cars at auction, but he acquired five acceptable trades. The Genius Used Car inventory contains twenty-five operational cars. Once the inventory falls to a certain number, we can close the car lot.

The fiasco at the funeral illustrated the nearly universal hatred of Gene, but it didn't present a clear suspect in his murder. I've been keeping notes on the possible killer, but not truly investigating. With Tiffany, I felt compelled to find her murderer. I'm curious about who Gene pushed over the edge.

The phone with the photos and the rankings could be the key. The deal jackets with numbers might be related. The deals marked with X's might be women who rejected Gene. That idiot Phoebe didn't seem to know anything about it. She displayed her lack of acting skills with her lack of underwear at the funeral. I assume she saw the deal jackets.

Butch hustled her out of the room, so I'm not sure if he knew. I watched Gennifer and Phoebe during the riot, not Dalton or Walter. They might have known something.

Gennifer and Cynthia had the phone, so they knew. The phone could also contain other evidence of Gene's misdeeds.

Sitting in Lando's wonderful library turned media room, I think about Gene's murder. Stillness makes me a cat jungle gym. Annika and Creamsicle have developed a civil relationship with each other revolving around crawling all over me. I review my notes about possible culprits, and Annika chases the pen. Creamsicle wraps around my neck and purrs with loud abandon.

My suspects list centers on the car lot. With all of the excitement, I didn't have a chance to talk to Walter or Dalton about their perceptions of the funeral. That reminds me of my questions regarding the woman Dalton brought to the funeral. She appeared to be so fragile. A funeral isn't my idea of a fun date.

I forgot to write my description of the event for Mac. I write four pages of my impressions of the funeral and the actions of its employees. The funeral director needs to return at least part of Cynthia's payment and apologize for making the situation more awful for her and Gennifer. If he fails to see the error of his ways, Mac will convince him.

I scan Lando's collection of DVDs he purchased for my enjoyment. I offered to share my copies when I arrived, but he had these waiting in the room for me. He told me to keep mine packed, because when I moved on, he would keep these to remember our times together. This sojourn at Lando's is only supposed to last one year while I prove I can work a regular job. I've experienced more excitement here than in my entire life combined to this point. I feel useful and important to other people. I'm not sure if attempting to return to academia remains my plan. Of course, in academia, I never stumbled across any dead bodies.

The spines of most of the shows I studied have dark, serious colors. I've never been a fan of happy, light situational comedies with light, happy covers. I notice a bright cover I don't recognize on the shelf. It's the first season of *Glee*. The show I watched about high school contains monsters and dancing demons, not singing teenagers. I feel like watching something effervescent, so I start at the first episode of *Glee*.

The alternate representation of high school reminds me even the car business is better than high school. The story lines and catchy tunes act like a siren's call which pulls me under the waves. My phone interrupts my bingeing when Lando calls me and asks several questions without waiting for my reply, "Where are you? Did you wander off for cat food and get lost again? You're confused enough, you can't add another boy to your messy dating life."

It's nearly seven in the morning, and we all planned to leave for Genius Used Cars early today. I run to the kitchen and grab a plain, dry bagel and a bottle of water. Lando and Sean glance at their watches, and Sean asks me, "Seriously, where were you?"

"I was in the media room. I woke up before dawn after sleeping for ten hours. So I started watching a new show and got caught by it. Luckily, I showered and got dressed before I started it." I turn to leave and a cat trips me. "I guess neither of you fed the cats?"

Lando points at Annika and replies, "You usually feed them and I thought the crying was a trick. I read a cat book that said cats are smart enough to pretend no one fed them to get extra food."

As he talks, I open the cat food can and split it between the two crying cats. They have dry food all day to nibble. The wet food makes them happy and content cats tend to be better behaved cats. If they start making messes in Lando's house, it'll be terrible.

Lando drives alone and Sean and I take his truck. Discovering a new television shows makes me giddy. Sean's uninitiated, and we talk about the show with side discussions about our own high school experiences. The car ride flies by without a single mention of anyone in the Johnson family or murder. We have a wonderful time. I can't wait for our date tonight. Maybe after the date, we can return to Lando's so I can introduce Sean to *Glee*.

Sean and I arrive at the car lot first, because Lando needs to detour to Lawrenceville to retrieve the Johnson women. I text Mac to see if she's coming to the lot today, but I don't bother Detective Andrews. I never communicate with Dalton or Walter outside work hours. I'm sure I'll see them both. It would be awesome if we sell enough cars today to start wrapping up this used car lot experience next week.

We park behind the service building for the first time since I found Gene's body. Sean's powerful white work pickup is catnip to working men. When they see it on the lot, several of them ask if it's available at a cheap price.

As we walk around the building to get to the trailer, I flashback to finding Gene. There's a car smashed into the side of the service building with the door hanging open. This time there's no body under the car, but splayed across the hood. Walter is crushed between the building and the car.

I collapse into Sean's arms. I've discovered four bodies all dead or near death by violence. This time I'm not alone and I want somebody else to be in charge. Sean responds immediately and competently to his first corpse. He holds me in one arm and pulls his phone out of his pocket by wrapping his other arm around me. He dials 911. Over my sobs, he answers the dispatcher, "I found a dead body at Genius Used Cars."

As he talks, he moves me away from the scene by keeping himself between me and Walter's body. Once he's moved us to the other side of the building, he rests his head on top of mine and sighs, "I don't know how you've handled this situation three other times."

On the end of a sob, I say, "It's easier if you don't like the person. This week hanging out in the service building with Dalton and Walter, I got to know them. I'm getting sick of being the unlucky one who finds the bodies."

Sean props me against the building. "Violet, I need to run over to him to make sure that he's past the point of help. Can you lean here for a little?"

I nod and he disappears around the building. Once I'm out of his arms, the shaking starts. I've responded in different ways to every body I've found. The boneless way Walter slumped over the car looked like a dead person. It must've been Walter. It was his car and the body had gray hair and the cheap suit Walter wore every day.

Sean returns and shakes his head at me. "There's nothing we can do to help him."

He holds me. I fight to swallow my sobs.

The ambulance beats everyone else to the car lot. Saturday mornings must not be busy for emergency personnel. Continuing my four for four body finding streak, Quentin and his silent female partner are on duty. I turn around but Sean keeps me anchored against his chest with his arms around my middle.

I point in the direction of Walter's body, "Hi Quentin, I think I was a cadaver dog in another life. As usual, I can identify the body."

He reaches out to pat my arm and ignores Sean. "I'm sorry Violet. It looks like this one hit you hard. Detective Andrews should be here any minute."

Sean tenses but he must decide this isn't the time to get into it with Quentin. Quentin's more comfortable at crime scenes and goads Sean, "Usually this is the time you're leaning on my shoulder, Violet."

Sean moves forward an inch. Everyone's on edge, and I can't handle conflict between these two as I deal with finding another dead coworker. Like Tiffany, I wasn't friends with Walter, but in this past week I'd gotten to know him well enough to care about him as a human being.

Based on his stories, I'm not sure many people in this world cared about him more than Dalton and I did. He was over sixty years old, and his parents were long dead.

Other than his older brother who died in Vietnam, he never spoke about siblings. If he had any, he didn't have a relationship with them. According to his stories, he never married and his female relationships were with strippers or prostitutes. He didn't even own a pet.

Detective Andrews arrives as I contemplate the loneliness of Walter's life while I'm trapped between two men. This time literally, not figuratively, the way I often am between these two.

Detective Andrews addresses me, ignoring the tension between Sean and Quentin, "Just to let you know, this is the reaction I expect from someone finding a body when she arrives at work. I don't need to introduce myself this time and I promise not to be as terse. I interviewed your coworker, Walter so you don't need to look at him again. I can identify him."

I nod. He says, "Violet, this needs to be on the record. I'm going need you to respond to my questions with actual words. Do you need me to call your grandfather or your delightful lawyer? I see you have a friend with you, plus the EMT for some reason."

He turns to Quentin and raises his eyebrows at him. Quentin takes the hint, "I guess I need to help my partner with the body. She's used to me disappearing to comfort you in these situations."

I sag into Sean's arms again. I straightened up during the tension of their silent confrontation. "I can answer your questions, sir."

He rubs his hand over his bald head, "Wow, you must be shaken up if we're back to sir. I guess I should be happy this time you aren't calling for your lawyer. For the record, what is your full name?"

I stare at the ground, "My name is Violet Landovic. This is the fourth body I've found since I moved to Pittsburgh. Sean and I got to work early because after yesterday, we all thought the publicity might make us busy. That reminds me, did you secure the scene?"

He laughs, "Thanks for learning the lingo, but I've got this. I have officers blocking access to the lot this time. They're watching for Lando's car, because no one wants him to panic, especially at his age. Is your lawyer on her way?"

I shake my head, "I haven't called Mac, and we never discussed her coming here today. Lando will have Cynthia and Gennifer with him. We got here first because he was picking them up. Can I break the news to Dalton? He, Walter and I have been talking all week. They worked together before I got here."

Detective Andrews nods, "Violet, you tend to get distracted when under stress. If we get this interview finished quickly, I can let you go. Please walk me through your morning."

I hate open ended questions from the police. I'm never sure how much information to give them. Mac always tells me to only answer the direct questions. However, this type of question confuses me. I want to tell the police everything I know.

I swallow and plunge into my description, "Sean drove the truck. I didn't check our arrival time. He parked his truck and opened the door to help me out of it. He always gets my door and the door of any lady. He learned good manners from his grandmother. We walked around the building and saw Walter crushed against it. He was sprawled on the hood. Thankfully, the car obscured my view of blood or anything else. He didn't look alive, but I didn't check. Sean propped me against the building out of the line of sight and went to see if he could help Walter. Sean checked on Walter and told me he couldn't find a pulse."

I glance at Detective Andrews and drop my head. I'm not sure what he wants me to say. I found another dead body.

Detective Andrews asks, "Do you know anyone who wanted to kill Walter?"

"No, I have no idea." I shrug my shoulders as I speak. "Tons of people wanted to kill Gene Johnson, but Walter was a harmless, pathetic old man. I don't think anyone cared enough about him to kill him."

The detective pockets his tablet. "I'll contact you if I have any further questions. I want to interview Sean. Why don't you go into the tiny restroom in the trailer and clean yourself up. I'll inform everyone there's been an incident."

I pull away from Sean's arms. As I trudge toward the trailer, I say over my shoulder, "When you talk to Lando please lead with the information that I'm okay. He freaks out if he thinks I'm hurt. He worries about me. He's also afraid my dad will put him in a nursing home for letting me get hurt."

After I wash the tears off my face, I stare at my reflection. I like living in Pittsburgh, except for all of the dead bodies. I wouldn't have been surprised if Walter had died in his sleep or even dropped over in the lot from a heart attack. I can't imagine who'd want to murder him. For Gene, there's so many suspects, but I can't think of a single one for Walter. I want to hide in this bathroom until Sean or Quentin or Lando comes to rescue me and take me home.

"You can trust me to get you into a car."

I'm stronger than an emotional collapse. I discovered three other bodies and faced down a murderer. I convinced someone to do the bad guy monologue and I survived several police interviews. When I go out there, I'll ask Detective Andrew Andrews if I can break the news to Dalton.

A text message from Lando appears on my phone.

What happened? The cops said you were okay and sent us away. We pulled into the first parking lot we saw.

I reply.

Sean and I are fine. I'm not sure what I'm allowed to tell you. I'll ask and get back to you.

Sean and Detective Andrews are still talking when I leave the trailer. Their body language doesn't appear to be adversarial. I approach the men to ask the detective if

I can tell Lando anything. For this dead body, the police arrived before any of the bystanders so they were able to secure the scene. Detective Andrews won't believe I need my grandfather's support since I have Sean and this is my fourth body discovery.

I tap Detective Andrews on the shoulder and when he whirls to face me I ask, "Am I allowed to tell my grandfather anything?"

He replies, "Usually we attempt to contain the information about a death until notification of the next of kin. Based upon your earlier comments, finding his family will be difficult in this situation. Your grandfather is Walter's boss and it happened on company property. I'll have my officers let him onto the scene. You can tell him about the possible homicide. Please ask your grandfather to go against all of his natural inclinations and be discreet."

I nod and text Lando.

> You can drive onto the lot. I'll meet you at the entrance.

Walter's death explodes the suspect pool. No one can solve this case. It must be related to a car deal gone wrong or maybe someone left something in a vehicle and blames Genius Used Cars. Lando will have to close the lot and auction the rest of the cars. It isn't safe for any of us to be here. This could be the work of a serial killer or someone with a grudge against used car salesmen or maybe a serial killer who hates used car salesmen.

Lando pulls into the lot as I reach the entrance. It's a small lot so he must have been close during our text exchange. Detective Andrews told me I could tell Lando but no one mentioned informing the Johnsons. I trust Lando's discretion, but I don't want more responsibility for those two.

Gennifer jumps out of the car before Lando can fully open his door. "Violet, what's going on? Why are all the cops here? Are you okay? Is Sean okay? Most importantly, is Dalton okay? Who isn't okay? Did someone break into the trailer? Is someone dead? Why do you look so bad? Your face is all puffy and red. Were you crying?"

I put my hand up with my palm facing her. "Gennifer, please stop talking. I got permission for Lando to come onto the scene. You need to get back into the car and close the door. You and your mom can sit here for a few minutes. Lando will leave his keys in the car, if you get hot roll down the windows. Detective Andrews will be angry if you get out of the car. You don't want to see him angry."

My speech to the rambunctious teenager gives Lando time to get out the car. I take his arm to pull him away from the Town Car. I'd rather have this conversation with him sitting down, so I lead him to the trailer. It's stuffy and smells like feet and nail polish remover in the trailer without the air conditioners running. Lando sits at the title clerk desk, and I turn on the wall unit.

He taps the metal desk with his cane to get my attention, "Violet, what's going on here?"

"Walter is dead. Sean and I found his body. Maybe it's me. Maybe I'm cursed. Everyone around me seems to die." My eyes fill with tears again, but I fight to keep them from falling.

"Sweetie, it's okay. He was old and kind of sick. I

know you've found several people cut down in their prime, but death can be natural." Lando stands and moves toward me. He pats me on the arm.

I wave my hand toward the door of the trailer. "Even though Walter was old, this didn't look like a natural death. He was run over by a car like Gene."

Lando steps away from me and flops into the chair. "Oh Violet, you found another murder victim? It's like you're a magnet."

I nod as the prickle of tears start again. I square my shoulders and look around the dumpy trailer as a distraction. According to the yellowed clock on the wall, the lot's open for business in thirty minutes. "You need to text Dalton and tell him not to come into the lot today. Based upon our past experience, it'll take hours for the police to process the scene. There's no reason to make him drive over here."

As he pulls out his phone, Lando says, "Good idea, I'm texting him now. He's eighteen and a Saturday off of work will probably make him happy so he won't question me." As he writes the text, Lando asks, "Do you think the same person killed Walter and Gene?"

I nod my head, "I can't imagine two murders in the same fashion, at the same location aren't related. Time of death should eliminate some of the suspects. I didn't go near Walter's body because I collapsed this time. Sean checked to make sure he was beyond help."

Lando grimaces and says, "I should drive Cynthia and Gennifer back to Lawrenceville. I'm not sure what I should tell them about this situation. They're both so fragile after yesterday."

I don't argue with him or say Cynthia is as fragile emotionally as a barracuda. I follow him out of the trailer. As he heads to his car to drive them away from the scene, I look for Sean. He remains next to the service building talking to Detective Andrews. I approach them but don't interrupt until Detective Andrews calls me.

He points at me and asks, "Did you tell Lando and ask him to keep it quiet?"

I wave toward his car as it pulls away, "I did and he's driving the Johnson women home. I'm not sure what he plans to tell them, but he'll keep the news from them to protect their delicate sensibilities. He also texted Dalton not to come to work today."

Andrews looks between Sean and I, "I'm finished with the two of you today. I have a key to the trailer, so I'll find Walter's address in his personnel file. I'll check his house for any clues. Thanks for your assistance. I'll call if I need anything else."

Detective Andrews acts much nicer than last week when I found Gene's body. He might've been more understanding last week if I'd behaved like a hysterical girl. This murder hit me harder than the other three because of Walter's insignificance. The other three murder victims who I found owned their strong personalities. Walter always acted like life had defeated him. The violence of his death shocks me.

Sean holds my hand as we walk the long way toward his truck to avoid the scene of the new crime. He keeps my hand after he helps me into his vehicle and kisses it. The text message chimes, and it's Quentin making sure

I'm okay. I respond that I'm fine and thank him for checking.

Sean gestures toward my phone and asks, "Was that Lando? Are we meeting him for lunch?"

I hesitate. Trying to date two guys at the same time is awkward. "No, it was Quentin. He was checking how I was doing after my breakdown."

Sean clenches his jaw and asks, "Did he ask you out again?"

I shake my head, "No, he wanted to make sure I felt stable. He's been here every time I've found a body. This time was the first time he saw me so upset."

Sean looks away from me and talks while he starts the car, "I don't like that guy. I might be willing to give him a chance if I didn't see him as competition. I get you need some time to decide who you like better, but I hate it."

Part of me wants to reassure Sean he's the one I want to date. However, his jealousy and overprotectiveness aren't attractive traits. He seems to try to fight his inclinations, but his competitive streak appears whenever I mention or communicate with Quentin. My relationship with either of them hasn't developed much beyond friendship. Quentin always focuses on me and acts like Sean amuses him rather than threatens him. I found my fourth body today so I'm not in the mood to placate Sean.

I tip my head back because I don't want to look at Sean, "I've tried to be honest with everyone that I'm not ready to be in a serious relationship. As I've discovered again today, life is short. I'll talk to you about Walter or Lando or even Mac or Detective Andrews. I refuse to discuss Quentin with you. If he's all you want to talk about, I'll rest my head on this window and close my eyes for a while."

Sean must be thinking about my statement because he doesn't respond. I lean on the window and close my eyes. The vision which pops into my head is Walter pinned between the building and the front of his car. How did someone catch him unaware when he was facing the vehicle that hit him? How fast was the car moving when it hit him? Did he feel a lot of pain? The questions whirl through my brain. I'd rather talk to Sean than deal with the thoughts running through my head.

Sean's driving and watching the road, but the traffic's light on a Saturday afternoon. I ask, "What're your plans for the rest of the day?"

"I'll work on your grandfather's addition. Trying to help run Genius Used Cars this week resulted in a riot at a funeral and another death. I lost a week of work on the addition. My guys kept working in my absence but we'll get more done with me on the job."

He doesn't elaborate on his statements or open another line of conversation. I don't want to be in the car with him anymore. The tension feels like bugs crawling down the back of my neck. When I first met Sean, I felt safe and comfortable with him. I no longer feel that way. It might not be fair to judge my relationship with him on the day I found another body. I want him to say the magic words that will make Walter's death make sense but he's too busy pouting about Quentin to comfort me.

I pour some fuel on the fires of his disapproval by texting. I fail to tell him I'm not texting Quentin. It's none of his business, and I want to annoy him. I text Lando to ask about his plans. He texts back he'll meet me at the house and we can talk.

Detective Andrews didn't tell me if I was allowed to inform Mac about the murder. She's my lawyer. I think privilege covers our discussions. It must be fine because I could've called her before my official onsite police interview. She'll berate me for not bringing her into the loop before my police interview. She enjoys striking sparks off Detective Andrews. I text her that if she's free, she should meet me at Lando's in about an hour.

Mac replies that it's a Saturday so she's at the law firm taking care of some stuff. She'd love a break. I hold my phone and stare at the texts I've already read because I don't want to talk to Sean. Phones are an awesome way to ignore people in real life. My phone chimes with the 'Grr argh' sound from *Buffy* to signify another text.

Sean squints at the road and says, "Wow, he just can't leave you alone can he? He must enjoy the chase."

I sigh and reply, "I don't know what your problem is today. I don't deserve you acting like a jerk."

Sean pulls over into the next open parking lot and turns to me, "You're right. I'm taking my frustration out on you. I've been trying to pretend to be the big strong man. When we found Walter, you collapsed. Everyone treated you like you were behaving the way they expected. When I saw Walter, all I could think of was finding my grandparents dead. They've been my foundation since my parents died when I was a kid. I'm lashing out at you because I don't know how to deal with my own pain and fear."

I move closer to him from my door hugging position

and put my hand on his shoulder, "I'm so sorry. I was so absorbed in my own reaction to Walter's death that I didn't consider your feelings at all."

He runs his hand through his thick red hair, "I'm sorry, too. I know finding bodies is difficult for you. I tried not to let my frustration boil onto you. I'm jealous of Quentin's ability to compartmentalize death because of his job. He also seems to know how to talk to you about your recent run of finding bodies."

I shake my head, "I may have misled you about who I was texting. The first texts were from Quentin, but the last few have been with my grandfather and Mac. I'm meeting them at Lando's sometime in the next hour. You're invited if you'd like."

He flashes a small smile that doesn't engage his dimple. "I'll drop you off at Lando's and then go check in with my grandparents for a little bit. Text me when Mac arrives, and I'll head back over for the meeting. I think discussing our week at Genius Used Cars with the four people who we know aren't murderers is a priority."

He pulls back onto the road, and we're silent for the rest of the ride. This conversation reminds me that I can be self-absorbed. I feel guilty for not saving Walter or even realizing he was in danger. He must have known something about the murderer which made him a target. I don't remember him mentioning anything that could've gotten him killed.

Sean walks me to the door when we arrive at Lando's. After the situation with the last set of murders, Lando installed a security system, and it doesn't show any intruders. The cats escort me to the kitchen and stare at the cupboard which holds their wet food. They split a can in the morning before I leave for work and at night when I get home. They must think they can con me out of another can of food at two o'clock in the afternoon, but I resist their entreaties.

I call the local pizza place and ask them to deliver two large pizzas, one white and one red. Leftovers can be tomorrow's breakfast. Then I head to the media room to watch an episode of *Buffy* as I wait for everyone.

The doorbell rings. It's the pizza guy. As I open the door, I realize I don't have any cash. In fact, I don't have my bag. I feel so rude. When I was in college, I always assembled the money for the delivery person when I hung up with the pizza shop.

I say, "I'm so sorry, I just realized I don't have my purse which has my card and all my cash in it. This is so embarrassing. I'll call my boyfriend who's at his house which is only a few minutes away. He'll be here really soon with money and I'll make sure to tip extra."

As I ramble, I dial Sean's number and thankfully there's an answer. As soon as the phone picks up I start talking, "Can you please hurry and bring some money. I ordered pizza and I can't find my purse."

Rather than Sean answering, I hear a woman's laughter. So I'm embarrassed in front of the delivery guy and whoever picked up Sean's phone. A lovely voice answers me, "This is Sean's grandmother. He left his phone on the counter while he's in the shower. I'll knock on the door and send him right over. By the way, I'm looking forward to meeting you young lady. Goodbye for now."

The delivery guy starts to shift his feet and asks, "Is

this going to take a while? I'm on a schedule. Did you think maybe you should have made sure you had your bag before you called?"

"I'm so sorry. I found one of my coworkers dead at work today. Someone ran him over him with a car. It's my fourth murder victim. I must've left my purse in the trailer when the police officer was interviewing me. At least the detective was nice this time. He was super nasty the last time and I needed my lawyer with me."

The guy widens his eyes and steps away from me, "If you found four dead guys, are you sure you don't have a different personality that's a serial killer? I listen to true crime podcasts. That's more murdered people than most people ever meet. Is this a trick to get free pizza or am I your next victim?

He looks ready to bolt and I feel like a complete idiot. Sharing my propensity for finding murder victims isn't the best way to get my pizza.

Then the pizza guy smirks and says, "You know what if this is a scam, it's a great one. Is there a camera somewhere? Are you filming for YouTube? These pizzas are already made so they'll get thrown away if I take them back. I'll cover the cost if you promise to repeat our conversation so I can film it. If I tell this story without proof no one will believe me."

The delivery guy is acting polite. I nod while he puts the pizzas on the ground. He pulls his phone out and starts to film, "I moved to Pittsburgh this spring. Since I moved here, I've found four of my coworkers dead at work. I think I'm cursed. I also leave my stuff at the crime scenes, so I don't have my purse to pay for the pizza."

A car screeches along the curb in front of the house, and Mac jumps out of it leaving the door hanging open and the engine running. She dashes up behind the guy and grabs his camera. He's so engrossed in filming me that he ignores the sound of her running feet. "No, no my client can be dumb but she's clearly overwrought. She can't be filmed and she has no comment on whatever mess she got into this time."

She puts her hand out to ward off the delivery guy and fiddles with the phone. "At least I know how to use this phone since I had one like it two phones ago." She erases the video and glares at me, "Violet, you're so lucky he wasn't posting this live anywhere."

He opens his mouth, and Mac points at his chest and says, "You are a jerk to try to take advantage of her stupidity and shock. Two pizzas can't be more than this." She reaches into her back pocket for her wallet and pulls out a fifty dollar bill. She hands him his phone and holds the fifty toward him.

Mac doesn't look like a lawyer this Saturday. Her long dark hair's pulled into a high ponytail. She's wearing jeans with a dark blue t-shirt with the Wonder Woman emblem on it. Her attitude shouts authority and demands respect.

She waves the fifty dollar bill at him, "I'm giving you a big tip and your phone back if you don't move for a minute."

He stares at the fifty with avarice gleaming in his eyes. She looks at me, "Violet, get my phone out of my purse and take a picture of his license plate and him."

He puts his hands up and says, "I'm not sure what

type of game, you two are playing. I don't want my picture taken."

She jabs her finger at him with the fifty crumpled in her fist, "Look bozo boy, I'm her lawyer and I'll give you this tip as a nondisclosure agreement. She's distraught. I don't want it broadcast all over social media. If you repeat anything she babbled to you today, I'll contact your boss and your boss's boss and have you fired. Who's going to be more sympathetic, her or you?"

He looks at me, at the beautiful house behind me. Then he glances at his beater car and his dirty clothing. He grabs the fifty and glares at Mac. "I'll take the fifty because without the whole story on film, she sounds crazy. I'll get out of here and forget I ever came to this house."

Sean pulls up while Mac and the delivery guy are arguing. He leans his tall, muscled body against his enormous white truck and yells, "Is there a problem here, my grandmother said you called."

The guy looks at Sean and back at me, "Is he your boyfriend?"

I nod as Sean crosses his arms and makes his biceps appear gigantic. The delivery guy runs to his car and calls over his shoulder, "None of you's worth the trouble. I won't tell no one nothing. I'll say I got caught in traffic."

Sean walks over to me and pulls me into his arms, "Did you notice you acknowledged I'm your boyfriend? You said it in front of your lawyer which makes it binding."

I lean into him and try to get some strength from his embrace. Mac interrupts, "Enough of the lovey dovey stuff, stop it. Violet, what were you thinking letting some pizza delivery guy film you talking about murders when you haven't told your lawyer, yet?"

I stay in Sean's arms but turn to face the wrath of Mac. "I'll admit I wasn't thinking. This morning, I found Walter my older coworker crushed between his car and the service building. I lost it and had a complete breakdown. I left my purse in the trailer after I talked to Detective Andrews. I didn't have any money to pay for the pizza."

"Nice attempt to bury the lead, but the important part of your statement is you talked to the manipulative police detective without your lawyer present." As she talks, she walks over to us and invades our personal space. "Were you alone when you had this lapse in judgment?"

As I debate throwing Sean under the bus so we can be there together, he answers, "Violet and I found Walter together. I also talked to Detective Andrews without a lawyer present."

Mac throws her hands in the air and waves them at us, "Didn't any of you learn anything from the last case? Police officers aren't your friends when you're involved with multiple murders. So far from one Saturday to another, Violet's found two dead bodies and been involved in a riot. If you add last month, the number of murder victims who she knows personally doubles to four. They're going to have to put you at the top of their suspect list."

As she paces and berates us, she doesn't look at her feet or the ground. I'm mesmerized by her energy and gestures. I don't see the danger until she steps in it. The pizza boxes remain on the ground where the delivery guy placed them in his eagerness to escape this circus. Mac steps right on top of them and stumbles. She jumps off the boxes and kicks them. The boxes skitter across the sidewalk in front of Lando's house. She chases them and jumps on them several times.

The physicality of her tantrum breaks the tension and the three of us start to laugh. The angst and guilt erupt from me in the form of laughter. I laugh so hard I can't breathe and tears stream from my eyes. Sean moves away from me because he's laughing so hard he's shaking. Mac sits down on the lawn to keep from falling.

Lando comes to the front door and yells, "You three need to get in here before someone calls the cops for you all disturbing the peace."

His ire makes me laugh harder. Neither Mac nor Sean can stop, but Sean's attempts make his muscles bunch attractively. Lando and his cane thump onto the front porch, and he grabs the hose. I foresee the danger, but I'm laughing too hard to move. Lando sprays all of us with the hose.

TWENTY-FOUR

"If you help me, I'll help you into a car."

The shock of cold water stops my hysterical giggling. Mac hiccups and falls backward onto the lawn. Sean looks fabulous in a wet, tight white t-shirt. One of the advantages of wearing dark colors is water makes them darker, not transparent.

Lando glares down at us, "You need to get your fool selves into this house and stop annoying my neighbors." He drops the hose, pounds his cane on the porch and slams the front door. It's a summer Saturday afternoon, so the drenching isn't chilling, just surprising.

Mac stands up, "Wet jeans aren't comfortable, but I'm not sure if anything of yours will fit me, Violet."

"I own sweatpants with drawstrings at the waist. You can borrow a pair and roll them up if they drag on the ground. Your fitted t-shirts always look so feminine, but my t-shirts will be too big on you." I turn to Sean, "Mac can wear clothes that are too big for her. I don't think we own anything that won't be silly on you because it'll all be too small."

He waves toward his truck, "I live so close and I ran out of the house to save you from the evil pizza delivery disaster. I can drive home to grab dry clothes. My grandmother made a bunch of cookies. I'll grab some and get two pizzas from the local place with better food and no evil delivery drivers."

Most of the time he wears his jeans a little baggy and his t-shirts a little long. The water makes everything cling to him. Mac and I both watch him climb into the truck and she sighs with appreciation. Once he's inside the vehicle, Mac says, "Violet, you snagged a fine specimen of man with your ditzy ways. I must salute you."

As I turn to walk toward the house, I say, "And he's bringing cookies. Now we need to go inside and face the wrath of Lando."

Lando sits at his desk in the receiving library. "It took you two long enough to get in here, even after you stopped cackling like the witches in Macbeth. I'll be here waiting after you two change into dry clothes. Your performance on the lawn shows no respect for Walter or pizza."

Mac follows me upstairs. When I move the bookshelf to get to my side of the house, Mac says, "That's the coolest contraption in the world. I need one. You have a sliding bookcase that opens into another house. It wouldn't work in my condo downtown. Once I open my own practice, I could buy two half doubles and use one for my home and the other for my office. Pittsburgh has tons of duplexes."

I throw open the door to my bedroom. "Lando renovated this room for me. I love the sunlight and the view of the backyard."

Mac walks to the window, "It's Pittsburgh, sunny days are rare and the backyard has an addition in progress."

I smile and tap the window, "Did you forget who's been building the addition?"

She peers out the window, "How long have you been sitting in your window, creeping on Sean and watching him work?"

I nod, "He saw pictures of me growing up. I watched him in his natural element for a few weeks before we actually met. Anyway, I have a ton of casual clothes, you can take anything you want."

I open a drawer full of sweatpants. Mac looks at it, "How many pairs of black sweatpants do you own?"

I shrug, "I don't know. In college and graduate school, they were the mainstay of my wardrobe."

She picks up a stack of them, "Why sweatpants? Why not leggings or jeans?"

I look through another drawer and pull out a pair of jeans, "I also own a bunch of pairs of jeans. I don't feel comfortable in leggings unless the shirt covers me to the middle of my thighs. In college and graduate school, I always dressed casually. At Roar Motors, I wore the polo shirts Lando collected for years. Lando believed in suits which meant the polos were like new."

"I can see you truly need a fashion intervention. Once this case is solved, you and I are blowing every penny you made at Genius Used Cars on clothing for you." Mac says as she rifles through my dressers and closet.

I lead her to my lovely bathroom. I want her to see even if I don't have any fashion sense, I have decorating style. Actually Lando has decorating style but I get to use it. She looks at the clean black and white tile, the enormous claw foot tub, the separate free standing rain shower, and the gorgeous stained glass window with the matching transom.

She nods at the room as I open the door with a flourish, "I'm having some bathroom envy right now, but you didn't decorate this place. I bet you don't clean it either."

"I get to use it every day and Lando designed it for me. He has a cleaning lady who comes in twice a week." I sigh. "I'll let you use the shower, change and go through all of the cabinets. I'll get dressed in my room."

As I close the door, she yells, "Try to find something cute. You should be inspired by the sight of Sean in his wet, clinging t-shirt."

Mac raises the bar on my fashion choices for pizza and cookies with her, Lando and Sean. She tries to distract me from my real worry. Someone murdered another car salesman. Most of the massive suspect list for Gene's murder wouldn't be interested in a broken man like Walter. Last week he shared everything in his life while he sat with Dalton and me watching the lot. Occasionally, he told us way too much. I can't imagine if he knew anything about Gene's murder, he wouldn't have told us. Toward the end of the week, he mentioned how much he appreciated us because no one had listened to him for years.

I run downstairs and grab the murder investigation notebook from the desk in Lando's favorite library. I don't see Lando, so I run back up to my room to take notes on my suspect list while Mac uses my shower.

Cynthia remains my favorite suspect but she still doesn't have a car. She might have been able to convince Walter to pick her up, so she could use his own car to kill him. Maybe Walter was her accomplice to kill Gene. He whispered something to her at the funeral. Then she could've used her trailer key to grab car keys to drive one of the cars on the lot as her getaway vehicle. I need to ask Detective Andrews if any of the cars are missing or I can check when I go to get my purse.

Butch, the repo guy, remains a gigantic jerk. However, I need to check with Detective Andrews if he and his paramour, Phoebe, were in jail for their actions during the funeral riot.

Gennifer or Dalton could have killed Gene, but I can't see either of them hurting a harmless old man to cover their tracks. Walter wouldn't have bonded with Dalton if he had knowledge Dalton murdered Gene.

Detective Andrews went through lists of customers and while most hated Gene with good reason, none stood out. I wonder if Detective Andrews noticed the codes on the deal jackets. If the killer was someone connected with Gene's scams at his corporate dealership job, they're also beyond our reach as amateur investigators.

I chewing on my pen and stare at the book when Mac interrupts me with her return. "Why aren't you wearing dry clothes and staring at a notebook like it contains the secrets of the universe?"

I tap my pen on the cover, "I got distracted thinking

about Walter's murder. I made a suspect list. Want to see it?"

She shakes her head at me, "Obviously, you failed to learn your lesson last time. Police solve murders not Popular Culture Ph.D.s turned car salesmen."

I slam the book closed, "Fine I won't show it to you now. I'll take it downstairs and discuss it with Sean and Lando."

She walks into the hallway but says over her shoulder, "Is it safe to keep getting your grandfather who is in his seventies involved in your true crime drama?"

She might be right, but Lando loves fictional mysteries and these actual murders keep occurring within his sphere. When we get to the kitchen, two fresh pizza boxes and a basket full of cookies distract me from discussing the murders.

After two pieces and several cookies, I glance at my phone to check the time. There's a text message from Detective Andrews. Texting with police officers because I've discovered so many bodies seems odd. Sean tenses when he sees me reading a text.

To avoid unpleasantness, I wave the phone and say, "Detective Andrews texted me he wants to talk to me. I left my purse at the trailer, so I'm going to meet him at Genius Used Cars. Mac, you can come with me because you're so worried about being present as my lawyer. However, I don't need an entourage."

Sean nods, "I understand. What could possible happen with your lawyer and a police detective present? Lando and I can go over to my grandparents. He can tell them about his adventures being back in the car business this week. I already cancelled our reservations for tonight. Murder in the morning doesn't set the best tone for a romantic dinner in the evening."

We take Mac's practical sedan because she wants to drive. During the trip, she makes me tell her everything I remember about finding Walter's body. She demands I recount exactly what I told Detective Andrews this morning, and any possible relevant conversations Walter and I had in my two weeks of knowing him. Then she proceeds to tell me she'll be there when I'm talking to Detective Andrews and I can't speak unless she approves it. I nod to her instructions but I'm not sure if I can be as guarded as she wants me to be.

TWENTY-FIVE

"After the sale, we will stay in touch."

When we arrive, Detective Andrews waits in his vehicle. He pops out of the car when he sees our car turn into the lot. Lando gave me the keys to everything so I unlock the trailer. It's nice he wants to talk to me at Genius Used Cars rather than the police station this time. He makes himself comfortable at the title clerk's desk where he spent most of the week. I stand across from him and feel like a child called to the principal's office.

If I'm the kid in the principal's office, Mac is the helicopter parent from hell. She glares at him and starts to question him. "Why did you text my client to come in to speak to you at such an unorthodox time and place?"

He smiles, "Violet answered nearly all of my questions this morning without you present. I wanted to go over her impressions one more time. I know she felt uncomfortable at the police station. I thought here would be more pleasant for her."

Mac strides around the desk and into Detective Andrews's personal space. He leans back in his chair to gaze up at her. "I appreciate that you both came at such short notice. I'm not sure what you were doing, but those sweatpants and oversized t-shirt look very professional on you Miss MacKenzie."

The tension between these two unsettles me. I glance around the interior of the trailer to see if my bag is anywhere in evidence. I may've left it in the service building. Mac and Detective Andrews laser focus on each other. I could disappear from the room. They wouldn't notice.

Mac puts her finger on Detective Andrews's broad chest and shouts, "I'm a professional and my professional status doesn't change based on my clothing. I notice you're wearing a t-shirt that's so tight I can see every ripple of your abs. Did I say anything?"

He grabs her hand and pulls her closer to him. The sparks flying between these two charge the air and change the atmosphere. They enact the attraction between enemies trope before my eyes.

Detective Andrews points toward me but never takes his eyes off Mac, "I bet Violet would never have noticed my abs. She's too busy being pulled between the EMT and her construction worker protector. I find it interesting my abs are the first thing you mention, counselor."

I inch toward the door of the trailer to escape whatever's happening between these two. I open the door and slip outside. I clutch my phone in my sweaty palm. If they need me or notice I'm missing, they can call or text me. I won't leave the premises. I'll just go to the service building to look for my purse.

Headlights illuminate the service building as I

approach it. On a June evening, the lot would've been closed by now even if we hadn't closed early for Walter's murder. It's odd to see a car sitting in front of the service building with its lights shining.

There's a muscular, confident police detective in the trailer behind me, but I can handle this. It looks like there's only one person in the car. I creep around the car and knock on the driver's side window. It's only Dalton, my surviving coworker. I move away from the car door and motion he should get out of his car.

In that excitement between Mac and Detective Andrews, I failed to ask him if I could tell Dalton about Walter's death. I'm sure the detective wouldn't mind, especially since I can walk Dalton over to the trailer after I'm done.

Dalton looks heartbroken. His man bun is askew and his wrinkled clothes look like he slept in them. He must know about Walter's death.

We can go into the service building so he can meet Detective Andrews looking neat. There's a tiny bathroom with a toilet, a sink and a mirror. He can splash some water on his face. I'll feel guilty if I cause an eighteen year old boy to cry while talking to the police.

I gesture toward the building and walk toward it, "Dalton, can you come into the service building? I want to talk to you."

He follows me. The only sound is the traffic and his dragging feet. I have the keys in my pocket. I take care of the doors and the light. I choke back a sob when I notice the three lawn chairs lined up facing the closed garage door. Walter's gone and Dalton appears to be broken.

I plop down in my chair and pull Dalton's chair across from me. I glance around the service area looking for my purse as Dalton goes to the restroom. I spot it on a work bench next to the restroom. I'll let it sit there until I'm done talking to Dalton. I don't want him to think I'm spying on him in the restroom. The door isn't thick and sound travels.

When he comes back into the service area, he stumbles over to his lawn chair and flops into it. The cheap chair shakes but doesn't collapse. I pat his hand, "You must've found out about Walter. I'm so sorry I didn't have a chance to tell you."

He jerks away from me, "What're you talkin about? What's wrong with Walter?"

Scooting my chair closer to him, I say, "I'm so sorry. I thought you were upset because you heard that the same person who killed Gene, came back and murdered Walter."

He shakes his head vigorously, and his man bun collapses, "You're lyin and tryin to trick me. Are you taping me?"

I sit up straight in my seat at his odd behavior, "Why would I be recording you? That's the second time today someone's asked me that. I'm telling you the truth. This morning when I came to work, I found Walter's body. He had been hit with his own car."

"That's impossible. I didn't kill Walter, so it couldn't of been the same killer." Dalton jumps out of his seat and pushes the lawn chair back so hard it skids across the floor.

I've uncovered another murderer, and I'm alone with

him. Sneaking away from the tension between the lawyer and the detective in the trailer seems like it was a bad idea. My cell phone's in my hand but with Dalton's attention on me, there's no way to call or text for help surreptitiously.

I need to distract Dalton, so I can call for help. I get out of my chair slowly because I don't want to upset him with any sudden movements. At this point, he's unstable but also unarmed. I move toward him, "You're overwrought. You'll feel much calmer if you sit down again."

He puts his hand up with his palm facing me and yells, "Stop using big words. You're tryin to confuse me."

Dalton paces around the service area.

The room contains random pieces of metal and heavy equipment. All of them are potential weapons. Dalton runs his hands through his hair and doesn't grab anything. He's only eighteen but he's several inches taller than I am with about fifty pounds more muscle. I'm afraid my self defense training from college won't help me against him.

Approaching him feels like a bad idea, but I can't stand still. I move toward one of the workbenches on the wall near the door. He starts to mumble, "I'd never kill Walter. He was always good to me. They're goin' to try to pin it on me. Two killings will mean the death penalty. Gene deserved to die but not Walter."

He confessed to Gene's murder to me. This destroys my plan to play dumb and pretend I didn't figure out he's a murderer.

The two in the trailer will have to get done arguing soon and notice the lights in the service building. The building was dark when we all arrived. Hopefully, they'll come to investigate before Dalton kills me to eliminate loose ends.

Dalton never seemed like a murderer. Maybe I can distract him with questions. He was on my suspect list, but not at the top. In as soothing a tone of voice as I can muster, I ask, "Dalton why did you kill Gene?"

He keeps walking around the room, but he answers me, "He hurt my sister. She had a baby and really needed a car to go to work. Her worthless ex took her car. No one could afford nothing, but she saw the sign here about no money down so she tried. It was a couple months ago, I was still in school. She got that worthless car, but she was so sad afterwards."

I swallow my sigh. I know how she got the car. I wish I didn't.

Dalton keeps speaking in a monotone and blaming himself. "I just wanted to have fun with my friends. I shoulda gotten a job to get her a car. I didn't even notice that she stopped eatin' and got real skinny. She went to work and cuddled the baby but stopped talkin' to the rest of us. One day, I got home from school and found her cryin' and rockin' the baby. There was blood on her and the baby. I grabbed the little guy and ran him over to his playpen. He laughed when I ran with him. She started screaming she didn't deserve her baby no more."

I gasp and cover my mouth. I want to ask about the baby's health, but I don't want to interrupt his story.

He stares at this hands and answers my unspoken question, "Baby didn't have a single scratch on him. He didn't have no idea his mommy hurt herself. She slashed up her arms. I wanted to call my mom, but I was so scared of all the blood. I hustled her into the ugly, beater car and put the baby in his car seat. I got them both to the hospital. They made sure the baby was fine. They kept her for a week in the mental ward."

He stops talking and moving and stares into space. He's standing between me and any possible escape. The stupid service building only has a single door and the closed garage door. He's distracted, but he's between me and the exit.

Approaching him seems like a bad plan, so I ask my burning question about the case. "Dalton, why did you put Creamsicle in Gene's car?"

He pulls his hair and moves toward me. "I started workin here to get Gene put in jail not kill him. I came that night to find the files to prove Gene was crooked. A guy I know was in jail and he loaned me his car for watching his dog while he was locked up. He got out and needed it back. I heard Gene was going to have that brute, Butch repo my sister's car.

Dalton walks away from me and stands in front of the garage door. He says, "I parked a couple of blocks away cause I was driving my sister's car. I had to take pictures of the files dat night. I took the key out of Phoebe's desk. Anyways, when I got to the lot, I seen Gene put down a can of something."

I nod at him, and he continues. "That orange cat came up to eat it. Gene jumped in his car, right by the cat. I knew he was gonna kill it. I snapped."

Dalton closes his eyes. "I ran right up to Gene and asked him what he was doin'. He got outta his car, he came toward me, and told me it was none of my business. I clocked him and he fell. It was so loud."

His eyes pop open and he looks me in the eye. "I got in his car, I put the cat in with me and I ran over him, four times. Then I moved the car so it covered everything but his head. It looked neater that way. I took off my shirt and rubbed it all over the car because of fingerprints. Then I left the cat in the car. I knew you would be here in the morning to help the cat and find Gene."

As if the confession drained every bit of energy from him, Dalton drops into the lawn chair and drops his head to his knees. This is my chance to escape. I want to hear more of the story. This is my second murder confession, and the last time Annika, my cat saved me. There's no cat to save me this time. I'm not competing in the too dumb to live sweepstakes. As he looks distraught, I dash for the door.

My running breaks him from his stupor, but I reach the door first and slam it in his face. It must hit him with enough force to stun him. I make it to the trailer with Dalton in pursuit. When I fling open the trailer door, Mac and Andrew stand locked in a passionate embrace. They're so enthralled with each other that the thump of the door doesn't break their connection.

I scream as I run behind the kissing couple, "I know who killed Gene, and he's right behind me."

Detective Andrews pulls away from Mac and says, "You two get in Gene's office, barricade the door and call 911 for backup."

I'm ready to follow his instructions, and I pull Mac into the office. She sees skinny Dalton and whispers, "I trust Andrews. You can call 911 but I don't think we need to close the door completely. Leave it cracked. I want to hear this interaction."

I dial 911 and whisper, "There's a police situation at Genius Used Car Lot in Whitehall. Detective Andrews is on-site. He told me to call for backup."

I hear loud sobbing but no sounds of a struggle as I stay on the phone with the emergency dispatcher. I tiptoe to the doorway and join Mac. Dalton doesn't have a gun or any weapon. He's collapsed at Detective Andrews's feet crying and repeating, "I'd never kill Walter. Gene deserved to die, not Walter."

Mac hustles over to the crying boy, and Detective Andrews tries to grab her arm. She shakes him off and asks, "Dalton, honey, do you have a dollar?"

He shakes his head in confusion, "Are you tryin' to shake me down."

She strokes his hair, "No, honey. You need a lawyer right now and if you give me a dollar, it's a retainer."

He puts his hand in his pocket and pulls out a quarter, a dime and a penny. "I got thirty-six cents, is that enough?"

Mac takes the change from his hand, "It's the idea, so yes."

She stands in front of Dalton, glares at Detective Andrews and says, "My client is exercising his right to remain silent."

Detective Andrews glares at her, "I know I told you two to hide in that office."

Raising my hand, I say, "I called 911 and help is on the way."

He sighs and shakes his head, "I don't think I need any help. It looks like my suspect has not only given up, he's retained counsel. Violet, do you know what's going on here?"

I glance at Mac who is still patting Dalton's head to comfort him. She's ignoring me, so I answer, "I can tell you fast what I'm pretty sure happened but this isn't my official statement. There's so much excitement. I might be in shock so I might not remember this if I have to go on the witness stand."

Detective Andrews points at me, "Fine, fine, this can be an unofficial statement because I want to know what occurred."

I lean on the desk. As the adrenaline fades, my strength disappears with it, "Dalton and I talked in the service building. He became hysterical when I told him about Walter's death. He insisted he didn't kill Walter. I don't have a poker face, and I may have gasped. I think he could tell I figured out he must have killed Gene. He launched into telling me about his sister getting a car from Gene. Then Dalton found her a couple of weeks later when she tried to kill herself. I put the puzzle pieces together based on his story. Dalton killed Gene to avenge Gene's victimization of his sister. I think it's completely justified. Dalton scared me, but he never tried to hurt me in the service building."

Detective Andrews runs his hand over his head and asks, "If Dalton killed Gene, who killed Walter?"

I tug on my ponytail, "I think he probably killed himself. I talked to Walter at Gene's funeral before the riot. Walter was so impressed there were so many guys at

Gene's funeral. Walter wanted people to remember him. He told Dalton and me we were the closest people to friends he had. He mentioned he preplanned his funeral last week. It seemed ironic but unimportant until Dalton insisted he didn't kill him."

Detective Andrews and I look at Dalton who remains cradled in the arms of his lawyer. She's petting his hair to try to calm him. The trailer door slams open again and two police officers barrel into the room with guns drawn.

Detective Andrews takes control. "It's okay guys. I solved the murder cases. The suspect in Gene Johnson's murder has retained counsel who's currently cradling his head. If you have a patrol car, we can move this party to the police station."

Mac interjects, "I'm not leaving my client alone. He's distraught and unstable. He also needs his mom."

Detective Andrews sighs, "He's legally an adult. He has an attorney. He doesn't need his mommy."

Dalton says through his tears, "Actually, I lied on my application. I started here after school left out for the summer, I'm only sixteen not eighteen. I don't think that's an adult, is it?"

Detective Andrews sighs again. Dalton's making him sigh like I usually make police detectives sigh. "Fine, call his mother. This complicates things."

Dalton and Mac go to the police station in the patrol car. I ride with Detective Andrews. On our trip, I suggest Detective Andrews take credit for solving this difficult case with too many suspects. No one cares that Gene Johnson, rapist, and swindler died. Dalton is only a kid. I inform Detective Andrews he could have a clean win if he went along with a plea bargain for a killer who is still a minor.

Detective Andrews shakes his head at me, "Violet, you do understand I don't get to make those type of decisions. You watched hundreds of hours of *Law and Order*. You are right about Dalton's status as a minor affecting the situation, but we will need to see what happens. I'm sure his shark of a lawyer will defend him well."

I look at him and ask, "Can I call Lando? I'm afraid he'll be worried about me when it takes me so long to get back. I forgot my darn bag again. It's in the service building."

When we stop at a light, Detective Andrews looks at me, "Of course, why don't you have Lando meet us at the police station and after you've given an official statement, you can swing by and get your bag. I think your lawyer friend will be busy for a while."

TWENTY-SIX

"Genius Used Cars fills all your needs!"

Lando and Sean retrieve me from the police station. The three of us stop at the crime scene to get my purse before it gets entered into evidence. We also get Mac's car and drop it off at the police station. She refuses to leave her client but at least she has her car.

The next morning Lando, Sean, and I go to Gennifer and Cynthia's house to take them to breakfast. It's a Sunday so the dealership would be closed even if there wasn't an active police investigation happening onsite.

I suggest we tell them about Walter and Dalton at their house rather than at Eat N'Park. I've been involved in too many uncomfortable public scenes to want to face another one. We park in the back, traverse the weed infested backyard, and walk on the narrow path between the houses to knock on the front door.

Gennifer opens the door and asks, "What's wrong? You look like you're on your way to another funeral."

Lando says, "Can we come in and talk to you and your mom?"

Gennifer opens the door without a word and gestures us inside the cramped, dark house. Cynthia smiles at us or more likely, at Sean.

Cynthia pats the seat next to her on the couch and continues to beam when Lando sits next to her, "I've had the best news in the entire world today and I want to share it with all of you. I thought my days were numbered last week. I tried to hide how sick I was. My doctor called me a half an hour ago on a Sunday to tell me it looked like the new treatment is working. My numbers are much better."

She grabs Gennifer's hand, "I was so worried I was going to leave my baby and she wouldn't have anyone so I pushed her away. Now I think I'm going to get better. I wanted to share it with you three because you've been so good to me, in spite of me being dumb enough to marry Gene Johnson. Now what do yinz have to tell us?"

My eyebrows raise because she's never used the Pittsburgh colloquialism in our conversations.

Before I can speak, Lando says, "We are so happy for you but we have some bad news. Walter's body was found at the dealership yesterday."

Gennifer gasps, but Cynthia nods her head, "He whispered to me when he offered his condolences he'd be joining Gene soon. He told me he had pancreatic cancer, and there was nothing they could do. He asked me not to say anything because he didn't want pity."

I perch on the edge of the worn couch and turn to Cynthia, "Your conversation with Walter at the funeral took like a minute. When did he share his feelings with you?"

"I called him after the funeral. I found his number in Gene's phone. I get how cancer messes with someone's brain. Was his car door open?" She asks.

Jolting forward at her question, I ask, "How did you know?"

She replies, "Someone needs to look for a big piece of wood attached to a fishing line. He planned to put it on the break and pull it when he was between the car and the wall. I guess he did it."

Her statement backs up my theory about his apparent murder being a staged suicide. I'm sure Lando will make sure his funeral is well attended. I don't volunteer about his manner of death. They'll find out soon enough.

Lando says, "I think we can send the rest of the cars to auction because the police are confident they have the right suspect for Gene's murder. There was a confession yesterday."

Gennifer starts to shake her head, "Not Dalton, please not Dalton. I wish everything would stop just stop."

Here phrase distracts me. Pointing at Gennifer, I ask, "Did you write anything on the mirror in the trailer with lipstick?

Gennifer pauses and slides into a chair. "The note was me, sometimes I write things when I get overwhelmed. Anyways, I need to get back to Dalton. When I saw him with a girl at the funeral, I was upset but she looked familiar. She was in Gene's phone. Her last name was the same as Dalton. Gene gave her a two. His notes said she was hot, but she cried too much."

I walk over to Gennifer and hug her. "I'm so sorry. Mac is his lawyer and I'm sure she's going to do her best for him. Dalton confessed to killing Gene. He's only sixteen and with the extenuating circumstances, I'm not sure what will happen."

Gennifer glares at me. "I'll do anything to help him. I'll testify for him. I'll write to him. I'll call him. I'm happy Gene's dead. I think we saw at the funeral so is everyone else."

Lando holds his hand up to stop her, "We will try to help Dalton and both of you. I think at this point an auction's our best bet and we can move on from this."

Cynthia reaches her hand out to Sean and leans against him after he helps her to stand. "Thank you all so much for helping us. When Violet found Gene's body, I felt happy because Gennifer wouldn't be forced to live with him. Then I realized we had nobody else."

She waves toward Lando, "I thought about Lando as an option. After spending a little time with him, I knew he wouldn't consider me. I'm too young. I switched my focus to Sean because he's a caregiver."

Cynthia looks up at Sean and pats his arm. "I flirted with you because I believed if I could convince you to care about me, you would take care of Gennifer when I was gone."

I can't believe Cynthia earned my sympathy.

Lando interrupts my thoughts, "You don't need to use feminine wiles. We are all happy to help you both. Gene committed terrible acts both financially and morally. He didn't trust anyone, so he didn't have any debts. When we send those thirty cars to auction, we should make enough money to fix this house, pay your bills, and help you both start fresh."

Acknowledgments

Thank you to everyone who read Death of a Saleswoman. Your encouragement and questions about book two have kept me writing. Thank you to my beta readers who read various versions of this book including Kathy Christmas, Lori Barden, Dana Armstrong, Suzanne Gausman, and Jelaina Jones. Thank you Kristian Beverly for helping with the formatting and creating the gorgeous cover. I love my husband Jason and my son Riley for their patience and support.

About the Author

Michelle Haring is a bookstore owner turned author. She started her book career in 1987 and has owned Cupboard Maker Books for over twenty years. Cupboard Maker Books has over 125,000 used and rare books along with several thousand new titles. As a bookseller, Michelle has won several awards including RT Book Reviews Bookseller of the Year, the 2018 RT Book Reviews Creative Initiative Award and the 2019 RWA Steffie Walker Bookseller of the Year Award. Because she has been so immersed in the bookstore and publishing world, she decided she didn't want to set her cozy mystery series within one. Thus, Death Motors was born. When Michelle isn't writing, you can find her reading and sorting through the plethora of books at Cupboard Maker Books. She's found all sorts of items in books, but has yet to find herself living in a cozy mystery scenario.

For more information, go to www.michelleharing.com, or follow her online @michelleharingauthor.

www.ingramcontent.com/pod-product-compliance
Lightning Source LLC
Chambersburg PA
CBHW071412200726
48294CB00002B/374